A KISS OF EMBERS

SYDNEY WINWARD

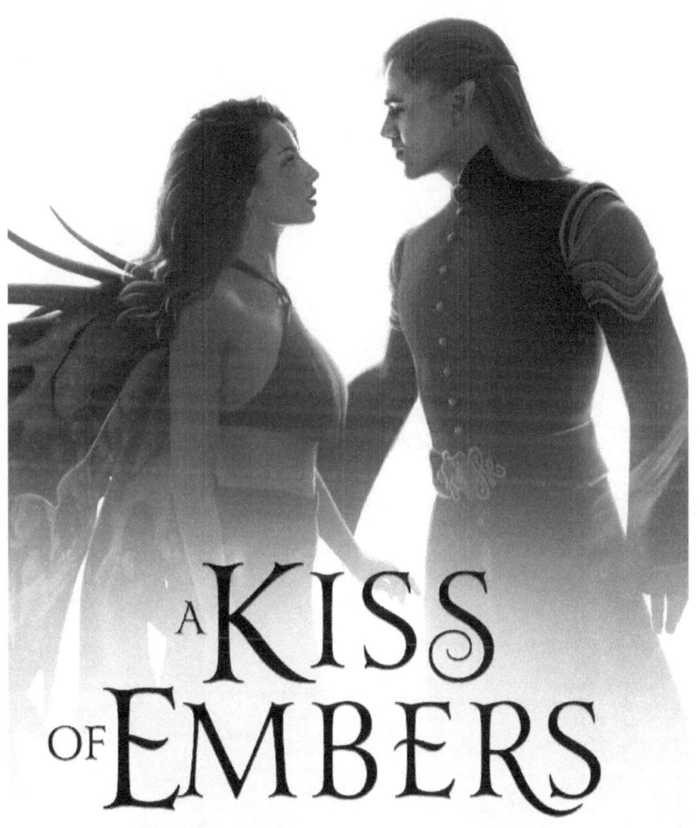

A KISS OF EMBERS

SUNLIGHT AND SHADOWS BOOK 4

A Kiss of Embers

Cover Design by MiblArt

Published by Silver Forge Books

Trade Paperback ISBN 978-1-960461-00-1

Digital ISBN 978-1-960461-89-6

www.sydneywinward.com

To my dad–

All those silly songs you sang as I grew up inspired a silly song of
my own.

BOOKS BY SYDNEY WINWARD

The Bloodborn Series
Bloodborn
Bloodbond
Bloodscourge
Bloodbane
Bloodcurse

Sunlight and Shadows Series
A Breath of Sunlight
A Taste of Shadows
A Glimpse of Music
A Kiss of Embers
A Balm of Healing

Letters to Love Series
Yours, Sterling
Forever, Mirabelle

Lord Death Series
A Waltz with Lord Death

Novellas
Through Wylder Meadows
Root Brew Float
On Silver Wings
Bloodmoon
Selkie

ONE

A terrifying silence ground its knuckles across the forest. Late summer leaves remained motionless in the towering trees overhead. Even the nocturnal animals held their breath, perhaps crouching in the darkness, waiting to spring from their hiding places. Each soft footfall on the foliage beneath her feet sounded like crashing boulders compared to the silence and her heart a pounding drum.

Pain rippled across Pri's torn wings, which hung limp and tattered against her back. She gritted her teeth when each movement across the forest floor consumed her with agony. Tears blurred her vision, but she quickly swiped them away to keep her eyes clear.

Awareness prickled across the back of her neck. When she turned to glance over her shoulder, only darkness stared back at her.

Shadows crawled from shrub to tree, accompanied by the faintest whistle of wind through the leaves. She blinked several times to dispel the distortion of movement and then continued to creep forward on the tips of her bare toes.

Please, she begged through the agonizing pain. *Don't let them catch me.*

Her older sister would never have allowed her to make this perilous journey if she had known her intentions. Not with an entire army at her back. And certainly not on her own. But if she did nothing, she would never fly again. She would rather risk her life than be bound to the ground for the rest of her days.

The sight of the waterfall leading to the top of the mountain spurred her heart into a hopeful frenzy. The Glades. Just across the rope bridge lay the entrance to the pool of healing. A little bit farther. Almost there.

A tingle from the back of her neck to her arms caused her to spin around once again. Darkness. Shadows. And the distant roar of the waterfall.

She stared into the shadows, eyes scanning every inch of the quiet cliffside. Trees. Grass. Leaves. But still, she moved closer to the safety of the darkness just in case. After several long moments of surveying her surroundings, she turned back around.

And yelped.

A man towered over her, wearing all manner of weapons on his person. Knives. A bow. Arrows. And the sight of the chupacabra skull covering his face like a mask melted her heart into a puddle of fear.

He was one of *them*.

A Forest Fae.

Her enemy.

Pri darted away, but the man moved blindingly fast as he grabbed the back of her clothing and threw her to the ground. An involuntary shriek escaped her mouth when she landed on her injured wings. She flinched, squeezing her eyes shut as she held her hands over her face to protect herself.

A second assault never came.

The man inhaled sharply, and she peeked through her fingers to find him pulling the bone mask from his face. White hair tumbled out from beneath the feathery skull, silvery blue eyes the color of a full moon staring down at her. His eyebrows furrowed while he took her in with one sweeping glance.

"You are just a child."

She whimpered. "Please. Don't hurt me." She wasn't a fighter like her older sister. All she knew how to use as a defense was her fire magic. Even then, it shied away in her terror.

Pri scrambled backward until her back pressed against a tree. She watched his hands. Instead of reaching for a weapon, they remained at his sides. He glanced over his shoulder at the darkness behind them. But even she knew anything might live within the shadows.

Finally, he growled, "Go. Run while you can. If they find you—" A pause, and then he swore under his breath. Seconds later, two other Forest Fae dropped from the boughs above, landing on silent feet.

"Well, well," one of them laughed, face hidden behind a bear skull mask. He probed her shoulder with the wooden end of his spear. "An Ember Fae. Good job, Bastien." He clapped the man with the chupacabra mask on the shoulder. "I was beginning to doubt your competence."

"Gael," Bastien murmured, his gaze flickering to her. "She's just a child."

"And?" The man now prodded her cheek with the blunt end of his weapon. Her pulse jumped in response, followed by frantic breaths. "They all grow up eventually. If we don't kill her now, she'll come back when she's older. It will be our people's blood on her hands."

Pri opened her mouth, desperate to beg for her life. But the words froze on her tongue the moment Gael held the sharp blade of his spear to her breast. She squeezed her eyes shut, silent tears trailing down her cheeks.

Seraphina! she screeched in her mind as she held the red stone strung around her neck. It burned hot in her hand at the tether between her and her sister. But her older sister wouldn't come to her rescue in time. She shouldn't have done this. She shouldn't have come here. She would die for her foolishness.

"Stop."

Her eyes cracked open to find Bastien with his hand closed around the wooden shaft of the spear. The man's eyes hardened. "Spilling her blood now will prove nothing. Take her to the village to face the council."

Gael frowned. "She will die there just as she would die here."

The third man with a snake skull mask, who had remained silent through the interaction, now spoke. "They can use her for information. Ember Fae attacks have recently become more frequent. She might know something."

No! Pri silently screamed. *I would rather die. I would rather die. I would rather die.*

In their distraction of conversation, Pri scrambled out from beneath the sharp end of the spear. Magic flung out of her fingertips, messy and uncontrolled. Flames burned the forest floor, lighting up sacred ground. Her bare feet sprinted across lush grass, patches of dirt, and rough branches. Fire trailed in her wake.

Desperate.

Frantic.

Terrified.

And then, as the Attleglade river came into sight, a large branch swung toward her. She turned her head just fast enough to catch a glimpse of a fourth man before her world turned dark.

TWO

Bastien Dalena crossed his arms, surveying his burnt home. In the space of a few months, it had caught fire.

Three times. First, when his older sister, Nyana, had stayed in Attleglade Forest with her family when they'd been attacked by Ember Fae. Second, when his best friend, Ashryn, had started the fire with a neat card trick.

Fine, fine. It didn't really count. But for being in the patrol guard like himself, she could often be a bit accident-prone.

And third, when that young girl's fire magic had traveled a bit too far...

Ashryn dropped down from the tree overhead in a flurry of brown pants and shirt, white hair like his, and warm brown eyes. She took off her saber-toothed cat skull mask and placed her hands on her hips to mimic his stance. Her voice deepened to further mock him. "You know, if I only made my home deeper within the safety of the settlement, it wouldn't be brown and crispy right now."

With a snort, he shoved her shoulder. "My house is fine. It just needs..." He opened the door, only for it to snap off its hinges. He grimaced when he found himself holding the door made of tree bark, almost his height. He often had to duck through people's doorways. Including his own. "A little work."

"It has always needed 'a little work.'"

Bastien gave his friend a mock frown, and when he attempted to flick her nose, she ducked out of reach. "I did a fine job hollowing out my own tree home. It looked great."

"Sure, it did. *Before* you got your hands on it."

Her laughter evaded him as he attempted to kick her in the back of the knee, but she ducked into the charred home. A laugh accompanied the roll of his eyes, and he followed after. And...*autumns*.

What a disaster.

Black soot stained nearly every inch of the dying tree. Tables were piles of ash. The stairs were unrecognizable, now fallen through like the fragile remains of a firepit. The acrid stench of soot stung his nostrils with every inhale, and he barely held back a cough. His eyes watered, but no amount of open windows could possibly save what was left of his home.

He scanned what used to be a kitchen connected to the front room within the enormous tree, now unrecognizable. And when he turned toward the stairs, he ran smack into Ashryn.

"Oof!" she said, her sooty hands on his chest. She grimaced after leaving two black prints behind and began dusting his shirt off.

He raised an eyebrow high. "So, are we on again or still off?"

She stopped her fussing to stare up at him. The woman was taller and stronger than most other females in Attleglade. He didn't know anyone who could swing a battle hammer as fast as she could *and* maintain a deadly accuracy. "Do you want to be on again?"

He shrugged and stepped away, kicking a charred piece of wood that he thought might resemble a chair leg. The tree groaned a weary sigh around him, slowly dying with little reprieve from its internal injuries. He shouldn't feel bad for a tree. He really shouldn't. But it hadn't deserved this.

Three times!

Ugh. He was the worst caretaker of trees. His father, on the other hand... Bastien was a great caretaker when it came to him.

Putting his worries at the back of his mind, he smirked as he ran a hand over his long, white hair he usually wore back in a bun. "I wouldn't mind a quick tumble in the woods."

She moved far too fast as she snatched the shoe from her foot and threw it at him. He barely managed to dodge its trajectory and watched as it smashed into what used to be a bookcase. The ashy structure crumbled to pieces at the impact.

"Watch it! That was my favorite bookcase."

"And now it's your favorite ash pile."

"Ha!" He grabbed her hand and pulled her close until she bumped into him again. She met his smirk with one of her own. "I take that as a 'no' then."

His friend's smile softened. "Someday, we have to stop this."

"We agreed until someone better comes along. For both of us."

Their friendship was a strange one. Not even his father understood it. Autumns, some days he didn't understand it himself. Laughing. Flirting. Sometimes something more. But never any feelings. At the end of the day, Ashryn was his best friend. He enjoyed spending time with her. They did nearly everything together. Inseparable. But not actually in a coupley kind of way. But sort of, yes, at the same time.

"You'll be waiting a long time then." Those brown eyes lit up with amusement. "You'll never find someone else."

They cringed at the same time.

"Oh, Bastien. I'm sorry. I didn't mean—"

"It's fine." He dropped her hand and scratched his nose to cover up the devastation in his expression until he managed to pull a grin from the deepest ravine of his soul. It didn't matter that he was only twenty-two. He hated that any type of future wasn't possible for him, including one that involved a wife and children. "I've made peace with it."

Except, he hadn't.

If his father, the chief in name only, ever left the settlement, the man would be killed. Bastien would never leave his father here by himself and, therefore, couldn't leave.

And it was against the law for a half-breed like himself to marry and reproduce in Attleglade. He would be either banished or killed, along with his family. Someday, when his father died, Bastien would be killed shortly after to end their bloodline of chiefs and start another. Of course, he couldn't let that happen. He just had to bide his time until then. And then he would figure out what to do.

The pity in her eyes told him she didn't believe him.

"You are more than just a half-breed," she insisted.

"But I'm not. You know as well as I do that there is little for me here." Friends. Family. A future. Ashryn was his only friend, alongside a few hesitant acquaintances. Aside from his father, he'd have nothing if he lost her.

How pitifully sad.

At least she was a good friend.

He stooped to pinch a page that used to belong to a book and rubbed the soot between his fingers. He should be angry about losing his home and many of his belongings. But instead, a pit of sadness welled within him.

"They will kill her," he murmured, glancing up at his friend. "That girl."

He grimaced and hunched his shoulders. He should have escorted the Ember Fae to safety himself, despite her being the enemy. She couldn't have been more than twelve years old. No child deserved to die in the feud between faekind.

"There is nothing you can do."

But wasn't there?

"I gave her more time to live by bringing her back to the settlement. I can't help but wonder if I should have just let Gael kill her in the forest to give her a swift death." He swallowed as he stood. "Now, they might do something terrible to her. What if they torture her?"

Ashryn didn't refute him. Rather, she gnawed on her lip and stared over his shoulder. "Killing her would likely bring Ember Fae retaliation. Surely, the council is smart enough to let her go."

Yet they shared a look, neither believing the council smart enough to make *any* rational decisions. No one except his father. But his father was wise enough to keep his mouth shut lest they maim anything other than his legs.

"Pardon me," someone said at the charred doorway, followed by a cough. They spun around to face the Attleglade messenger. "Bastien, the council has sent for you. They expect you to arrive within the hour."

With a dip of his head, the man disappeared, leaving dread in his wake.

"Ash." He ran a hand over his face, the icy dread climbing his body until it settled in his chest. "What if they know what we did?"

More specifically, when they—mostly him—had snuck his sister into the Glades to enter the sacred healing pool in secret. If anyone found out, he would be punished, likely with a swift death. But he would deny Ashryn's involvement to his very last breath if he must.

"They don't," she reassured with a hand on his arm. "It's been months since Nyana was here. If they were to find out, they would have done so by now."

"I hope you're right." He blew out a long breath, steeling his nerves, and then he resumed his teasing grin. "Save a tumble for me later?"

Her second shoe flew at him, but he ducked out the door before it made contact, his laughter filling the stuffy, burnt air.

But then he sobered as he made his way through the settlement. Enormous trees towered over him. Vibrant green grass and rich brown earth greeted each footfall. The scent of smoke lingered in the skies, blocking out the usual crisp forest air. Most Forest Fae with white hair and brown and green clothing ignored him as he passed, while others stared at him distrustfully.

Ashryn was literally his only friend. Although no woman would dare have an open relationship with him lest they get dragged down to his level, a few had been willing to keep involvement with him a secret. At least until they got scared. Their fear of getting caught with a half-breed fae often sent them running.

But Ashryn… She was the only person willing to love him publicly. If only in a friendly manner. She stayed by his side through the hardships and happy times. He never should have crossed that line with her. He regretted it. But he also didn't because she meant the entire world to him.

Even if they had no romantic feelings toward one another despite trying to unsuccessfully develop something a year back.

As he neared the meeting house, an uneasy sense of dread climbed his spine. It was one of the largest trees within Attleglade, hollowed out to create a dwelling but also living and breathing just like the other tree homes.

Two average guards standing on either side of the door leading into the meeting house instructed him to shed all his weapons, a standard procedure, before they permitted him entrance. At first, his eyes needed to adjust to the dimmer light. But then he took in the crystal sconces on the walls lighting up the large room, the rows of benches carved straight from the tree, and the long table at the front of the room…

…housing the entire council of seven.

His father, Emeric Dalena, sat in a wheelchair, situated in the middle of the council and acting as presiding chieftain. Unlike Bastien, his father's white hair was cropped short, accentuating his silver eyes and the stern yet worried wrinkle in his brow.

Father had fallen in love with a Sun Fae, and breaking almost every rule known in Attleglade, he had run away to marry her. Together, they'd raised his older sister Nyana and himself, at least until the council had found them and threatened Father to return as Chieftain...or die.

Bastien still remembered the sobbing goodbyes as his father had taken him back to Attleglade with him, and his sister and mother had stayed in the sun kingdom of Heulwen. They hadn't been able to come with them to the forest. Because his mother had been an outsider, and Nyana had looked too much like a Sun Fae to be accepted in Attleglade.

His fists clenched as he recalled the day the council had pinned his father down as he'd screamed, stealing his magic and maiming both of his legs just for trying to visit Nyana years after.

The anger fueled him as he looked into each of the council members' eyes, remembering why he trained and fought and played by the rules.

Because one day, he would kill them all.

"Bastien Dalena," his father said in a stern tone despite the warning flashing in his eyes, a warning for him to be on his guard, "do you know why you have been called to the meeting house today?"

Despite the anger crawling through his blood, he adopted an easy smile, his face relaxed, all while he seethed inside. "For my rotation change, I assume."

The council member he liked to call Cranky Cricket because of his creaking knees held up a small item, and Bastien narrowed his eyes in an attempt to discover what it was.

His blood froze over, and his stomach rolled.

"Can you explain what this is?" The elder held up a hairpin no larger than his index finger. But it was no ordinary hairpin. Upon closer inspection, Bastien recognized the elegant metal bend, a flawless shimmering gold, as Cranky Cricket turned it between his fingers.

He would be a fool to claim a lack of knowledge. "Well," he shrugged, "it looks like it is Sun-Fae crafted in design."

The man nodded slowly, eyeing him with suspicion. "It is. And the only Sun Fae to walk Attleglade's forests was your sister and her family months ago."

Father's stare burned with warning again, as if he, too, felt a predator in calm waters.

"And? It probably fell out of her hair. Or one of her daughters' hair."

"We found it in the Glades. *Inside* the sacred healing pool."

Shite!

Somebody would get killed over this, whether it be him, his father, Ashryn, or all three of them. Their survival depended on his ability to lie. And if that didn't work?

He swallowed as he realized all his weapons were with the guards stationed outside. He couldn't fight all six of the elders with only his hands *while* protecting his father.

He was in so much trouble.

"And?" he tried again, adopting another smile. He even added a faint snort to the mix. "Are you telling me *Nyana* would have been able to sneak past an entire village, two vigilant and armed patrol guards, brave the rickety bridge, and bathe in the pool? Only to do it all again on her way out?"

He sat on the arm of one of the benches to portray a more nonchalant appearance as he swiveled his gaze toward Grumpy Grasshopper. "You, yourself, said we have the best defenses of any Forest Fae settlement out there, second to none. Even the Ember Fae. An outsider unfamiliar with the settlement would never have been able to accomplish the feat."

Stinky Socks raised a suggestive eyebrow. "Unless she had help."

Bastien's mouth fell open in mock disbelief as he pointed to himself. "You couldn't mean me. What do you think? That she would fit under my shirt?"

Quiet murmurs echoed throughout the meeting house as the elders turned to one another to discuss. Bastien vaguely heard someone whisper that the tale sounded incredulous to begin with, but Cranky Cricket still didn't appear convinced.

The man's wrinkles deepened with a scowl. "The hairpin ended up in the pool *somehow*. Listen to me, half-breed. You are on thin ice. If I discover your involvement in any form, you will be punished. Do you understand?"

He dipped his head in acknowledgment as his pulse raced with unbearable heat in his veins. "I understand."

"Good." Cranky Cricket stood, his knees screaming out in protest as they creaked. "You are dismissed."

Bastien didn't dare spend another moment lingering in the room when even a second longer could mean his or his father's death. He moved toward the door at a leisurely pace despite how his body longed to flee. The guards returned his weapons, and he strapped them on his person as he walked the remainder of the way to his father's house while paying extra attention to the boughs above. The patrol guard often spent their time in the trees, and he didn't want any of them to surprise him.

Finally, when the large, sturdy structure of his father's home loomed over him, he opened the door and ducked inside.

His heart continued to race as he pressed his back to the wall and closed his eyes. Any day at any time could mean a brutal death. He was only buying time. He knew that. But how much remained?

Minutes later, the door opened again, and he tensed, fingers reaching for one of the many knives on his belt.

But the squeak of his father's wheelchair relaxed his tense muscles, and his hand fell to his side.

The door shut behind his father, and for several long moments, they stared back at each other in the dim light of the tree. At least until his father touched one of the crystals in the sconces, lighting up the main floor.

Bastien had recarved new sconces into the walls after his father's "accident" to allow him to reach them in his chair. The only thing not wheelchair-friendly were the stairs leading to the upper floor to his own space. Now that his tree had burned down, he reckoned he'd have to start sleeping here again.

"I can't keep living like this," his father finally said, hands shaking from the ordeal. Bastien watched as he wheeled himself to the kitchen, poured himself water into a cup made from animal bones, and downed the entire thing in seconds. "If you die, I will have nothing left."

Releasing a long breath, Bastien sat on one of the stools beside the counter, also carved straight from the tree, and rubbed his face with his hands. "There is no other way to live."

What more could he possibly say? There was no reassurance to give. No hope for a brighter future. Nothing could change the fact that they both lived on borrowed time.

After a long pause, his father waved his cup at him. "You need to leave in the dead of night. Get far, far away from the settlement. Go somewhere they can never find you."

"I won't leave you."

"I *beg* you."

"No."

His father slammed his cup onto the table, water sloshing out of the sides while fury blazed in the man's silver eyes. "Why won't you see reason? They are so close to finding out what you did, and when they do…you're a dead man."

"And if I leave, *you're* the dead man."

A long sigh followed his words as his father hung his head and stared into his lap. He said nothing, even as Bastien waited and waited. And waited. Heartbreak lived in each of his father's frown lines around his mouth, his sallow face telling of a man whose spirit had died long ago when Bastien's mother had died of heartbreak after their separation.

"Don't do it," his father finally murmured, still staring into his lap.

"I wasn't planning on leaving, like I said."

Slowly, the other man shook his head. "Don't break the Ember Fae out of jail. I know you, Bastien. You stick your nose where it doesn't belong and take risks that will get you killed one day."

"She's just a *child!*" Bastien smacked the table with his hand, and the tree groaned as if protesting his treatment of the living structure. "I've seen far too many heads roll, far too many bodies dangle, and I refuse to allow her to become one of them."

His father closed his eyes and sighed again, rubbing his temples with his fingers. "Then you better prepare to run. Because you will be on the top, if not the very first, of the suspect list when the child is discovered missing."

"I'm not leaving you."

When his father lifted his head, he and Bastien stared each other down in a glaring battle of wills. A long time ago, his father had taken risks in the name of love. Why couldn't Bastien take risks in the name of goodness and justice?

"You cannot choose both," his father finally answered as he wheeled past him and maneuvered himself onto the cushions sitting on top of the wooden sofa, leaving his wheelchair within reach. "I attempted to long ago, and I lost the most precious woman in my life. Don't make the same mistakes I did."

Silence filled the tense atmosphere as his father brooded, and he fumed. He clenched and unclenched his fists as he debated whether to argue further or drop the subject. In the end, he could do neither and therefore left the tree house with an exasperated huff, slamming the door shut behind him.

The tree groaned again, and it almost seemed to shake its branches, as sunlight managed to sneak through the thick boughs overhead.

He fingered the knives on his belt as he stormed toward the training grounds. He needed to release his steam, and fighting was the only way he knew how to do it.

Besides, he needed a clear head if he was to figure out how to break the fae child out of the jailhouse.

THREE

*S*eraphina!

Pri's cries for help still echoed in Seraphina's head days after she first realized her little sister had snuck away from home, and she didn't know who to kill first—her sister, the damned Forest Fae who had captured her, or the entire Attleglade village. Because if anyone killed the child she had helped raise since birth, there would be hell to pay.

And plenty of it.

She reached for the Ember stone hanging around her neck and clasped her long fingers around the cool, smooth surface. Seeking. Searching.

Nothing.

The communication between them had gone cold, which likely meant Pri had shattered her stone. Not enough remained to keep the communication strong over a great distance.

Fear crawled up her spine that her sister may already be lost. But she batted it away with the same hand she swiped at an overhanging branch with.

Her eyebrows drew together in concentration, her semi-translucent, leaf-like, emerald-green wings draping down her back as she hopped onto a log stretching across a raging river. Her bare feet created no sound in the dim light of early morning, her movements muffled further by the coursing water. All the while, her gaze carefully scanned the area for enemy fae.

But if someone attacked her, she was ready.

She fingered the blow-dart gun tied to the sash around her waist, stashed with a variety of darts ranging from poison to sleeping powder to vivid hallucinations and everything in between. Two daggers lay sheathed on the band strapped around her right upper thigh, barely visible under one of the two long slits of her dark turquoise dress. Most of her legs showed through the slits, as well as most of her arms. She was unarmored, exposed, yet the black scales on her hands, feet, shoulders, outside arms, and outer legs protected her.

A fierce breeze tugged at her clothing and pulled her long black hair out of her tie. She didn't dare let her guard down for a single second, not even to secure her hair.

The breeze settled when she hopped down from the log on the opposite side of the river, her feet landing on plush pine needles. She paused to listen to her surroundings.

Birdsong lifted into the skies above. The river rushed by behind her. But what lay in front of her?

Her jaw set as she tightened her fists. If a single white-haired fae crossed her path, she would show no mercy.

She kept to the shadows of the forest, moving swiftly as she weaved through the tree trunks. But knowing the Forest Fae often kept watch far above, she flitted her wings, her body momentarily as light as air before she silently landed on a thick tree branch. Far above the forest floor, the branches created a winding path of their own from tree to tree. Perfect for watching, sneaking, and catching the enemy before they caught her.

The Forest Fae possessed keen hearing, especially the patrol guard who traveled the forests day in and day out. The Attleglade Guard was vigilant, skilled, and ruthless. One well-aimed arrow could ground her. For good.

Dusk settled in the sky, which cast shadows around her as she crept forward as slowly as she dared, relying on her wings to camouflage her with the forest leaves. The shadows jumped and danced with each lift of the breeze, and she moved along with them.

Scuff!

Seraphina halted in her tracks and tipped her head to the side as she listened to her surroundings. Faint birdsong. A distant river. Rustling leaves.

But then a dagger made of bone swiped at her head, seemingly from nowhere. She ducked beneath the attack and drew her own dagger, striking against the other weapon in a lethal dance of blades.

She found herself facing a tall woman with white hair, most of the strands hidden beneath a saber-toothed cat skull ensemble. Fierce brown eyes glared at her behind wicked, sharp teeth.

"You had no chance of sneaking into our territory, Ember Fae," the woman growled as she struck again.

Seraphina blocked the attack and snarled back. "I never intended to. Rather, I planned to fight through each and every one of you."

"Fat chance of that."

The woman withdrew a second dagger and attacked again with a ferocious spin that forced Seraphina to retreat a few steps along the thick branch they shared. She unsheathed a second dagger of her own and fought back. When the woman proved herself a strong fighter, she clenched her jaw. The patrol guard always traveled in groups of two to six. Another would show themselves, and she preferred to be long gone by then.

With renewed determination in each confident step, she changed fighting styles and jabbed forward repeatedly. The fae woman managed to keep up with each of her strikes, but the attacks forced her backward until her back rested against the tree trunk behind her.

"I am growing tired of games," Seraphina hissed. "Get out of my way."

She jumped backward as she reached into the pouch on her belt and fisted a pinch of black powder in her palm. With a gust of breath, she blew the powder into the woman's face.

The Forest Fae breathed in sharply before blinking sluggishly as her body swayed back and forth. Within moments, her body tipped precariously to one side, and she wasn't able to catch herself as she slipped off the branch and fell the hefty distance from the tree branch to the ground.

Thud!

The woman lay still, unmoving below.

"Over here!" a male voice shouted, and she cursed under her breath as she spotted the blur of three other Forest Fae wearing masks rushing in her direction. She had hoped to avoid the patrol, at least until she spotted one of their tree dwellings.

No matter. She came prepared for such a fight.

The blurs of their movements quickened until she lost sight of two of them within the dense foliage. She sheathed her knives and reached for her blow-dart gun from her sash. Knowing the Forest Fae expected her to use her poison darts, she pretended to fumble with tugging it free and even allowed herself to take a hit.

One of the fae smashed a fist into her stomach, and she doubled over with a grunt. He moved close enough to stab her with a dagger. He swiped at her, but she flattened herself to avoid getting nicked by the blade. She pulled a dart from the quiver, and thrust it into his thigh.

A curse escaped the man's mouth as he, too, swayed from the poison's influence. Unlike the woman before him, he had the good sense to jump while his legs still worked, latching onto the tree with his arms, and slid the entire distance to the ground before he keeled over, breaking his mask upon impact with a boulder.

Two more.

Too late, Seraphina heard the rustle of leaves above her moments before a fae jumped on top of her and kicked her forcefully with both feet. She cried out at the impact between her shoulder blades. The momentum kicked her off the branch she stood on. Her dart gun flew out of her hands and landed somewhere in the bushes below.

Wind whipped at her hair as she fell, a surge of panic engulfing her with her scapula momentarily stunned. However, she managed to flip over in the air. Her wings spread out on either side of her, slowing her descent a good amount, but not entirely. She hit the ground on her hands and knees, the shock traveling through her wrists and up her arms to her shoulders.

She didn't have time to reflect on the pain because the two Forest Fae jumped down after her. She rolled out of the way of another woman attacking with her spear and dodged when the man team-attacked her with a bone blade. The tip of the blade scratched through her armored shoulder, and she hissed as blood ran down her arm.

"Surrender or die!" the fae man with the snake skull mask cried as he jabbed forward with his blade once again, but she thwarted the attack with one of her daggers.

Seraphina smirked. "You are not capable of killing me."

She spun blindingly fast as she kicked the woman in the stomach, causing her to stumble backward. The man lunged with his blade, nearly piercing her wing, but she managed to avoid the hit when she completed her spin, grabbed him by the arm through his momentum, and pulled him toward her.

And then she kissed him.

The fae man grunted in surprise and tried to pull away, but she jumped on him and latched her legs around his waist, causing him to stumble backward with her weight. The embers in her core stirred as she called upon her magic. Her entire body heated as if she were on fire, burning hotter, hotter, hotter.

And then she breathed flames through his mouth and into his lungs.

He screamed as he ripped away from her. She jumped off him, darting in the opposite direction just as the remaining female fae threw her spear. A second scratch cut swiftly across her leg and embedded itself in the trunk of a tree in front of her.

With a swift tug, Seraphina pulled it out, spun around just as the woman charged at her with her knives drawn, and thrust the end of the spear into her belly.

A look of shock crossed the woman's face before her knees buckled, and she fell to the ground in a heap.

Finally! The way was clear to—

Shouts in the distance caused her to clench her jaw until her mouth ached. She rushed in the direction where her blow-dart gun had fallen, and after sifting through rows of stiff, sharp foliage, she located it within the center of a bush. Thorns scratched her hands as she pulled it free of the barbs. But the shouts and voices drew closer, becoming louder by the second.

She swore under her breath and darted the way she'd come, only to hide behind a tree with large vines climbing the thick trunk. Her heart thundered against her ribcage as she spotted six more patrol guards darting in her direction through the boughs overhead.

She folded her green wings over herself, camouflaging her body with her surroundings and attempting to control her labored, panting breaths. Taking on four patrol guards had been difficult enough. Facing another six would exhaust her resources and put her in danger of losing her sister altogether.

Therefore, she needed to find another way into Attleglade.

And fast.

FOUR

"Ash!" Bastien gasped. His eyes widened as he spotted the limp figure lying on the ground below, her saber-toothed cat mask lying haphazardly beside her while her limbs were tangled beneath her.

He leaped the distance from the tree to the ground, stomach clenching and wind whipping at his clothing until he transferred his weight from his heels to his toes and rolled into the fall to keep from injuring himself. He unfurled onto his feet and dropped to his knees beside Ashryn.

Eyes closed. Pale face. Bruised cheek.

He took her by the shoulders and shook her all while his chest tightened. Although he knew he should face the threat that had managed to take down four trained patrol guards, his eyes glazed over, attention focused on his friend.

"Wake up," he begged, shaking her again and gently slapping her cheek. "Wake up!"

"Stop slapping me," she protested weakly, eyebrows scrunched together and eyes squinting as if the light was too bright.

A sigh escaped him, and he carefully helped her sit up as he assessed her for damage. She didn't protest as he bent each of her extremities in search of broken bones and inspected her scalp for bleeding or bruising. Nothing seemed to be broken, but she sported plenty of bruises.

"What happened?"

He glanced up to find half of the other patrol members seeing to the wounded and the other half scouting the vicinity. A couple of them glanced their way as if waiting for her answer.

Ashryn placed a hand to her head and took several deep breaths. "She was like nothing we've ever faced. She was fast and cunning and...angry. She acted alone and wore no armor."

"She?" His lips pressed together. "You don't mean..."

"An Ember Fae." Ashryn winced once again. "But she didn't look like the others. Not quite."

"What do you mean?"

His friend skimmed a finger over the side of her face from her temple to her cheekbone. "She had tiny horns on her face and scaled skin."

All at once, the entire forest seemed to hush as fear spiked in his blood. Judging by the tension in the air, the others made the same connection. "They sent the Ember Queen." He ran a hand through his hair as disbelief shrouded his vision. "And she was alone?"

Ashryn nodded. "Two knives, a dart gun, and some sort of poison powder. She used nothing else. Not even her fire magic."

Bastien sat back on his heels as he stared at Ashryn, hardly able to comprehend the new threat they faced. The Ember Queen was rumored to be powerful, able to harness the very power of a volcano if she commanded it.

If the queen was here, Attleglade was doomed.

"Bastien!" Achille shouted, waving him over to where Tobie sat propped up by two patrol guards. The man's breaths escaped as wheezing rasps, each sounding labored and pained. He appeared fine on the outside, but his lips...

They were tinged black with white flakes huffing out with each breath.

"He was burned from the inside out," Achille explained as he spread a clear salve across his lips. A healer in Attleglade would be able to do more. Or the Glades if an Elder permitted it.

"How is such a thing possible?"

"I don't know. I've never seen anything like it."

Tobie lifted a trembling hand to his face. His mouth opened, and several moments passed as if he were trying to speak. "Ki—" The man winced as the syllables wheezed from his mouth. "K-k-ki—" He sobbed, tears of pain trailing from each corner of his eyes. "Kiss."

"Autumn's glory," Bastien choked. "She *kissed* you? What kind of mother-blasted magic is this?"

Silence reigned in the forest once more before Achille gave the order to clear out. They each helped carry or support the wounded, and naturally, Bastien wrapped an arm around Ashryn's waist with her arm around his neck.

"You're not going to carry me?" Ashryn joked feebly.

He returned her jest with a disbelieving look. "You weigh a *ton*! Of course, I'm not going to pick you up."

She smacked him but winced as if the action pained her. "It's all muscle, you know."

"I know," he laughed. Despite his good humor, he glanced over his shoulder and immediately sobered. The Ember Queen was still out there somewhere, and the patrol needed to be extra vigilant.

Lest his entire village meet an untimely end.

Bastien exited the meeting hall with a pit in his stomach, hardly paying attention to his surroundings when his mind spun with everything the patrol had discussed with the elders within.

It was no coincidence that the Ember Queen had chosen now of all times to make an appearance in Attleglade. The Ember child they'd captured was someone important. Nathalie, another member of the patrol guard, had suggested she was the Ember Princess, but Cranky Cricket had shot her suggestion down quickly, as the princess had no scaled armor nor horns on her face.

But the good news? The council decided to delay her execution.

He glanced up the moment his thoughts returned to him, and he found Ashryn standing beneath a nearby tree, this one much smaller than the surrounding trees.

Exhaustion rested in her eyes and the sag of her shoulders. The previous bruise on her jaw was glaringly purple. But a fire lived within her expression, a determination to protect their people.

"How are you doing after your fall?" he asked as he settled in the space beside her.

"For the love!" she exclaimed, throwing her hands in the air. "If someone asks me that one more time..." But when he simply tipped his head and gave her an exasperated stare, she cracked a smile and shook her head. "Fine enough. Just some bruising. Nothing broken."

They shared a look of understanding. Being in the patrol guard was a dangerous occupation. Of course, Bastien didn't want his best friend to get hurt. But he also knew cautioning her against such danger would only spark an argument. Ashryn was one of the three females in the patrol guard, and she was blasted proud of it.

For several minutes, they watched the other Forest Fae go about their day, not yet aware of the danger lurking in the woods. Several booths in the market drew his attention. The smithee sold weapons made of metal and bone. A carver, a man unfairly blinded by the Elders and also a good friend of his father's, sold bone instruments and other trinkets. Behind another booth, a woman drew plenty of business with the mouthwatering aroma of her famous sticky buns, a mixture of cinnamon, butter, and some other spice he couldn't quite recall.

And then his thoughts shifted from the threat of the Ember Queen to his current predicament with the council.

He absently pulled out his small sketchbook and began etching the memory of the Ember prisoner onto the parchment the night he'd run into her in the woods. He stared hard at the page as he shaded in her hair, his eyebrows drawn as he contemplated all the ways he and his father could be punished for sneaking Nyana into the Glades. And all for what? A measly hairpin! Months had passed without questions or incidents. So why now?

His stomach tightened as he lifted his gaze to glower at Cranky Cricket, where he smoked his pipe outside the village hall. He couldn't possibly have found out earlier and only decided to play his cards now.

Right?

Beside him, Ashryn whistled.

He glanced from her grinning face to the new Forest Fae named Sylvain, who was visiting from Albrasia, the snowy region of their territory. The man was likely in his late twenties with straight white hair reaching the top of his shoulders with the top of his hair pulled back in plaits. A serious note rested in his hard eyes, and he carried himself confidently and showered himself in a wide range of weapons. In that regard, he and Sylvain were much of the same.

"Who's the new fae?" she asked. "I haven't seen him around."

Raising his brows, he once more scanned the newcomer from his white hair to his silver-tipped boots. "You're into *that?*"

"Who wouldn't be?" She eyed the fae while biting her fingernail, casting a coy glance at his turned back. "He's *gorgeous.*"

Bastien rolled his eyes. "His name is Sylvain, one of the five Ancel brothers from the snowy regions. He transferred from their settlement to ours. He's new on the patrol guard."

"Oh really?" She blatantly ogled him again. "Sounds like we'll be working closely then."

"Not too closely, I hope."

She snorted. "You jealous?"

"As much as anyone would be getting their casual tumbling partner taken away."

They stood in comfortable silence, one born of years' worth of trust and friendship. Ashryn was his best friend, yes, though he wondered not for the first time what would happen when a serious relationship would inevitably drive a wedge between them. Sure, they'd both had a few flings, but one of those flings was bound to become permanent.

At least for her.

Ashryn broke the silence first as if attuned to the direction of his thoughts. "Do you ever wonder who our someone better will be?"

"All the time."

"Me too."

She glanced at him from the corner of her eye. "But I'm more concerned about you."

He shrugged one shoulder. Secretly courting as a half Sun Fae-half Forest Fae was one thing. Marriage was another. "I've already accepted that something serious isn't for me."

"Why give up?" However, she already knew why because they'd had this conversation several times already.

"To marry, I'd have to leave the forest. I can't leave my father, and I can't take him with me." Besides, leaving the forest was deadly for him, something he didn't want to mention to his friend. Despite the trust between them, he still kept a couple secrets of his own.

Silence reigned over them again, but this time it was a heavy, contemplating silence as he thought about his future. Or lack of.

Ashryn inhaled sharply, her hands flying to her hair to smooth it down. "He's coming this way! Oh, autumns. I forgot to bathe today. Do I stink? How does my hair look? By the autumn star, I look hideous with this bruise."

Bastien chuckled. "You stink like a silver goose. Your hair looks ghastly. And your clothing is rather unflattering."

She elbowed him hard enough to knock the air out of him. "Oof!"

"Good afternoon," Sylvain said hesitantly as he approached, his hand gripping and releasing the hilt of his sword and a strain of nervousness in his rigid posture. His gaze moved from him to Ashryn, lingering a little longer on her. She blushed under his stare. "You must be the chief's son, Bastien."

He nodded. "And you're the new patrol guard recruit. We don't often get transfers to these woods."

The man shrugged, once again glancing at Ashryn. "Dire times call for dire actions. We cannot allow more of the Ember Fae to destroy the sacred woods. Several volunteers from our settlement came to help defend the territory."

Tension crackled through the air. Not awkward but filled with heated glances and hopeful intentions. Bastien barely resisted rolling his eyes as he squeezed Ashryn's shoulder, urging her forward a step. "I don't believe you two have met. Sylvain, this is my good friend Ashryn. She is one of the patrol's best." Heat could have sizzled in the air between them with the intensity of their stares. "I'll see what strings I can pull to pair you two up for your first patrol here. No one can teach you the ropes of our settlement better than she can."

Sylvain nodded and finally broke eye contact with her. "I look forward to it."

After the man bid his farewell and disappeared from sight, Ashryn released a whoosh of breath and fanned her face with her hand.

"Huh…" he started teasingly. "I think he likes you. Though, I have no idea why." When she tried to elbow him again, he laughed and twisted out of reach. "See you tonight, Ash."

"But we're not on again," she hissed as she glanced around them to make sure no one heard his comment.

"I meant for patrol. We're taking the new transfer out for training, sooo…best to bathe. You really do stink."

She scowled and threw a pinecone at him. He dodged, laughter trailing after him. But when he passed the prison tree where the Ember girl was being held captive inside, his good mood instantly vanished.

His quiet footsteps slowed. His mouth puckered in a frown. The air around him silenced while his gut tightened with dread. Children shouldn't have to die in the feud between Ember Fae and Forest Fae. The thought created an ache in his soul.

The prison tree towered over him, its long brown trunk reaching high and disappearing into a plume of green leaves. The base itself was as large as a cottage, hollowed out into a livable dwelling like many of the trees in their settlement. On the outside hung a signpost carved from the hip bone of an elk with a star-like etching to differentiate the tree as a prison.

He took one step forward and paused. The girl was none of his business. She would die at the gallows just like many before her, and he could do nothing to stop it.

Yet…

Internally, he cursed himself as he glanced over his shoulder to find Forest Fae going about their day, no one paying him any attention, especially with the excitement of receiving new visitors to Attleglade.

He took a deep breath and cursed his stupidity once more before opening the front door to the prison and slipping inside.

An eerie darkness stole across the front room where one of the prison guards sat in a chair, carving into animal bone. The man shot to his feet, his hand resting on his sword. At the sight of him, the man's shoulders relaxed, and his brows smoothed into a thin line.

"Bastien. I apologize. I'm a bit jumpy considering our current prisoner." The guard nodded toward the darkness on the opposite side of the room, and through the dim haze, Bastien barely made out the silhouette of the girl huddled in the corner behind thick bars.

"She's been questioned?"

"Multiple times. Won't say a word."

Then the only other option is death.

"How long will they hold her prisoner?" *You know, before they snap her neck.*

The guard shrugged. "Likely not much longer. I can't speak for the council. Although they want to delay her execution, Ember Fae never last more than a week behind bars."

The man's words rattled him, despite not being surprised by them, but he didn't let it show. Instead, he nodded casually toward the gloom of the cells. "I was there the night we captured her. Mind if I try to speak to her?"

"Go ahead. Just leave your weapons."

Bastien unhooked his spear from his back and set it on an empty table still attached to the living tree, followed by his chupacabra mask residing on his back, two daggers, five knives, and he finished with his bow and quiver of arrows. It may be a lot of weapons, but as a member of Attleglade's patrol guard, he was the first defense for his people should the enemy attack.

He snorted quietly to himself. He protected his people. He served them. Yet, he was still "that half-breed." It only served to prove that whatever he did would never be good enough.

When the guard returned to his seat, Bastien slowly approached the cells, his eyes quickly adjusting to the dim light.

His throat constricted.

The girl crouched in the corner, her entire body shivering from her shoulders to her legs to her tattered wings. Black hair draped over her face as if to hide her when she could otherwise not hide at all. She appeared small and frail. *A child.* This time, his people had gone too far.

He crouched on the opposite side of the cell. The way she slightly turned her body toward him indicated she was aware of his presence.

"What's your name?" he asked.

No answer.

His gaze traveled from her black hair to the magical brand on her wrist shaped like a cluster of leaves. As long as the brand marred her skin, she could not use her magic. It was pointless now. There was nothing left of his tree home to catch fire anyway.

"Why were you in the Glades?" he tried again quietly. "Was there anyone else with you?"

Will anyone try to save your life?

Although the fae girl didn't answer, she lifted her head enough for her hair to part to reveal the terror in her eyes. For several long moments, she stared back at him as if capable of sifting through his soul.

Her gaze darted to his feet and back up to his eyes. He followed her gaze to find red dust sprinkled at his feet. The texture felt coarse between his fingers, and he held his hand up to his face to get a better look. The substance felt like sand yet glinted like jewels.

"Her stone necklace exploded before we managed to snatch it," the guard explained across the room without looking his way. "I'll get around to cleaning it up after the execution."

Autumn winds, he swore in his head. *A child, you bastard! Do you not care?*

The Ember Fae met his eye again, her gaze intense. *Don't react.*

Her voice echoed in his mind, and he almost gasped. Almost. But he swore his pounding heart nearly gave him away to the guard across the room. How could the girl speak to his mind?

As if hearing his thoughts, she said, *Where I come from, a single Ember stone can be cut multiple times to allow each person in possession of a piece to communicate telepathically.*

In the hand she marginally opened, she revealed a scattering of red stone dust on her palm.

Not wanting the guard to become suspicious of their telepathic conversation, he asked, "Why did you come on our land alone without a weapon?"

No answer, of course.

You tried to let me go, the girl said. *I can't trust you, but you're the only one I have. Please. Tell me of a way I can escape. I don't want to die.*

It's impossible to escape, he answered with regret, hoping the girl could hear his thoughts. *If the guard doesn't catch you, someone from the settlement will. If they don't catch you, the patrol guard will.*

Her broken wings fluttered slightly before she winced. *Please. Out of the goodness of your heart, don't let them kill me.*

"Answer me!" he added gruffly before saying silently, *It's my life on the line. They will execute me if I'm found out, which, I promise you, they will catch me.*

Please, she simply begged again, her voice inside his head much quieter than before and filled with hesitancy and doubt.

He stood and turned his back to her to avoid looking into her eyes, but not before placing more stone dust in his pocket. *What's your name?*

Pri.

Only just barely holding back a sigh, he replied, *Give me two days. I'll try to find a way to break you out.* Oh, his father was going to kill him. But his conscience would not allow this death to transpire.

Thank you, thank you, thank you.

Instead of answering, he returned to his pile of weapons and began strapping them on once more. He allowed his words to escape as a frustrated growl. "I can't seem to get anything out of her either. Let's just hope she acted alone to save ourselves the trouble of tracking others down."

The guard grunted in agreement but otherwise ignored him as he left the prison. The first thing he'd usually do is track Ashryn down and tell her everything. But this time?

If he got caught, he would be killed, and he wanted his best friend in complete ignorance should his impossible task sink into the deepest mud puddles of Anadari.

He frowned as he thought of the Ember Queen once again. Perhaps if he managed to break the Ember child free, it would protect the people of Attleglade.

The very people who couldn't care less about him, but he wasn't going to allow that to stop him from trying.

FIVE

The woods were quiet.

But Seraphina knew it meant nothing, as no place in Attleglade was safe as long as the guards strutted about with their bone masks and their bone weapons. Any of them could lie in wait, jumping out at her when least expected. Unfortunately, she had no idea how many were in the Guard. At least ten, it would seem. Four of those ten were injured, likely unable to patrol tonight.

Her gaze scanned the ground below as she hopped lightly onto a branch in the waxing darkness. The rough bark brushed against the bottoms of her feet, but the sharp pressure didn't hurt against her scaled, armored skin. Several deer lazily passed by below, unaware of her presence above. She winced as their hooves crushed sticks and dried leaves. Even the smallest sound might give away her presence.

Sure enough, two Forest Fae leaped out of the higher boughs and dropped silently to the ground to investigate the sound.

Blazes!

She held perfectly still as she cursed their presence. After her fourth journey sneaking around the settlement, she realized it was surrounded by vigilant patrol guards. They knew she was here.

And judging by the number of guards she'd spotted within the past five hours, they knew who she was.

Silent fury clenched her fists, and she glared at the guards now moving farther away from her location. There was no way into Attleglade, at least none that didn't involve burning the entire village to a crisp. But she didn't dare risk the safety of her sister by attacking. Ironically, Pri was safer without her involvement. At least for the time being.

She clutched the ember necklace hanging from her neck and tried once again to reach out to her sister. *Pri. Can you hear me?*

Silence.

Even if Pri possessed pieces of her shattered stone, she was still too far away to communicate.

Her brows furrowed as she headed in another direction, away from the Forest Fae but closer to the settlement. After her hours of spying, she knew of one way to get what she wanted. It was a huge risk, but so was attacking the village.

Hold on, Pri, she begged silently as she fingered her dart gun. *Just hold on.*

"And he fell into the water!" Ashryn doubled over with laughter while Bastien scowled at her, arms crossed as they traversed through the dark forest in their patrol team of three.

"I would have won that skirmish had the rocks not been slippery beneath my feet."

Ashryn rolled her eyes and shoved him in the shoulder, and he pretended to stumble to the side as if her strength far outmatched his own sturdiness. "You just can't handle the fact that you were beaten by a girl."

With a huff, he turned back to his companions and gave Sylvain a mock pout. "She thinks the world of herself. She just can't handle the fact that I let her win."

She kicked the back of his knee, and he retaliated by grabbing her in a headlock and rubbing his knuckles along the top of her head until she shouted for mercy. When they broke apart, both of them were laughing after their bout of playfulness. He draped an arm around her shoulders and squeezed.

But then he froze when he noticed the uneasiness in Sylvain's expression as he eyed them. Bastien quickly dropped his arm. To outsiders, his and Ashryn's interactions likely looked a lot like flirting. But it was all in friendly playfulness.

However, if Ashryn was interested in the fae man, then he didn't want to do anything to discourage the relationship from progressing.

Bastien cleared his throat and took several steps away from his friend.

"What are the northern regions like?" he asked to recenter the conversation, all while he eyed every shadow that crossed his path. The Ember Queen was still out there. It was better to catch her sooner rather than later.

Or at least Stinky Socks said as much, quadrupling the patrol for the next week or more. But it would be unnecessary.

Because Bastien planned to break the Ember girl out of prison. Tonight.

"Snowy," Sylvain answered in a light accent. "By the end of each shift, my eyelashes would be coated in a layer of frost. My homeland is beautiful, surprisingly colorful despite the snow. But I do enjoy the cold quite a lot. I plan to return in a few months." The man cast a sideways glance at Ashryn as if gauging her reaction.

But her nervousness seemed to get the better of her when she didn't answer and instead wrung her hand over one of her knives strapped to her chest. She was getting nervous now of all times? Was she hoping to fail?

He clapped her on the shoulder. "Ashryn loves the winter. She complains tirelessly during the summer about the hot temperatures. But the snowy season? I caught her stargazing in the snow once."

"The cold was refreshing." She laughed, and the outer shell of her anxiety cracked at his jest. She glanced at Sylvain and held an arm around her torso, which revealed yet another shell layer. "I would love to visit Albrasia someday."

Sylvain perked up and delved deeper into the culture and traditions, especially when he had an enraptured audience. Ashryn clung to his every word.

Bastien hid his smile by glancing in the opposite direction to survey his surroundings once again. As the moon hid behind a layer of thick clouds, the way through the forest was almost indiscernible. Without his years of practice familiarizing himself with the landscape, he would have been lost.

Aside from the occasional patrol group crossing their path, the forest was silent. No activity other than hooting owls and a bubbling brook marred the stillness of the atmosphere.

They decided to stop for the night to eat supper and sleep, each agreeing to take turns for watch. Cranky Cricket wanted every group to patrol throughout the entire night. And, naturally, they needed to get sleep at some point while other patrols were awake.

He and Sylvain gathered firewood and sparked a fire while Ashryn laid out their bedrolls around the contained flames. The other two sat across from him with their backs against a log while he sat on the other side of the fire, cross-legged on his own bedroll.

Although he focused on adding sticks to the fire, he couldn't help but notice the way Sylvain shared his meal of dried elk meat and hard bread with Ashryn. The sight warmed his heart. But it also invited a pit of deep loneliness into his soul. If their relationship worked out, Ashryn would likely settle in Albrasia with the man.

And Bastien would be alone.

As if sensing his sobering thoughts, Ashryn lobbed a piece of meat at him, smacking him on the side of the head.

"Oops," she said innocently while she smirked. "I missed."

He threw it right back at her, but she caught it in the air. They both laughed, effectively silencing the bout of loneliness screaming for attention.

Sylvain glanced back and forth between them, the same serious expression from before. Instead of remaining quiet about the exchange, he motioned between Bastien and Ashryn. "You two don't have a thing, do you?"

He grimaced at his carelessness and met Ashryn's gaze across the fire. Her eyes silently pleaded with him, taking him by surprise. Of course, he knew she liked the man. But *like-liked*? They'd only just met.

He and Ashryn had agreed to a casual on-and-off relationship until someone better came along. Perhaps, after all these years, this was her someone better.

Once again, he grimaced to downplay their casual involvement in the past. "Me and Ashryn? Autumns, no. She's my best friend and will never be anything more."

"Ah," the man grunted, though Bastien didn't miss the faintest relief in the corner of his upturned mouth. "I see."

And when Sylvain turned his attention to his hard bread, Ashryn mouthed *thank you* to him. He simply replied with a genuine smile and slowly stood as he brushed crumbs off his pants. "I'm going to do another patrol round to make sure the area is safe before we settle down for the night. I should be back in..." He glanced between the two of them. "...an hour."

He wasn't shocked when neither protested against him being gone longer than he really ought to. He could sense when his presence wasn't wanted.

Making sure he carried all his weapons, he stepped out of the small clearing and walked straight ahead until the flickering light from the fire disappeared altogether.

Only then did his shoulders droop.

What kind of life was this? To forever be alone. Without a wife. Without children. Without a true purpose in life other than to follow orders and protect people who didn't care about him. A part of him resented his father for bringing him here as a child instead of allowing him to stay with his mother before her death. With his sister. Nyana had a great life with children and a good husband to care for her.

And him?

He had nothing. And he never would.

Because he loved his father too much to leave him.

Not wanting to despair over his lack of future, he focused heavily on his surroundings. He listened to the leaves swaying in the breeze. He studied each shadow and silhouette hiding in the darkness. And when he decided approximately an hour had passed, he followed the path back to the camp, dragging his feet on the ground to announce his presence just in case…well…just in case things were getting heated. Knowing Ashryn, they probably were.

The moment he entered the clearing, he chuckled at finding the two cuddled together. Their legs were tangled together, their bodies close as her head rested against his chest in sleep. Both breathed deeply with eyes closed, arms around each other.

He hoped for the best for them. He truly did.

"I suppose I'll take the first watch." He chuckled again and shook his head when neither answered. But then his eyebrows furrowed when he spotted something small protruding from Sylvain's upper shoulder. However, when he moved closer to inspect it, something sharp stung the back of his neck.

He hissed, hand flying to his neck. And slowly, his eyes widened as he plucked the sharp item out, only to study it in front of his face. A dart. It was an Ember dart.

He attempted to spin around, but his surroundings swayed with the movement. In one moment, he stared at a dark forest. In the next, his body crashed to the ground as his limbs failed him.

His tongue refused to work as he attempted to cry out. His body lay limp even when he tried to lift himself from the ground.

A flutter of wings jolted his heart into a frenzy, but no matter how hard he tried to thrash, no matter how frantically he urged his hands to reach one of the weapons attached to his belt, he could do nothing but lay still like a man trapped beneath a guillotine.

A breath of wind caressed his face, followed by the faint sound of footsteps swallowed by the pine needles littering the ground. And then suddenly, the noise ceased altogether.

His breath faltered in his lungs as he took in a pair of bare ankles and followed the path up to a slender calf and then a knee. Legs.

And then he looked into the face of the woman with the attractive, shapely legs. Straight, black hair tumbled over her shoulders. Black-red lips matched the hue of her hair. Light green eyes with an orange flame-like center stared down at him with hatred burning in their depths.

Oh, shite! His lips tried to form the words, but they felt numb and useless. An Ember Fae. Not just any Ember Fae, but the Ember Queen judging by the small horns protruding from the side of her face and the patches of black scales that adorned her body like armor.

The orange ring in her light green eyes flickered and danced in tune with the fire now crackling through her fingers.

He attempted to struggle away from her, but his body refused to obey him, and his lips remained motionless. Rather, he found himself eyeing the flames casually dancing across her skin. A weapon capable of immense destruction.

A single bare foot kicked him onto his back and pressed against his chest, pinning him to the ground. The woman leaned closer until her hair brushed against his cheek. Heat burned his ear as she traced the pointed tip with her finger.

"Not quite Forest Fae. Not quite Sun Fae. You're him. The chief's heir."

He might have laughed if his mouth could move, but all that managed to escape his throat was a strangled noise of mixed amusement and fear.

A grin pulled up on her red-black lips. "You are going to get me my little sister back."

Then she pulled a dagger out of the belt cinched around her waist.

The blade moved lightning-quick as she stabbed him in the shoulder.

Strangled agony caught in his throat, unable to escape in the form of a cry but rather an unflattering garble. Tears of pain leaked from his eyes, the only response his body allowed with the Ember Fae's poison inside him. Hardened eyes glared down at him as she pressed her fingers to his wound, inciting more agonized tears to trail down the sides of his face. Her fingers came back bloodied, which she promptly smeared across the grass beside him.

"Your friends can hear me." The weight of her foot crushed his ribs further before she addressed the other two. "If you want your heir back, you will exchange him for my sister in our territory on the Burning Cliffs. If you hurt or kill her before the exchange..." Now her foot ground into his wounded shoulder. A shout escaped as a garbled moan. The fire in her eyes danced with hate. "I will torture him. And then I will end his life."

With unnatural strength, she closed her fingers around his ankle and dragged him away from the others as if he weighed little more than a potato sack. He reckoned his blood smeared for several paces, at least until the fae woman spread her large wings and leaped into the air.

Bastien's surroundings distorted with a stomach-churning dip as he dangled upside down. She methodically weaved around trees and through tangles of boughs, a tactic he recognized as trying to lose not only their scent but their tracks as well should someone spot his drops of blood.

He fought against the poison in his body with all his might but lost in the end when it continued to render him immoveable.

After several minutes of flying, the woman dipped suddenly, and he released a slurred cry moments before they both splashed into a frigid river. The only mercy she showed him was holding his head above the surface as the water's icy claws dragged them downstream.

When his body shivered involuntarily, only then did she drag him back out of the river, down a grassy bank, and then stopped when they reached a small clearing. She dropped his leg and glared at him.

"Is my sister still alive?" she asked, black hair dripping with water to make it appear even darker.

His only response was a moan.

She sighed and knelt beside him. She unclasped the pouch on her belt, pulled out a smooth, black volcanic rock, and rubbed it along his head, face, and lips. His skin crawled with tingles, and then the numbness disappeared altogether. But only for his face.

"What in the blazes is wrong with you?" he coughed, wincing when the action tugged on the stab wound. "You did all this for the Ember Fae trapped behind the bars of our prison? I was her only ally. And now she has no one."

"Quiet!" she hissed, anger blazing in her eyes at the mention of her sister.

But if his lips worked, he refused to remain quiet. "What do you think the council will do? Trade her for me?" He laughed, ignoring the stinging pain shooting through him. "You made a poor bet on me. I'm half-Forest Fae. Essentially an outcast in Attleglade. They won't care to come after me."

"No?" She leveled a pointed stare at him. "That girl will. The one snuggled up with the fae male. I sense a deep bond between the two of you. She'll do whatever it takes to keep your life intact."

Curses.

Ashryn needed to stay away. "That *girl* has no romantic attachment to me."

The woman raised an eyebrow. "Did I say romantic? I don't believe I did. A strong bond of friendship will do just as well."

The woman smeared white powder over her palm and covered his eyes with her hand. He tried to argue against her touching him in any manner, but the protest died on his lips as his world suddenly turned dark.

57

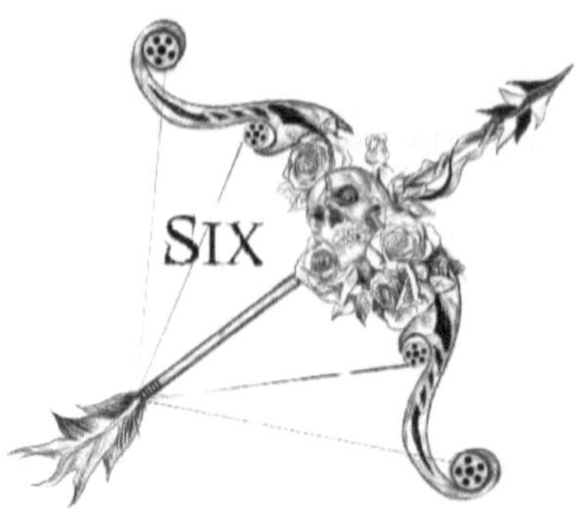

SIX

Seraphina stared down at her fae male captive, unconscious at her feet. Like all of the other Forest Fae, his hair was white, his tied into a knot at the back of his neck, bringing attention to the long, pointed ears on either side of his head. The man had a strong jaw to match his strong build, with an expressive nose and surprisingly attractive lips. His skin was tan, as if he spent a lot of time outdoors, a stark contrast to his hair.

Trading him for her sister was a huge risk, but she'd seen no other option when she hadn't been able to get past the patrol. Now Pri's life depended on a fae woman to go to the ends of the earth to rescue the heir.

She'd followed the group for an hour, watching them interact. The woman had obvious feelings for the second fae man. But it was as clear as moonglass that the heir and this woman had a history of a strong friendship…and a romantic past, no matter how much the heir wanted to deny it.

The heir.

Bastien Dalena.

Her lips curled into a snarl as she thought his name. She hated the man almost more than she hated anyone in Attleglade. How many people had she lost over a prideful war? All because the Forest Fae refused to share what was the Ember Fae's birthright?

But now?

They had gone too far. Would it truly have killed them to allow her sister into the Glades?

She only wished Pri hadn't tried to go at all…

Flashes of her perilous fall burst through her memory. Of Pri's limp, broken body. Her tattered wings. The weeks when she lay in bed on the cusp of death.

Flames flared between her fingers as heat boiled her blood. She wanted justice. She wanted revenge. It would be too easy to light the fae man on fire and watch as her flames consumed him.

The flickering light of her magic died, replaced by a chill as a brisk wind pulled at her damp clothes. Gooseflesh crawled up her arms, and she ignited her magic within her core to keep her warm in the cooler temperatures.

Bastien, on the other hand, began shivering in his sleep, his clothing soaked and damp strands of hair falling haphazardly across his forehead and cheek.

She wanted to stab him again. But she also needed him to live.

Grabbing onto his wrist, she dragged him farther through the woods, over lush pine needles, across rocky terrain, and through snaggly branches that caught onto his clothing and ripped small holes in his shirt and trousers. Aside from the howl of a wolf or the scrambling of a small creature in the foliage, she didn't notice any signs of pursuit.

However, she continued her journey until her body drooped with weariness. Her wings brushed against the forest floor, demanding she stop and go no farther.

And she obliged.

After her heaving breaths subsided, she sprinkled white dust over Bastien's eyes to wake him. He blinked sluggishly at first before his eyes snapped wide open when he spotted her. She barely managed to hold back a smirk at the discomfort pinched around his mouth.

"What did you do to me?" His words escaped as a nearly incomprehensible slur.

Instead of answering, she gathered firewood and stacked the branches neatly into a pile with kindling on the bottom. A flicker of magic sparked in her hand and caught onto the kindling, the growing light illuminating Bastien's flaring nostrils and his wide, distrustful eyes.

"Who are you?" he demanded.

"Why don't you take a guess."

His jaw clenched next, revealing the fear hiding behind his defiant eyes. "The Ember Queen."

"Mmhmm." She tossed sparks toward his face, and he flinched by squeezing his eyes shut. But the sparks flickered out before they managed to burn him. A pity.

"And your sister is the Ember Princess."

At the mention of Pri, anger burned within her. She crossed the space between them, latched her fingers around his shirt, and pulled his limp body up to sitting so he was eye level with her.

"Don't ever mention her again."

"Pri, was it?"

Seraphina shoved him backward, and he landed with a thump on the ground. The sound was eerie, like a dead body hitting the floor, but Bastien was very much alive.

"You never told me your name," he grunted, and she only wished she'd kept him unconscious. But he needed to eat to keep him alive.

She enunciated every syllable as she tossed smoked pheasant onto his chest. "Seraphina Nova. Otherwise known as the person who is going to kill you."

"I thought you planned to trade me for your sister."

"Of course. But I do want you to be somewhat recognizable when I'm done with you."

She felt his raw fury like threads of tension strung tight in the air. She rubbed her volcanic rock over his right arm from his shoulders to his elbow to his wrist and fingers.

The moment his arm regained movement, his hand darted toward his belt as if he expected to find his weapons there. She smirked.

"Looking for something? Surely you don't think I'm idiotic enough to allow a patrol guard to keep his weapons."

He glared. "What did you do with them? That was my favorite hunting bow."

"I discarded them in the river," she lied, her fingers playing with another pouch on her sash where she'd stored a smaller version of his belongings, shrunken using magic. "I figured the weapons you used to kill dozens of my people only deserved a watery grave."

Bastien's lips pressed tightly together as he leveled her with a stare. "You cannot possibly tell me your hands are clean. No one's hands remain unbloodied in this feud."

Unfortunately, he made a good point. No one enjoyed killing another person. But they did it to protect the ones they loved.

"Release me," he demanded. "I can break your sister out of jail, and then there will be no need for bloodshed."

"I'm afraid it's too late for such actions to be taken." Her fingers flirted with her knife as she imagined Pri lost and alone, cornered by the Attleglade patrol, and now hunched in a jail behind bars. If they harmed Pri in any way, she would burn down the entire village, even if she met her own end by accomplishing the dark deed.

Leaving her own people without a leader...

She clenched her fists and turned away from her enemy. "Eat. You might not get another chance until we reach our destination."

"What did you do?" He scoffed and threw the meat into the bushes. "Poison it?"

"Poison is my specialty." She moved closer until the hem of her dress brushed against his leg. "But I don't need to sneak poison into your food to do the job effectively." She leaned even closer. "Believe me, I can make your life a living nightmare with very minimal effort. And I'd enjoy it, too."

In a movement faster than her eye could follow, Bastien lunged at her with his one working arm and managed to grab her around the neck. The strength behind the attack took her off guard, and he took advantage of her momentary shock to flip her over, holding her against his chest as he tightened his arm around her throat in a chokehold.

She clawed desperately at his arm, but no matter how hard she tried to free herself from his grasp, he proved much stronger than her.

The ring encircling her finger pulsed faintly with the magic to make her stronger, but without sunlight to charge it, she was no stronger than the average woman.

Kicking and clawing quickly proved futile, and as black spots danced at the edges of her vision, her fingers desperately fumbled toward her belt. She spilled powder. She dropped a knife somewhere in the dirt. But then her fingers clasped around a small dart. She had no idea what was in it. The substance inside could give Bastien hallucinations, or it could kill him.

In a single movement he was unable to dodge, she thrust the dart into his arm as the light faded from her vision. Just as her arms drooped and her head fell to the side, Bastien's grip loosened on her enough for her to gasp in a breath of air and shove his arm off her.

She leaped to her feet and put distance between them, inhaling breath after rapid breath as she watched Bastien's body convulse in a seizure. Her hand flew to her aching throat. Disbelief trembled through her core. Had he held onto her for only a few more seconds, she would have died.

He was fast and strong. She wouldn't make the mistake of underestimating him again.

A gasp escaped the fae man's mouth as he convulsed, his body shaking and thrashing as if a demon possessed him. Even from his current symptoms, she had no idea what she'd injected him with.

At least until she glanced down at the dart gun strapped to her sash and realized what was missing. Although Bastien likely wouldn't die from what she'd injected him with, it was going to be a rough night for him.

As if to confirm her words, he stopped thrashing for only a moment as his eyes lurched wide open. His mouth formed an "o" shape as terror leaked from every facet of his expression. He inhaled deeply.

And screamed.

SEVEN

Tingles shot up Ashryn's arm as her body slowly regained movement. Agonizingly slowly. She itched to leap to her feet. She was desperate to reach for her weapons and rush after the Ember Queen. But judging by the dwindling flames several paces from her giving way to a dark forest, several hours had passed since the woman had taken Bastien.

Anything could have happened during that time.

A sob stuck fast to her throat as she spotted the blood smeared across the grass as if the victim of a murder had been stabbed and dragged away from the scene. She'd heard Bastien's grunts of pain, and it had killed her not being able to do anything about it.

How foolish she felt. She should have been watching out for the threat. Not flirting with a man she fancied.

Her fingers twitched, followed by her toes. Slowly, her body thawed out from its petrified state like an icy lake giving way beneath warm sunlight. Raw determination worked through her as she fought for feeling, for movement. Beside her, Sylvain stirred as if he, too, battled the poison in his body.

She begged another patrol to pass by overhead. She willed her voice to work to allow her to scream for help.

But her tongue was as numb as the rest of her body. And no one came to their rescue.

"Ash...ryn," Sylvain choked out beside her. A silent question. A pleading prayer.

She swallowed. And then swallowed again. Until her mouth thawed enough for her to speak. "I'm...fine." She attempted to clear her throat, but it only came out as a garbled grunt. "Are...you...hurt?"

When her neck thawed enough to move, she turned her head, only to realize she was resting heavily against him, each tangled up with the other. Despite the seriousness of their situation, her cheeks heated as she recalled the feel of his body pressed against hers, the taste of him on her lips. She'd never felt a spark with anyone like she did with him.

And it ached knowing she needed to throw it away.

The man shook his head when his neck seemed to work better than his voice. An impatient, desperate silence ensued as they both struggled for movement. First, her fingers moved freely, and then her wrists, followed by her arms and torso.

Her legs still felt heavy, and she didn't dare attempt to stand when she knew she might topple over.

"Please," Ashryn begged, turning to face Sylvain more fully. "Find another patrol. Tell them we were attacked by the Ember Queen."

Sylvain stiffened beside her, his white hair shifting slightly before resting at the top of his shoulders once more. "You are planning to go after him."

"Of course I am. I love him." She winced and shook her head, amending with, "Not in a romantic way. He is my best friend."

A hardness rooted within his eyes as he gazed at her with a deep intensity as if studying the very workings of her soul. "Tell me you feel nothing for me."

The demand took her aback. She inhaled sharply, eyes wide as she pulled away to better take in the rigidness of his shoulders, the intent in his eyes. "I cannot."

His jaw jumped as he reached for her hand. "Then I will come with you."

A breath trembled from her lungs as she stared back at him, trying to figure out if he meant what she thought he meant. "I will be damned in this society. And I will damn you with me."

"Because you plan to take the Ember girl."

She nodded mutely. What more could she say? Bastien's life meant more to her than her acceptance in Attleglade. But she refused to bring Sylvain down with her. "I must do it tonight while the patrols are still occupied and their attention is diverted from the settlement. While everyone is still asleep." She squeezed his hand in earnest. "You must protect yourself. I will not strip you of your career, of your home, just to appease me."

Sylvain ran a hand up her arm and cupped the side of her face. "I cannot pretend we don't have an *étincelle permanente*."

"What does that mean?" she whispered.

"In my culture, we use the term to describe a spark we find with our soulmate. I have found it with you, and I am not willing to let you go." He moved closer until she spotted a dark gray freckle in his silver eyes. "I am with you to the end."

The declaration thrummed through her like a steady beat of a drum. They'd known each other for less than a day, and already he was willing to go down fighting by her side.

And she knew she couldn't deny the spark between them. She'd felt it the very moment she laid eyes on him.

They linked their fingers as they wobbled to standing, her legs still heavy but working, nonetheless. Whatever poison the Ember Queen had used on them was potent. She feared what she might have used on Bastien. What she might use in the future on him.

When their legs worked enough to walk without tripping, they crept through the forest and back toward the settlement. She knew every patrol group. She was aware of their rounds, where they would stop for the night when their shift ended, and where they wouldn't be as well. She followed her own path through the trees, successfully evading each patrol.

And then they stopped at the edge of the settlement, the village quiet aside from the occasional footfall as the two inner patrol guards made their rounds. Sneaking past them would not be easy. She was ill-prepared, but there was no other choice in the matter. It had to be now before anyone found out what happened to Bastien.

She turned to Sylvain and found his eyes in the darkness. "Are you sure you want to help me?"

He nodded. "I am."

Blowing out a long breath, she nodded toward the prison where the Ember Fae was being held captive. "I will need to break in, subdue the guard, and escape with the girl." She reached into her pocket and pulled out the dart that had pierced her own neck only hours ago. Although she didn't know if anything remained inside, she was going to try to use it anyway. Besides, the "evidence" would hopefully absolve her and Sylvain from blame.

"What is my part?"

In an equally hushed tone, she replied, "Raise some hell. We want this to look like the Ember Queen's doing. It will be the easiest way to try to get out of this intact."

"You want me to light up the woods?"

Ashryn released a shaky breath and nodded. "Create a distraction. But try not to hurt our own. I will grab the girl and leave quickly."

They gazed at each other for several long moments as they both came to the same conclusion—they might not see each other again for a long while.

He grasped her forearm, his expression filled with fervor. "May we meet again soon under the frost trees of Albrasia. It was a pleasure to know you."

Her heart trembled as she caught his meaning. The people of Albrasia married beneath the frost trees in the citadel. Somehow…the idea seemed fitting. And she looked forward to when they could continue exploring their courtship in the future.

If they made it out of this heist alive.

Ashryn waited several more minutes for the guards to move farther away from the prison, and only then did she slink forward while Sylvain started in the opposite direction. She didn't know how he planned to start a fire, but she trusted him to follow through.

Chirping crickets filled the summer night, the only backdrop to her furtive footsteps. Taking a deep breath, she glanced around her to make sure no one was watching before she grabbed the door handle and slipped through a small opening. The guard leaped to his feet and drew his weapon.

Drat.

"Thank the autumns, you're here!" Ashryn gasped, and in his confusion, the guard lowered his weapon and tipped his head to the side as he studied her.

"What are you doing here? No visitors allowed until sunrise."

She shook her head, trying to feign a frantic urgency with her wide eyes and gaspy breaths. "The Ember Queen is here."

On the opposite side of the prison, a sharp inhale pulled her attention to the dim interior of a barred cell, followed by a faint rustle as the silhouette of a young girl moved closer to the bars.

The guard's expression turned serious. "The queen is here for the girl."

With a nod, Ashryn gestured to the cells. "The council has ordered us to kill her and dump her body in the river for the queen to find."

The guard's mouth flickered with an obscure grin as if excited to finally do something other than sit and guard an enemy fae. He strode toward the cell, and in the man's momentary distraction, Ashryn leaped forward and jabbed the dart into his neck.

He gasped and reactively swung his sword at her. She jumped backward, the tip of the blade slicing through her sleeve but not making contact with her skin. Her heart pounding wildly when he didn't faint immediately, she drew her daggers and eyed the man's longer sword. Regret pinched her mouth. She should have stabbed him in the neck rather than rely on the flimsy dart that was likely empty. Avoiding bloodshed was high on her priority list.

But Bastien was worth every drop shed.

Within the small space of the prison, Ashryn struggled to dodge the man's heavy blows. Each time he swung at her, she barely managed to evade the attack even when her training as a patrol guard far outmatched the man's experience on prison watch.

Parchment scattered at the slice of his blade. The tree groaned when the man's sword sliced through its timber. But then he cornered her in front of the Ember girl's cell, the exit far out of reach. He brought his sword down fast and hard, and she crossed her daggers to block the attack. However, his strength outmatched hers. Her arms gave out, and she crumpled to the ground.

Ashryn scrambled for her weapons when her mind spun in disorienting waves. The guard lifted his sword above his head to prepare for another attack. But before he brought the fury of his weapon upon her head, red dust shimmered directly above her and into the man's face.

He breathed in the dust and choked on the air. His sword dropped to the ground as he hacked and coughed, clutching at his throat as he struggled to breathe. The man stumbled backward over a chair and crashed to the ground in a heap of broken wood and flailing limbs.

But after a few more moments, he lay still and silent.

There was no doubt about it. He was dead.

"What did you do?" she gasped as she spun around to face the Ember girl.

A handful of red dust lay in her palm as she eyed Ashryn with distrust, and not wanting to contend with the deadly red dust, she slowly backed away toward the lifeless guard and checked for a pulse.

Nothing.

"Did Bastien send you?" she asked in a small voice rather than answering her question.

Ashryn stared at the girl. "Bastien?"

She nodded. "He promised to break me out tonight. Did he send you?"

Her mouth fell open as she gaped at the girl, trying to make sense of her words. Had Bastien truly promised such a thing? Of course, she knew her friend had lamented over the Ember Fae's inevitable demise. But he never kept secrets from her, especially not one of this magnitude. Why had he left her in the dark? And what other secrets was he keeping?

She shook the thought away and fumbled with the keys on the guard's belt. Five keys jangled together as she wrestled the ring off the man and cautiously approached the cell. The girl continued to stare at her warily, but she didn't blow the red dust into her face.

The fear of getting caught in the act lodged a lump of trepidation in her throat as she tried each key in the slot, continuously glancing toward the closed door. All was still, and a part of her worried Sylvain had either fled his dangerous task or got caught by one of the patrol guards.

But until someone caught her, she would continue to hope.

Finally, a key fit into the lock, and the metal door swung open. "Hurry," she ordered the girl. "We must get you to your sister."

"Why?" the girl gasped as she stumbled out of the cell on clumsy legs as if her head spun from the blow she'd received days ago. "Why are you helping me?"

Ashryn's eyes hardened as she glared at the Ember Fae. "I'm not helping you. I'm saving my friend. Your sister captured him and is threatening him with death unless I trade him for you."

The girl's mouth fell open as she reached out to steady herself against the cell bars. "I don't understand. He was trying to save me."

"Rotten luck, I suppose. Bastien attracts misfortune wherever he goes. The poor sap."

Quietly, she crept toward the door and opened it just enough to peek outside. Chickens clucked softly nearby, and a rooster perched in one of the trees overhead, stretching its feathers against the waning darkness of early morning. The creature squawked in annoyance as a patrol of two passed by in the boughs, quick and agile and on their guard.

A breath escaped her lungs as a defeated tremble. They would never clear the forest without someone discovering them. Sneaking the girl out was an impossible task.

But she vowed to risk her life trying anyway.

"Stay close to me. You won't have a chance of escaping this forest alive if you stray from my side."

The girl nodded, eyes wide and shoulders stiff. "I will never fly again, will I?"

She glanced toward her wings and winced at the tattered membrane. Beautiful with an emerald sheen but completely useless. Only then did she realize the girl must have entered Attleglade territory to heal her wings in the Glades. It was a shame she got caught.

"I know very little about your people," she replied as she turned her attention to the outside world through the crack in the door. "On my signal. One…two…

But before she finished her countdown, a loud explosion pierced the air, a shockwave slamming into the door and trying to force it open. Orange and yellow flames burst upward from across the village in a wild dance of hope and determination.

Ashryn spared no second, and she rushed outside with the girl on her heels, darting in the opposite direction while keeping to the shadows. Confused and fearful shouts echoed behind her as they ran, everyone's attention now on the plumes of smoke and fire instead of the fleeing prisoner and the traitorous fae who broke her out.

The guard's death is on my hands, she lamented.

But then she steeled her emotions against the man's inevitable death. He'd delighted in the chance to kill a child. It was unforgivable.

And for Bastien, the man's death had been worth it.

EIGHT

Bastien screamed.

Thick, barbed vines wrapped around his immobile body and squeezed, the thorns piercing his arms, his legs, his torso. And then they dug into his neck and face. Breath escaped his mouth in pained huffs, and when the barbs dug deeper, he screamed again. But instantly regretted the action when the vines shot toward him like tentacles bursting from the ocean. One of the vines entered his mouth, the others through his ears.

His jaw shattered. His lungs seized. Blood flooded down his neck and seeped into the coarse dirt beneath his body.

He released excruciating sobs as the vines tore his body apart. His legs. His arms. Then they ruptured his stomach, blood spurting in every direction.

He wanted to scream. He wanted to fight back. But all he managed to do was watch as unbearable heat flashed through his body. Hot, painful heat.

One of the vines dug through his open chest and cut his heart from his body, squeezing it in front of his face.

Fading…fading…fading…

Darkness pulled him beneath the waves of consciousness, but instead of the pain dispersing, agony continued to course through him like a curse that refused to break.

And then he started falling through the ground. No matter how hard he willed his broken body to clutch onto tree roots or fallen leaves, it refused to obey him.

He landed hard on compact earth before dirt rained over his head, burying him alive.

It covered his lower half and then his chest, followed by his face. Panic clawed through his open chest as he fought for breath. But the dirt was too heavy, and all he managed to do was choke.

Bastien gasped in a sudden gust of air, his chest heaving as his eyes snapped open.

His gaze darted around frantically as he tried to make sense of his environment. Forest trees surrounded him in the morning light, creating a protective barrier between him and the terrifying creatures lurking within the woods. The scent of earth and pine wafted beneath his nostrils with each inhale of breath. The pop and crackle of logs brought his attention to the flames billowing upward several paces away.

And behind those flames...

Green eyes stared at him, the expression behind them showing no emotion, only guarded emptiness. The woman's legs were crossed, her dress falling to the side to reveal the long slit that reached her upper thigh.

Weariness flushed through his body, and he glanced down to find himself still intact. His heart beat within his chest. His ears were no longer stuffed with vines. Breath entered shaky lungs and exited as tremoring rasps.

He was alive.

Warm moisture dripped down the side of his face, and he tried to move an arm to find out if it was tears or blood. But his body was once again completely immobile.

With his head turned to one side, more warm moisture dripped from the corner of his eye and over the bridge of his nose before plopping on the ground.

Tears, he decided.

And he couldn't stop them no matter how hard he tried.

"I thought you said you wouldn't torture me," he mumbled as a frosty breath escaped his mouth despite the fire billowing before him. Autumn lurked around the corner, and the nights were getting colder. His entire body shivered, whether from the images still haunting his mind or from the morning chill, he wasn't sure.

"You attempted to kill me," Seraphina replied after several moments of silence. "I think I was well within my rights to protect myself by any means necessary." Out of the corner of his eye, he spotted her holding up a silver and black woven band around her finger to the light of the sun. An onyx gem rested in the middle of the jewelry, soaking in the sunlight like wet hair desperate to dry.

"Of course, I tried to kill you." He coughed, flinching when he expected excruciating pain to jolt through his lungs. But it didn't. Rather, only a deep ache burned his shoulder. "You said you planned to kill me eventually."

The woman smirked. "No loose ends. I'm sure you would do the same in my place. Down with the queen, no? Or, in your case, down with the heir."

He snorted and turned his head away—the only thing he could move. The tears on his face turned with him, and he only wished he could swipe them away rather than put them on blatant display.

"You know nothing of our culture if you think they would let me sit in the chieftain's chair. I would meet an untimely 'accident' long before then."

Her hand dropped to her side as she returned her stare toward him. "Then I'm glad I didn't ransom you to the council but rather to your friend." A glowing amber surrounded the pupil of her eye like the fire separating them. "At least you matter to *someone*."

He remained quiet instead of engaging her. It seemed she was intent on dragging him the entire way to the Burning Cliffs because she refused to give him even an arm back. And if she was planning on stubbornly keeping him as her limp potato sack, then he planned to annoy her until she snapped.

By any means necessary.

He adopted an air of levity rather than one of hatred and disdain. "It's a shame you have to resort to dragging me across the entire forest. It would be much easier if you at least gave me the use of my legs."

The woman tipped her head and gave him a pointed look. "And offer you a chance to either run or strangle me with your thighs this time? I'd be a fool."

Smoke drifted into the sky, followed by a *hiss* as she extinguished the flames, and he watched them with longing as they disappeared. The frigid morning chill seeped into his crusty, bloodied clothes. The wound must not have been deep. Otherwise, the bleeding would have been worse. But he still feared infection. If he could only find an antiseptic plant to help ward it off...

But as he glanced around the immediate vicinity, he found nothing other than a few clusters of wildflowers and several patches of vines climbing through the earth and scaling the trees.

He tried to shy away from the vines, but his body refused to move.

With a silent glare, Seraphina grabbed his ankle and dragged him forward with a grunt. "This ring hasn't charged all the way. You are heavy."

"I assure you," he replied with a wicked grin, "it's all muscle."

She stopped momentarily to glower at him before she kicked him in the side.

"Ow!"

"I recommend you remain silent. No one wants to hear you speak."

Pine needles softened the blow of getting dragged, but the jostle of each of her steps pulled on his wound. He winced but refused to allow her to witness the agony in his expression. Instead, he lifted his lips in a merciless grin as his gaze dipped to her backside, the shape flattering beneath the fall of her dress, nearly hidden behind green wings he could have mistaken for enormous leaves.

"At least I have a good view from here."

Seraphina's head turned sharply until she glared fiercely at him over her shoulder. She dropped his leg, which landed with a *thump* on the ground, circled him, and grabbed him by the wrist instead. She stooped and yanked him closer to her eye level until he noticed the faint sheen on her otherwise matte black lips.

"I am flattered you enjoy my figure so much." Her lip curled in a snarl. "Now you get to admire the dirt."

Again, she yanked his arm, pulling painfully on his shoulder socket, before dragging him once more. Thankfully, his back found reprieve from the harsh patches of rocks and wood chips. But his legs weren't so lucky.

He sighed heavily as he stared at the passing trees, bushes, and small pockets of running river water. The leaves were starting to take on a redder hue, signaling the start of fall. As he turned his head in an attempt to glance over his shoulder, he noticed the sway of Seraphina's wings once more. They, too, took on a more reddish tint as if changing with the seasons.

Incredible.

But absolutely annoying.

He scoffed as he challenged the stare of a tree in front of him, slowly moving out of sight. "You rely heavily on your potent poisons. In a real fight, you would never have beaten me."

"In a real fight, hmm?" It seemed as if she couldn't help but respond to his goading. "I bested four of your own. I'm quite certain in a real fight, you would be on your knees, begging for mercy."

"Give me back the use of my limbs, and we'll find out for certain."

Something like a mixture of a huff and a laugh reached his ears. "Do you want me to stab you again? Quiet."

His lips twitched as he realized she was close to her breaking point. Only a little more provoking... "So you are saying without your powder, your poisons, and your magic, you can best me in hand-to-hand combat? I'm quite sure I proved you wrong, and I only had one arm available to me."

Her fingernails dug into his wrist. "Do you never stop talking?" the woman growled. "I'm getting tired of hearing you yap."

"The only way to get me to stop is with your mouth."

Faster than he managed to blink, Seraphina dropped his arm, jumped on top of him, and held a dagger against the soft flesh of his throat. The orange in her eyes danced like fire, burning with her anger and seeming to grow hotter through her hand and into the blade pressed against his neck.

He held perfectly still, afraid the smallest movement might cut him.

The fae woman's wings flared out on either side of her, both a magnificent and terrifying sight when paired with the fire of hatred literally burning in her eyes.

"Not another word from you, Bastien," she snarled. "You don't need your lips in order to be *mostly* intact. Tempt me one more time."

"So you *do* know my name," he rasped.

She shoved his shoulders and stood, tucking her blade into the strap on her thigh. His gaze followed her movements. The way her bare feet padded against the soft earth. The way her calves flexed when she stood on her toes as if absently navigating the terrain. The way the black scales on her shoulders rippled against the sunlight, matching the sheen of black in each strand of her hair.

Why did his worst enemy have to be so blazing beautiful?

He hated it.

He hated *her*.

The burning hatred flared within his chest when she snatched his limp wrist from the ground and dragged him forward once again. The Ember Queen had almost killed Ashryn. That was unforgivable. On day one of patrol training, they were taught how to fall. Starting from a lower branch until they learned from the very top of a tree in the Attleglade forest. If Ashryn hadn't received such training, she likely would have been dead or so broken as to be hardly recognizable.

But she'd only received a few bruises. She was both lucky and skilled.

He frowned when he realized Seraphina hadn't killed *any* of the four Forest Fae she'd battled. She'd only wounded them enough to be completely incapacitated. And after witnessing the aftermath of the fight, he realized she was skilled enough to have ended each of their lives.

But instead, she'd fled the scene and allowed each of them to live.

"What do you want?" he asked, feeling silly for addressing the trees rather than her…um…back.

"You know what I want."

Pressing his lips together, he shook his head but winced when the action tugged on the tender skin around his stab wound. "You are the queen. You have the power to stop this bloodshed. Why don't you?"

"Because once upon a time, the Glades were a part of our territory."

Of course, he already knew as much. But it still didn't make sense. "Aside from the healing properties of the water, why in autumn's name would you want to live there? It gets cold. I doubt you could manage without the heat."

"Ha!" She snorted. "Do you have no idea that the Glades rest directly beneath a dormant volcano? It did not used to be so cold in Attleglade. But it is still our land, our birthright."

Bastien was startled at the newfound information. A volcano? Did no one in Attleglade know about it? Because he certainly hadn't.

But then he rolled his eyes. No doubt Cranky Cricket and his lackeys were well aware of what the Glades were sitting on.

A painful silence filled the next stretch of time as Bastien fought against the throbbing ache of his shoulder and the churning hunger of his stomach. However, he wasn't about to accept food from his enemy and suffer through a stomachache so terrible he'd only wish for death. Seraphina could poison him, paralyze him, and give him hallucinations, but he refused to accept any of her torture willingly.

"Are we there yet?" he asked in a tone that was sure to annoy the autumns out of her.

Her only response was to dig her fingernails into his wrist.

"No, truly," he continued. "Are we? For some reason, I can't see the path ahead."

"You know very well how long it takes to reach the Burning Cliffs," she hissed. "You battled our people there. We lost twelve men and women in that battle. One of them was a ten-year-old boy."

A dull throb pulsed through his chest for the ceaseless bloodshed on both sides of the war, which had lasted for decades already, starting long before he'd been born. "My job is to secure our borders. Not venture out of our territory and take lives. Besides, you can't possibly think you can drag me for another two days."

"Watch me."

The woman possessed a stubborn spirit. He'd give her that.

They reached a stretch of rocky earth, and Bastien braced himself for the accompanying pain along his legs and backside. The rough terrain was as unforgiving as he expected as rock after rock dug into his skin. But his clothing protected him for the most part.

Seraphina dragged him until she struggled with pulling his weight through the forest. Their journey slowed astronomically, and her breathing escaped as labored puffs. Whatever magic kept her strength up, it seemed to be fading and fast.

He glanced up at the skies overhead only to find thick clouds blocking out the sunlight, the gray hue promising rain in the near future.

At last, she dropped him and gasped in breaths, perspiration dotting her hairline. But otherwise, he noticed nothing more from his poor vantage point. He listened to the whispering winds and the rustling of leaves along the forest floor. Unfortunately, he found nothing out of the ordinary, especially not the presence of another fae.

So far, he'd had the privilege of moving his head and his lips. He wanted to save the opportunity to shout for help.

He frowned at the thought. The Ember Queen was a fierce adversary. Would he only be risking others' lives if he screamed for help?

He inhaled sharply as Seraphina suddenly hauled him upright with her arms beneath his shoulders and balanced him against a tree. His eyes widened as she pulled a large rope from what appeared to be a small pouch on her belt.

"What are you doing?" he growled as she started to tie him to the trunk.

"Sleeping." She pulled the rope tight, and he winced when it tugged on his wound. "I will take no chances of your escape. And I wouldn't scream for help if I were you. This part of the forest is dangerous. You never know what beast you might attract."

Bastien rarely ventured this far into the woods, especially when it neared Ember territory. Discomforting heat spiked in his blood and throbbed in his temple as he glanced about. Of course, he didn't want to run into any dangerous beasts. But he also didn't want to find himself anywhere near the border of the woods.

His heart thumped painfully, the deadly claws of warning squeezing his chest with each beat. He was close to the border. He could feel it. And if he crossed the line...

He swallowed.

Falling over dead would help no one. But giving the Ember Queen the very secret to kill him? He wasn't sure if he should risk giving her the knowledge.

When he returned his attention to Seraphina, he found her lying down with her knees tucked beneath her stomach and her arms folded to give herself a pillow for her head. Her wings draped over her back like a blanket, and her eyelids were closed.

Unable to help himself, he snorted. "There is no way you actually sleep like that."

Her only response was to turn her head away from him.

He sighed deeply. "Can you at least push me to the side? Something is digging into my back. Probably a rock."

She ignored him.

"Fine. Pretend I don't exist. I will sing at the top of my lungs until you acknowledge me."

Her wings twitched. Otherwise, no response.

He inhaled a deep breath before belting out to the skies, *"I once knew a fairy who walked on the moon. She danced, and she sang, and she drank from a spoon—"*

All too suddenly, Seraphina smashed her palm against his mouth to silence him, her eyes two glaring daggers that could rip out his soul. She moved closer until only a breath separated them. And usually, when he might offer a jest or lick her palm to get her to retreat, he remained frozen as he gazed back into her eyes. His heart beat a disjointed rhythm, his pulse skipping through his veins as he stared back at her.

She was beautiful. Deadly. And far more alluring than he was comfortable with. The irrational, dumbstruck side of him wanted her to lower her hand and kiss him with lips that likely tasted of fire and smoke. The rational part of him fled entirely, especially when her thumb slipped on his mouth and brushed his bottom lip.

Seraphina's eyes widened as she jumped backward, a haunch to her wings as she avoided eye contact. "I told you to be quiet," she hissed, turning away from him entirely.

The woman settled back down in the same position as before, and his gaze couldn't help but glide over her smooth hair, the bare skin around her wings, her flattering form. He asked the one question plaguing his mind since his capture.

"Why did you come alone?"

Her eyes appeared far away, her fingers clenching into fists before she maintained a neutral expression. "Because I ordered my people to stay behind. It was the only way I knew how to save Pri."

She said nothing more as she turned away from him again with finality. But he supposed her logic made sound sense. If it had been him, he would have preferred going alone or with a small, trained group to keep out of notice.

In a quieter voice, he continued his tune, *"Her hair was like gold, and her eyes were like gems. She plucked up the sun as if right from the stem..."*

"What is the song you are singing?" Seraphina asked, and he found he held her captive attention as she shifted from her knees to her side, her knuckles resting beneath her head.

"A folk song." He grinned. "About the most beautiful woman in the valley."

All too quickly, her mouth dropped into a frown, and she tossed a pinecone at him. It thumped him in the chest.

"What?" he groaned, giving her a mock pout. "You don't want to hear the rest? I think I'll end it with something like..." He raised his voice and belted out another verse. *"There were flames in her eyes and more flames in her hands. And when she got mad, she would tighten my bands!"*

"Bastien!" She kicked his foot and glared at him, but he didn't miss the mirth dancing in her fiery eyes. "Stop singing."

He opened his mouth to start another verse but froze when a deep groan shook the entire forest around them and turned his blood cold. Seraphina shot to her feet, both of them staring in the direction the sound had come from.

Wind picked up the leaves around them, scattering them about the forest floor as if a storm brewed overhead. The temperature dropped exponentially in the space of seconds until a chill raked up his arms and dotted his skin in gooseflesh. His limbs began shivering despite his lack of control over his own body. His teeth chattered enough to rattle his skull.

But still, he watched the path behind them with hard eyes. His hands itched to reach for a weapon. Frustration clawed at him when his body refused to obey his command to move.

The wind ceased moving, and all was still on the path as the leaves settled with the faintest whisper of warning.

Frost crawled along the ground, curling its fingers around scattered leaves and weaving around vines and branches. The temperature dropped further until frosty breaths escaped Bastien's mouth.

He dared not utter a sound, and behind him, neither did Seraphina.

Yet, the frost continued to claim their surroundings little by little, climbing over fallen tree logs, squeezing the life from once-thriving grass, and creating a stinging, brittle texture to each breath he drew into his lungs.

A screech loud enough to pierce his ears filled the skies, and an icy mist curled around the translucent figure standing on the path ahead of them, wearing a cape of ethereal frost and a hood of translucent mist.

The creature extended a long, misty claw and released another death-defying screech.

Fear jolted through Bastien's body when he remembered a similar creature killing eight patrol guards only seven years ago before they'd managed to bring it down.

Ice wraith.

NINE

"Blistering fire!" Seraphina cried as she hurried to untie Bastien from the tree. He tipped over without the additional support and dropped to the ground with a thud. She leaped in front of him just as a fierce, blizzardy wind shot toward them. She held her arms out on either side of herself and created a wall of fire to combat the chill, knowing just one touch of the ice wraith's magic could freeze them entirely and kill them quickly.

Her fire battled the unforgiving blizzard, and she grunted with the effort it took to keep herself from being thrown backward at the force behind the attack. Hair whipped around her face. Wind tugged at her clothing. But she remained steady.

"Unfreeze me!" Bastien shouted through the shrill wind, a tinge of panic in his voice.

"No!" she grunted back. "I can't have you running away. I need you!"

"You can't need me if I'm dead!"

For a moment, she entertained the idea of cutting him loose from his paralyzing bindings. But either he would run away and leave her to fight the wraith by herself, and she would lose her bartering piece, or he would join her fight and then lodge a knife between her shoulder blades the moment she turned her back to him.

She ignored his pleas and instead decided to face the wraith on her own. When the blizzard ceased momentarily, she dropped her wall of fire.

And gasped.

Snow piled up around her, filling her surroundings as far as she could see. The white powder climbed the base of trees. It layered the ground up to her ankles. And it successfully blended the ice wraith against the white backdrop.

She spun around, eyes searching for the faint shimmer of a translucent robe. But no matter how quickly her eyes searched the vicinity, she could not spot the terrifying creature.

Which meant they needed to run while they still could.

But as she eyed the man lying wide-eyed on the ground, she huffed out a breath of long-suffering. As much as she hated to admit it, the Forest Fae *was* solid muscle. Transporting him would either be so difficult as to slow each of her steps, or he would crush her entirely.

Bracing herself against his inevitable weight, she grabbed his arm and stooped enough to duck beneath him as she barely managed to lift his top half. Her legs protested as she draped his large frame across her shoulders and held on tight. Her legs shook, threatening to collapse. But raw determination pushed her forward.

Labored breaths escaped her mouth as frosty puffs as she trekked through the snow, cursing her bare feet. She rarely wore shoes in the spring and summer. But winter was another matter entirely. Her feet could outlast sticks and thorns and every manner of rough surface. But they were not impervious to cold.

She moved off the path in an attempt to make herself more difficult to locate. Between the barrier of trees, she noticed a hillside nearby. Knowing she couldn't carry Bastien for long, she started toward the large mound of earth with the intention to hide behind it, or if she was lucky, within it.

"You must pierce the creature through its eye," Bastien murmured as if he, too, felt its presence somewhere nearby.

"What do *you* know?" she gasped back, struggling to walk, let alone speak, when his weight crushed her spine. "No one can kill them. Only discourage them from continuing their fight."

"They're near impossible to kill. But I've done it once."

Her heart skipped at the startling realization. Although she'd never fought against Bastien in a fair fight, he was strong, fast, and smart. Though, she refused to declare it out loud.

Despite her desire to remain hidden, she couldn't help but argue. "In order to pierce it through the eye, you must allow it to get close. Too close. You would die long before you defeated the wraith."

"Not unless you have impeccable aim with a bow."

Ah, yes. The bow she'd *discarded*. Of course, it had been a lie on her long list of misdemeanors, but she lived by the mantra to never throw something out if it still offered some use.

A shrill screech grated against her ears and reverberated across her forest surroundings. It seemed to come from everywhere and nowhere at once.

She cursed under her breath.

"I am *not* going to die like this!" Bastien hissed near her ear. "Let me fight. Then you can continue dragging me around like a ragdoll to your heart's content."

"And give you a chance to run?" she shot back. "I need my sister back, and I will kill you a thousand times over if I have to."

Another snarl, this sounding closer to her ear than before. "I get it. She's your kin. But you are acting like she's your *baby*."

Seraphina clenched her jaw when he hit the nail on the head. Rather than entertaining him with the truth of the situation, she remained silent. Which seemed to confirm his words in his mind because he inhaled sharply.

"She *is* your baby! No wonder. It all makes sense."

"Shut it!" she cried but winced when her voice betrayed her location to the frost continuing to climb the trees. The blizzard started up again, fiercer than before, as it battered against her relentlessly and threatened to tip her over beneath the fae man's weight.

"Oh, now you've done it." Bastien tsked. "We're both gonna die, and you're too stubborn to give a man his legs back!"

Wind howled in her ears, nearly drowning his words, though she wished it would have. The blizzard thickened around her and distorted the path ahead. Her steps faltered when she couldn't tell if she stood upright or started tipping to one side.

Outrunning the creature would be impossible. She had to face it or die trying.

The snow thickened further until it brushed against her calves. She didn't dare set Bastien down lest she lose him entirely in the powdery chaos.

Slowly, she turned in a circle in an attempt to locate the wraith, but no matter how hard she squinted through the haze, the shimmer of its energy evaded her.

A sudden screech rushed past her, and she barely managed to side-step to avoid getting hit. She gritted her teeth, breathing heavily as her gaze jumped about. She reached for her magic but quickly realized that in order to use it, she needed both of her hands free. Either that or try to breathe flames from her mouth. She'd never attempted such a feat, but now she wished she had.

"In case we die," Bastien said, his own voice quavering, "I just wanted you to know that it was an honor to hate your guts."

"The feeling is mutual," she grunted. "I only wish I could have ended your life rather than for a wraith to finish the job for me."

"Such a charmer." A wry chuckle shook against her back. "I think I'm swooning."

"Swoon later." Another grunt as she stumbled beneath his weight but barely managed to find her footing. "We have a wraith to vanquish."

The wraith screeched behind her, and she barely caught a glimpse of its translucent hood as it rushed past, leaving a trail of frost in its wake. The frost caught onto her elbow and climbed her arm. Her magic melted it within a few moments until it dripped off her as droplets of water, turning into ice pellets before hitting the ground.

This time, as the wraith flipped through the air, it gave her no warning as it rushed toward her. She was unable to dodge in time as it crashed into them, Bastien taking the brunt of the attack and throwing them both into the snow.

Frigid cold rushed over her as the snowy powder engulfed her entirely. She gasped and spluttered as she broke the surface, but then her heart fell to her toes to find that Bastien had disappeared beneath the white plume.

"No, no, no!" she gasped.

But the wraith didn't allow her to sift the contents of the snow in search of him because it rushed toward her once more with a death-defying screech. Its icy fingers raked the air just over her arm and barely missed scratching her.

Her jaw set as she leaped backward and unlocked the floodgates of her magic. Fire shot up her arms, causing the wraith to pause as if contemplating whether to fight or flee.

Seraphina didn't give it a chance to decide as she shot a ball of fire from her left hand and then her right. The first attack shot over the creature's head. The second smashed into its translucent shoulder, and the wraith jerked backward as if the fire had hit a solid being rather than one made of icy wisps.

"Die!" she shrieked. "You are greatly inconveniencing me, and I want you gone!"

She shot a few more balls of fire, and with each attack, the wraith dodged, moving closer and closer until it floated only a few paces away. The creature tried to grab her with long, sharp fingers at the same moment she unsheathed a dagger from her thigh strap and stabbed at its face.

The wraith screeched just as its hand grazed her arm, burning her with its frigid touch.

She dropped to the ground as otherworldly pain shot through her arm. She focused on breathing. In and out. In and out. All while her fire magic combated the chill from spreading through her body.

Although the wraith disappeared, and she didn't know if she'd hit it directly in the eye, the blizzard continued to whirl quickly until she could barely see her hand directly in front of her.

Another wave of panic washed over her. *Bastien*! If she didn't find him, he might only have minutes to live.

"Bastien!" she gasped, frantically digging through the knee-deep snow to search the spot she thought she'd last seen him. "Bastien!"

When she couldn't find him with her hands, she resorted to using her entire arm as she swam through the bitter-cold substance. She desperately scanned the surrounding area in search of a single glimpse of him. But she only found white snow and brown tree bark.

"Blast your hair! Why couldn't you have red hair? Or black? Or even *blond*! White is the worst color in this scenario."

The faintest glimmer of distress echoed from within the confines of her Ember stone, startling her upright. It faded like the sound of a dying note until it disappeared entirely.

Just when she thought she might have imagined it, the same note of distress played but even quieter than the one before it. She latched onto the note and pulled against the thread. It wasn't Pri's distress, though it originated from her Ember stone.

Seraphina gasped when she realized it was Bastien. She lurched forward, following the thread, until she knelt beside the base of a tree and began scooping the snow away with her hands. The bitter cold gnawed on her skin and threatened to drown her within the prison of its icy fingers, but she ignored her numb hands and continued to dig.

Until she brushed against frozen clothing.

"Bastien!" she cried as she brushed the remaining snow off him, only for her heart to sink to the bottom of a cliff when she noted his pale skin, his blue lips, his frosted hair.

"You can't die on me now," she snarled. "I already told you that if anything was going to kill you, it would be me."

She grabbed his wrists and dragged him off the path and toward the small hill, barely visible through the blizzard, while glancing over her shoulder. The ice wraith could have suffered mortal wounds when seared with her fire or her dagger after fleeing, but it might still be alive. She couldn't afford for the creature to find them again.

Without the sunlight to charge her ring, the man's weight became too much of a burden. But the sight of his blue lips and frosted eyelashes gave her the strength she needed to drag him around the hill and into the small outcrop carved into the side by nature. The rocky ceiling sheltered them from the elements, but not entirely.

Bastien didn't move, not even to blink, as she knelt beside him and smacked his face to try to get him to stir. His eyes moved faintly to let her know he was alive and conscious, but if he didn't receive warmth soon, he would die.

"Hold still," she whispered as she climbed on top of him and straddled his waist. She almost rolled her eyes at how silly the demand sounded, as he couldn't move anyway if he tried.

Her insides trembled as she took either side of his face in her hands and met his eye. Her fingers shook when she knew he could see her, hear her, feel her. But if she didn't act, he would not survive.

She lowered her head and allowed her body to thrum with her fiery magic. The man's eyes danced as if panic rushed through his frozen veins, because she had no doubt he'd witnessed the aftermath of what she'd done to his friend.

She touched her lips gently to his, and instead of billowing her flames into his lungs, she allowed the warmth of her magic to slowly seep from her mouth to his, filling his lungs, fueling his body, giving him warmth.

However, she was not prepared for the warmth dancing in her own belly as she became painfully aware of every place their bodies touched, the strength of his jaw beneath her hands, the hardness of his belly where she sat, the frozen sweetness of his cold, soft lips.

Never in her life had she bestowed a kiss of embers upon a man, one that gave life instead of taking it away. Bastien was her first.

She broke away from him and next kissed his throat, allowing her magic to heat his frozen bones, his frozen blood, his frozen skin.

Carefully, she pulled on the leather strings of his shirt to loosen it enough to expose the smooth, hairless skin on his chest. Next, she kissed him over the heart, feeling with her lips the languid rhythm beating within. At her heating touch, it started to beat faster and with more purpose.

Instead of calming like she'd hoped, her hands trembled more. Not from the cold but from the entirely foreign sensation of kissing her enemy.

She removed her hands from his face and slipped her fingers into his, warming them with her touch. Magic coursed through her as it bounced and swirled within her, begging for more release. But she held it in and instead flared her wings on either side of her to trap the heat within.

Snow battered mercilessly against her wings, against her back, as she lay on top of Bastien, her body flush with his. Hand to hand. Arm to arm. Chest to chest. Leg to leg. His body was no longer as cold as ice as he slowly thawed from the inside out. But as he moved his lips the slightest bit, no sound escaped.

"Shh…" she whispered, placing their intertwined fingers against his lips. "The wraith might still be out there."

And as the snow continued to spray her with icy pellets, she felt a tingling sensation ripple through her, suggesting her wings were changing colors to mimic her surroundings. For now, they were safe. From the elements. From the wraith. From certain death.

When her head grew heavy from keeping it aloft, she dared to lower it to rest against Bastien's shoulder while keeping her gaze on his jawline, his chin, his throat, just to make sure he didn't succumb to death.

His throat bobbed with a swallow, followed by the slow blink of his eyes.

Seraphina pressed her lips together as confusion clouded her mind. Bastien Dalena was her enemy. She despised him for what he represented, for all of the suffering of her people. But here she was, keeping him alive with her heat, with her magic, with her kiss.

And she didn't hate it.

astien stared at the low, rocky ceiling with wide, disbelieving eyes. He swallowed once, twice, but the lump in his throat remained.

The Ember Queen lay on top of him, her breaths deep when sleep had claimed her hours ago. Her fire magic seeped into him, keeping him warm as the blizzard outside transitioned from a chaotic tempest to a peaceful snowfall to a cloudless sky.

His hand rested on her bare back below her shoulder blades where her wings jutted out. The paralysis poison in his blood had long since dispersed. Rational thought warned him to flee. But the confusing emotions jumbled within his chest kept him inside the small outcrop with his arm lightly wound around the fae woman.

A slow breath escaped his lungs as he studied her without her knowledge. Black hair fell away from her face, revealing her rounded ears—ears like a human's, with a waterfall of piercings running down one of them. Although she was of fae blood, her ears did not resemble his at all. While hers were rounded, his were long and pointed, with a slight droop at the tip to mark him as a Forest Fae.

Her red-black lips puckered in her sleep, reminded him of when she'd hovered over him before her kiss. For a moment, he'd thought she would kill him.

But she hadn't.

Instead, she had saved his life.

The woman's long, dark eyelashes fluttered in her sleep, and her wings followed suit as they shuddered during a small stretch. Instead of green with traces of brown, they were now white, edged with a rich mahogany hue.

His gaze traveled between the creamy complexion of her skin to the black armored patches of scales on her shoulders. And on the side of her face, the small black horns proved to be softer than they looked as she rested her head against his shoulder.

Autumns, Seraphina was a beautiful woman.

Run! The voice inside his head urged him to leap to his feet and get a running start from the woman who had captured him.

But she was so warm, and outside was so cold. Soft and warm, and she smelled oh so good, like sweet flora and autumn winds.

All too suddenly, she froze against him, not moving even to breathe. Slowly, he closed his eyes but kept his breaths deep and even to feign sleep. A part of him wondered what she might do after discovering themselves in such a position. Because he wasn't sure what to do himself. The woman had shown him compassion. But did that mean he could hand her a sliver of trust?

The action was nearly indecipherable when she moved quickly, but Bastien was ready. Right as Seraphina tried to slam another poison dart into his shoulder, he flipped her over and pinned her hands down with his knees while he held his forearm firm against her throat. The dart clattered across the rocky floor before coming to a standstill beside the cave entrance.

"I gave you a chance," he growled in her face. "Why would you squander it?"

She snarled right back. "You can't truly tell me you would come to the Burning Cliffs willingly. You are my prisoner, not my friend."

"You kissed me."

"I saved your life."

"I never asked you to."

Seraphina wriggled beneath him, trying to free her hands, but he held her tighter. "You are a means to an end. My sister needs me. This is the only way."

He laughed dryly and shook his head. "You mean your *child*."

She lifted her lip in a snarl. "I told you not to speak of her."

"Why not? Pri spoke to me through some sort of crystal dust. Asked for my help. Do you know what I said?" When Seraphina glared, he continued, "I told her it was impossible. But still, she begged. And I relented. I thought it was an impossible task. Ashryn is skilled and resourceful, but even she's no match for a dozen patrol guards."

He shoved her throat one last time before he stood, stalking away from the Ember Queen. A thin layer of snow still lay on the ground, but the sun beat down on the earth, making quick work of the remaining snow and melting it as he trudged through the numerous puddles and small streams surrounding him.

A part of him knew he was mad for facing his back to the enemy. It might earn him a dart to the neck. But he was feeling in a particular mad mood, with anger and annoyance as the backdrop to its symphony.

Behind him, Seraphina released a war cry, moving too quickly for him to turn around in time before she jumped onto his back and latched on. "I hate you, Bastien Dalena!" She pounded once on his shoulder. "You irk me, and I hate you more than you could ever know!" She pounded on his back.

Prying her legs off from around his waist proved difficult, but he finally managed to flip her over his shoulder and threw her toward a puddle of mud. She caught her balance in time and landed with an airy flit of her wings.

"More than I could know?" he shouted back. "You dragged me halfway across the blazing forest! My back is scraped up. My clothes have holes. And you single-handedly shattered my dignity." He laughed humorlessly once again. "I know exactly how much you hate me because it's a perfect reflection of my contempt for *you*."

The woman took him off guard as she untied her sash from around her waist and tossed it onto a patch of damp grass. "Fine. You want a fair fight? Come and get it."

The entire situation felt wrong. After what seemed like a twisted sense of camaraderie after the wraith attack, the thought of trying to hurt Seraphina didn't sit well in his stomach.

As if noticing his hesitancy, she charged at him, which forced him to block an attack to his throat. He swiped her hand to the side and lashed out toward her shoulder. She twisted at the last second to avoid the strike.

They grappled with one another, and just when one had the upper hand, the other would escape their grip like soap beneath water. His shoes slipped in slick mud, making his task of subduing her much more difficult.

She jabbed her elbow into his ribs, causing him to stumble backward. But his foot skidded to the side when he misstepped, and she was quick to take the opportunity to lash out at his throat once again. He grabbed onto her wrist and twisted it behind her back. In the process, he lost what little footing kept him balanced and crashed face-first into the mud, bringing her down with him.

Mud flew in all directions as they wrestled one another. Her green dress quickly became brown. His white hair turned brunette. And when he flipped her into the mud, and she rolled over with her face covered in the brown substance, he couldn't help but burst into laughter at the absurd sight.

"No!" she gasped as she smacked his shoulder. "Stop laughing. This isn't amusing. I'm trying to kill you."

Yet, even as she spoke the words, a giggle tumbled out of her mouth, and she slapped a muddied hand over her face as if in an attempt to quell the sound.

A soft smile pulled against his lips as he grasped Seraphina's hands and pulled them away from her face. And then he proceeded to wipe the mud from her cheeks and chin, followed by her armored shoulders. The scales were rough against his fingers, the edges pointed and beautiful.

The tension took a sharp turn as his hands trailed down her arms to her palms, and then he lightly touched the tips of her fingers. He watched as rapid breaths escaped her mouth, as her throat bobbed with a swallow, as her red-black lips parted beneath his stare.

The Ember Queen was his enemy. But for a moment, he couldn't help but imagine a world in which she wasn't. What if instead of fighting with one another, relationships between their people flourished? What if their people traded wares instead of blows? What if their people laughed with one another and created lasting friendships?

Of course, it wasn't reality. But what if, one day, it could happen?

"I think I won," Bastien murmured in the thick, charged silence. "You've been pinned for more than ten seconds."

She laughed again and shook her head wryly as she pushed him off her and stood. He couldn't help but watch as she spread her wings, now back to their previous green and brown hue. Mud flaked off the thin membrane, and he found himself mesmerized by their unique leaf-like patterns and the crisp, golden shimmer lining the edges.

"You can hardly call that winning." She rolled her eyes. "I could have felled you within seconds with a well-aimed knee to your crotch."

"But you didn't," he pointed out, subconsciously shielding himself with one leg. "Thank you for that." And then he nodded toward her back. "Your wings."

She glanced behind her, following his gaze, to also take in the shades of green, orange, and gold. "Camouflage," she answered. "My wings transition with the changing seasons. Even if one of those seasons comes far too early." She laced her words with dry annoyance. Thankfully, most of the snow had melted.

Within moments, her expression once again became guarded as she edged toward her sash and strapped it around her waist. They stood silently while assessing each other. One single question lay heavy in the air.

What now?

"Are you hungry?" he asked, and her eyebrows shot up upon taking her off guard with his inquiry.

"We need to settle this." She gestured between the two of them and fingered the dart gun on her hip.

There was no way in the seven suns he planned to get pricked with one of those despicable poisons again. But something had changed between them in the past day. He couldn't abandon her now.

"There is nothing to settle. I refuse to get dragged any farther, and we both are nearly unrecognizable. First, a bath. Then a meal."

"I will not turn my back to you while I bathe."

He raised a suggestive eyebrow and grinned. "By all means, turn your front to me."

Seraphina scowled and crossed her arms, bringing his attention to her—ahem—hands. "I cannot trust you for a single moment. Never forget we are enemies."

"You saved my life, and then you kissed me. If we are still enemies, why did you do it? All you need is my dead body. You don't truly need me alive if you are resourceful."

Slowly, her arms dropped to her sides as she gazed back at him with a troubled expression. "Are we being candid?"

He nodded.

She continued. "You and I…we are more similar than you might think. I suppose I didn't want to leave you helpless."

"Plus, you kinda like me. Admit it." He waggled his eyebrows in an attempt to irk her. But instead of a scowl, she simply stared back at him with another troubled expression etched into the worry lines of her face. Suddenly, she looked far older than…

Actually, he wasn't sure how old she was.

"Tell me your age," he said as she did, indeed, turn her back to him and tromped down a path parallel to a small stream. He followed after like the fool he was. His father always said his stupidity was going to get him killed one day.

"Twenty-five."

His lips twitched as he stepped over a puddle of mud before he realized keeping himself clean didn't matter when he was already covered from head to toe in the thick, gooey substance. "An older woman, huh?"

"Older?" she scoffed, glancing at him over her shoulder. An unexpected thrill shot through his body when she scanned him up and down, her gaze lingering a little longer on his arms and shoulders. "We are likely the same age."

"You are three years my senior."

He pushed a branch aside in time to witness the tail end of her surprise before her expression became an emotionless mask once more.

"You fight too well to be barely a man."

"Now you are insulting me." Bastien leaped over a log but hissed when the movement pulled on his wound. Only then did he notice the dark red joining the mud covering his shoulder. "I completed patrol guard initiation a long time ago. Years ago."

"Ah, yes. Your mask." Despite her obvious reluctance to give him any type of praise, he noticed what could only be awe in her eyes. "A chupacabra, was it? I've heard they're ruthless blood-sucking creatures that travel in packs. What did you do with the other chupacabras in the pack?"

"You want to hear the story?"

When she didn't answer but simply glanced back at him as she crossed the stream, he grinned from ear to ear and followed closer. Though, it didn't help that she moved quickly through a forest she was obviously well-accustomed to traveling.

He laced his fingers together and flipped them upside down, each knuckle cracking as he started his tale. "As you likely very well know, Attleglade is known for its skill in bone carving. Usually, we collect bones from elk, fish, and other game that we use to feed the settlement. But the patrol guards?" He popped a particularly stubborn knuckle before continuing. "We must kill something fierce and take on its skull for our mask. I hunted down a pack of chupacabras stealing our pigs in the dead of night. One of them even stole a child." He paused for dramatic effect. Seraphina slowed but didn't stop entirely as if engrossed in the tale.

"What happened to the child?" she asked.

"I'm getting there." Though, he didn't miss the pinch of concern around her mouth over the welfare of the boy. "I tracked the three chupacabras to their den and killed the two weaker beasts while they were feeding on the pigs. The third one was guarding the boy, wanting to keep its prize." Another pause, though Seraphina slowed to a stop beneath a copse of trees, behind her the silhouette of a small lake. "The chupacabra was no easy kill, and I have the scars to prove it." He lifted his shirt just enough to show the three scratch scars resting over his hip. "But I managed to defeat the creature and rescue the child. The boy was in bad shape but still alive. If we ever become good friends, I'll introduce you to him."

Seraphina snorted and stared at him pointedly. "We will never be friends. And our people will never be allies."

"Mmmhmm. If you say so."

She stepped out of the trees, and when he moved to follow, he stopped suddenly at the beautiful scenery. Pine trees surrounded the small lake. A cliff jutted out over the lake, and between two boulders at the top, a waterfall crashed into the water below.

Pixies darted back and forth across the clearing, a spark of light that left a shimmer in their wake. Birdsong flitted in the treetops, the perfect melody to the soothing crash of water.

But then his heart stilled when he focused on Seraphina again. She tossed her sash and dart gun close to the shore and pulled one arm out of the sleeve of her dress, followed by the other. She held the garment to her chest as she waded clothed into the lake. And only when her entire body was submerged did she shimmy out of the dress and toss the soaked frock beside her sash.

And then she scowled at him. "I would appreciate it if you turned around."

Bastien shook his head and leaned against a large boulder, arms behind his head as he basked in his muddied glory. "I turned my back to you *once* and ended up getting dragged across the entire blasted forest. I won't do it again willingly."

"Then it seems we are at an impasse." She held his gaze with a challenging stare as her hands glided over her wet hair to dislodge the mud from the black strands.

"It seems so." He challenged her back with an unblinking stare as he stripped himself of his filthy shirt and dramatically dropped it to the ground. Her gaze dipped to his chest moments before her nostrils flared, and her eyes found his once again. He silently dared her to keep watching as he reached for his belt and unbuckled it. He slid his trousers an inch off his hips and then another.

Her attention didn't waver from his face, but neither did she turn around.

Who was going to break first? Stubborn Seraphina? Or himself?

He pulled the remainder of his trousers off in a *whoosh*, and only then did she spin around to face away from him. Laughter burst out of his mouth as he waded in after her, and only when his bottom half was covered did she face him once again with a fiery glare in her unique orange and green eyes.

"Looks like I won yet another battle." He swam around her, closer to the two boulders with the small waterfall crashing into the lake between them.

"You won only *one* battle, might I correct. The mud fight didn't count."

A grin lifted on his lips as he continued to circle her while she turned with his movement. "Why not?"

"W-w-well," she stuttered. "You cheated."

"How?" Of course, he knew exactly how—by making her as mesmerized with him as he had been with her.

Seraphina's only answer was to splash him in the face. A chortle lifted into the air between them when he couldn't help but laugh, loving to tease her to get a reaction. Well, as long as it didn't involve one of her poisonous darts or a kiss that burned him from the inside out. Despite their unspoken, tentative truce, he didn't dare let his guard down for a single second. She was a dangerous woman.

But then her gaze dipped to his shoulder, and a frown of concern pulled her mouth downward. "Your shoulder looks terrible."

"Oh, really?" he scoffed and rolled his eyes. It ached something fierce, especially after their mud fight when what little healing progress he'd made had ripped the wound open again. Tendrils of blood slithered into the water and disappeared. "I wonder who stabbed me."

"It was necessary to convey the gravity of my disposition. I was willing to wound you before taking you. It would make your friends think you were in grave danger if they didn't hurry."

"I don't feel like I'm in grave danger." He swam slowly toward her, but she flinched away.

"No!" she gasped. "Don't come any closer."

He paused upon noticing the hint of a tremor in her voice, the smallest inkling of fear in her eyes as she held up a hand as if to erect a barrier between them.

Rather than advancing farther, he swam backward to put more distance between them. "All right. If you really don't want me to see your nasty mole, I won't come any closer."

The fear in her eyes disappeared in favor of amusement. "I don't have a nasty mole."

He laughed, which promptly turned into air bubbles when he dunked his head beneath the water to clean the mud from his hair, and then he flipped his hair back so it lay slick against his scalp.

"Why do you keep your hair long?" Seraphina asked as she studied him.

With a shrug, he answered, "Culture, I suppose. My father keeps his shorter to defy the constraints of our culture. Don't tell anyone I told you. Everyone else simply thinks it's easier for him to manage when…"

He trailed off and turned his head to avoid looking into her eyes. He didn't want to speak more on the subject. But at the same time, he wished to share his thoughts with the woman he once called his enemy.

No, she was still his enemy.

Then why were the lines blurring so rapidly? Why did confusion swirl in his mind each time he looked at her?

Because he realized she didn't feel like the enemy. Not when his people had wronged her so greatly. Just like they'd wronged him and his father, too. Perhaps he was not looking in the mirror like he should.

"When...?" she prompted softly.

Releasing a long sigh, he focused on scrubbing the mud from his skin rather than witnessing her reaction. "The council maimed my father's legs because he'd attempted to make contact with my sister outside the settlement." He paused and glanced up with a tortured expression. "I'm sorry my people took your...Pri. If it's any consolation, I wish to kill them just as much as you do."

Stunned silence.

And when her open-mouthed gape became too much to take in, he returned his attention to scrubbing his body down. "When my father dies someday, they will kill me next. I'm planning on killing as many as I can before someone cleaves my head from my shoulders. It will be a glorious death filled with justice for what they did. My only regret is I won't be able to see my sister, Nyana, one last time."

"You will kill your own people?" she asked in a raspy tone.

"Don't mistake my words. I want to kill the *council*. No one else. They've done so many terrible things. Maiming my father's legs. Blinding a family friend. Beheading a woman who had run away from an abusive marriage. Hanging a boy who had just come of age because he'd befriended an Ember Fae." He squeezed his eyes shut to try to block out the image of the last death, forever imprinted in his memory. "If those things don't anger you, then you should know they also killed the Ember Fae friend."

He opened his eyes to find Seraphina's fists clenched where they floated in the water in front of her. When he realized he could see the distorted color of the rest of her body beneath the surface, he looked away and instead studied the way water droplets rolled off her wings, similar to that of a bird's feathers.

"Well then." Seraphina spoke quietly enough for him to have to lean forward to hear her words. "Perhaps we do have more in common than I realized after all."

When she began swimming toward the shore, this time, he turned his back to give her privacy. Besides, if she wanted to hit him with a poison dart, then she'd have to be ready to search the entire lake for his body when he lost control of his limbs.

Still, the thought gave him little reassurance. Seraphina played dirty, and he still wouldn't put it past her to do such a thing.

"I have spare clothes for you," Seraphina called to him. "I'll set them on the boulder."

"Where could you possibly be keeping those?" he gasped, but she only laughed.

"In the same place as all my other stolen items. I'll never tell."

Temptation tried to coax him into turning around, but he forced himself to keep his back turned. Perhaps she wouldn't tell, but he planned to find out one way or another.

ELEVEN

Fire crackled in the cool night air as Seraphina watched Bastien turn the pheasant they'd hunted on the spit over the flames.

Usually, the warmth, the light, the crackling soothed her spirit. Today, it did nothing as she contemplated the mysteries of the man beside her. What was she supposed to do with him? For her entire life, the Forest Fae of Attleglade had been her enemy. But she couldn't very well drag him the rest of the way to the Burning Cliffs. Not after everything they had endured.

And the things he had confessed…

How was it she'd managed to capture the one fae who hated his leaders as much as she did? Either every Forest Fae harbored a secret hatred, or his was a special case.

As if feeling her gaze on him, Bastien glanced over his shoulder and nodded toward the ground. "You should sleep."

"And let you sneak off? Not a chance."

She crossed her arms as she surveyed him up and down. The Sun Fae clothing he dressed in looked nothing like his former Attleglade uniform. Instead of white and light brown, he wore a dark blue vest over a white tunic that might have been loose in the sleeves on another man. But on him, the fabric was straining at the seams. His dark brown trousers fit near to perfection, but her gaze tried not to linger too long.

As for herself, she now wore a spare set of clothing she'd stored away in her enchanted pouch, a similar v-neck and thigh-slit style to her last outfit, but this one was a deep red in color. Like blood.

In all honesty, she wanted Bastien out of his old clothing as they entered Ember Fae territory. Dressed as a patrol guard, he would be killed on sight. But the half of his blood that made him a Sun Fae might protect him should they be discovered. *If* her people didn't make an immediate connection that he was also a Forest Fae.

However, the shape of his ears gave him away. No matter what she dressed him in, she feared he was still in danger of an immediate skewering.

Slowly, as if to keep her from leaping into action, he reached for the strap on her thigh and slipped one of her daggers out of its sheath. She inhaled sharply as he cut his palm just deep enough to draw blood. "On my life, I swear to you, Seraphina Nova, that I will not run unless you run with me. I will not stay unless you stay with me. Until you release me from my oath, I am bound to you. This, I promise."

Her only response was to gape. "Why would you swear a blood oath to me? I am your enemy."

"But I don't want you to be. I know how important it is to get Pri back safe and unharmed. If I can help you do it, I will."

Emotion clogged her throat as she stared back at him, and she didn't flinch away when he picked up her hand and drew blood from her palm with her knife. Though, she couldn't help but wince at the sharp burn of accompanying pain.

He softly cradled her hand in his, gazing at her expectantly.

She wanted to trust him. She truly did. But years of contempt and heartache prevented her from pushing him away, from declining his blood offer.

Finally, she nodded. "I accept your oath." And then she scowled. "But I will still sleep with one eye open. Heed my warning."

"Warning noted." He laughed and dropped her hand before wiping his small injury on his trousers. He returned his attention to the fire as he rotated the spit to roast another side of their catch.

When it finished cooking, they split the meal and ate in silence. She couldn't help but watch as Bastien's ears twitched slightly at every sound. Despite his carefree demeanor, she saw past the carelessness and instead noticed his focused expression, the way he crouched on the balls of his feet as if ready to spring into action at any moment, how his gaze slowly scanned the area every other minute.

Although he had no weapons on his person, he was ready to fight.

"Soooo…" Bastien said slowly as he held up his hands as if in a show of peace. "Pri truly is your daughter?" He grimaced. "I apologize. I'm not trying to sound judgemental in any way. But if you are twenty-five and she's, what, twelve? Or is she really your sister?"

"Pri is eleven."

"Ah." He nodded, though confusion still lingered in his expression. He didn't inquire further, and a part of her wanted to maintain the silence. But Bastien had confided in her about his father. And she found herself wanting to confide in him as well. Because she couldn't tell anyone else. It was too dangerous. And she wanted to tell *someone*. Even if that someone was her enemy.

Her mind whirled with how to approach the topic. The situation was unique and filled with immense heartache and sorrow.

She stared into the flames with her arms wrapped around her knees, expression somber. "I got assaulted."

His head shot up. "Pardon?"

She released a long breath, not daring to meet his eyes as she repeated herself. "I got assaulted. But I suppose I need to delve deeper into Ember Fae customs for you to understand how terrible that is."

"It's already terrible. You never should have had to go through that."

With a shrug, she tightened her grip around her knees as she momentarily relived the fear, the devastation, the vileness of the act. "In my culture, the Ember Queen is literally the lifeblood of their people, the one person whose magic can keep them alive. There are three clans, and each used to fight mercilessly against another for a spot beside the queen. Eventually, it was agreed upon that a male from each clan would become the queen's concubine." She dropped one hand from her knee to absently drag her finger through the dirt. "After the three were chosen, each would go into the queen on the night of the full moon, and should she conceive, no one knew who the father was, therefore, strengthening the ties of the clans when each was considered the father. Until that night, the queen must remain untouched." She finally raised her gaze to meet his eye. "Or die."

Bastien pressed his lips together as he stared back at her with sympathy in his eyes, but he said nothing, allowing her to continue the tale.

"One of the leaders' sons from the three clans decided he didn't want to share in the next generation. He wanted to be King, not just a concubine. So, he assaulted me when I was only thirteen, just a girl barely become a woman."

"Did your clan try to kill you after what happened?" he asked quietly.

She shook her head. The memories were terrible, and she tried to block them out, but it had been the worst day of her life. "That man was the first person I ever killed, and my mother helped me make it look like an accident to redirect the blame. The clan witch used her magic to place my child into my mother instead, to not only save my life but to protect my future position as Queen." She paused to release another long breath filled with aching sadness. "My mother died in childbirth. I've helped raise my sister since." Finally, the guilt of her actions crashed down on her, and her finger ceased its exploration through the dirt. "Pri doesn't know the truth. I refuse to tell her until she is old enough to understand why we did what we did. Because she will be killed promptly after me should anyone find out, and the Ember Queen's power will transfer to the next person in line. If you thought your people were cruel, the Forest Fae don't hold a flame to what mine are capable of."

"But..." he rasped. "You are the queen. You should be their leader. Not their puppet."

"I am. But politics run far deeper than mere titles, especially where peace is concerned. You, of all people, should understand."

He ran a hand over his jaw, now covered in stubble from their three-day journey through the forest. "How many concubines have you chosen?"

"None yet." Her wings drooped as she leaned on the log against her, head rested on a fist as she now more brazenly gazed at her enemy. "It is customary to choose on one's twenty-fifth birthday." She paused. "I turned twenty-five the night Pri got captured. I feel guilty for the relief I feel for delaying the choosing for another full moon."

Bastien moved closer until they almost touched. Almost, but not quite. She couldn't fathom why she wanted to feel his warmth, his solid presence, his calm, comforting touch. It was silly that when his arm brushed against hers, her insides trembled in the most pleasant way.

"Because of your past?" he asked quietly, patiently.

After a long few moments of staring into the flames, she nodded. "It would be the assault all over again, but with three men instead of one, despite the change of circumstances and the fact that I would be choosing it no matter how much I don't want it." She swallowed, but her voice escaped as a raspy whisper anyway. "I want love. I want kindness. I want to know what it's like to be touched with a gentle hand." She sighed. "But it's too late for me. I never bothered with forming relationships with the opposite sex within the three clans. So each of my concubines will be little more than strangers."

He scratched his head before combing his fingers through his long hair, working to unravel a knot in the snowy white strands. "I can't fathom what a…situation…that would be like. We have monogamous marriages in Attleglade. Many of them are arranged, especially with how exclusive the council likes to keep our settlement." He frowned, though she wasn't sure if it was because of the direction of his thoughts or because his knot was being particularly stubborn. "Marriage candidates have to be thoroughly winnowed with their background, blood origin, and even physical traits before they're considered worthy of the marriage pool. And to avoid inbreeding, of course."

Surprisingly, she laughed and shook her head. "A monogamous marriage? I can't imagine what that's like. I had three fathers growing up. Two of them are still alive."

"That is the strangest thing I've ever heard of. Three? Truly?"

"Uh-huh." She laughed again at his incredulous stare.

"And how many siblings do you have? Not counting Pri, of course."

She shrugged. "In a way, she is both my daughter and my sister. But stranger things have happened within my family." And then she held up four fingers. "I have two older brothers and two younger. But unlike other cultural traditions, the first female inherits the power and position of Ember Queen."

A long pause passed between them as if he were trying to grasp the nuances of her culture. "Wait, wait, wait. So if you died, would Pri inherit the power? Does the power transfer through blood? Or birth?"

"For her sake, I desperately hope it passes through birth. Because her life would be put in danger if anyone found out the truth."

Another stretch of silence followed, and Seraphina couldn't lie. She hated the quiet tension and preferred Bastien's quips and attempts at flirtation.

"You became Queen at fourteen years old," he finally said.

"Like I said, stranger things have happened within the family. This is only one of them."

Guilt over her mother's passing hunched her shoulders. Her death had occurred many years ago, but Seraphina could never forget it was her fault her mother was dead. But what alternative had there been? She was a frightened child back then. Her mother had saved her life, sacrificed her own to save them both.

Bastien startled her out of her thoughts as he moved even closer until their legs and hips touched one another. She glowered at his shoe resting against one of her feet and glanced up at him with furrowed brows.

"I will kiss you again," she warned.

"Is that a threat?" He lowered his voice to a whisper, his gaze shifting to her lips. "Or a promise?"

"A threat, I assure you. What happened in the cave is not usually how my kisses transpire."

He tipped his head and offered her a charming smile. Butterflies fluttered in her stomach at the saucy look, and she hated it. "No? Then it seems you reserve such kisses only for me. I must be special." His fingers lightly traced the scaly patterns on her shoulders before following the creamier complexion of her lower arm. "The first thing they teach us as patrol guards is how to fall." Her breath hitched when his gentle touch moved to the back of her hand. "The second is how to flirt."

"Ha!" she laughed. "I don't believe it for a single second. You were born that way. None of the other guards flirt like you do."

"You've been watching us?"

"I've followed each of you around." And then her breath fled her entirely as he picked up her hand and cradled it in his lap. "Release my hand," she demanded half-heartedly.

"Why? We're friends."

She laughed again at the absurdity of the situation. How had it come to this? Within a matter of days, he'd managed to charm her, to get under her skin, to get her to speak of things she hadn't told another soul other than her mother.

"We are *not* friends."

"Friends laugh together." He paused and glanced down at their intertwined fingers. "And they hold hands sometimes, too."

Immediately, her thoughts jumped to the Forest Fae woman he called Ashryn, and an unexpected surge of envy heated beneath her skin. "Call friends what they are," she hissed in an accusatory tone. "They are your beaus." She pulled her hand from his and hid them beneath her arms. "Or are you telling me all you're doing with your fae *friend* is holding hands?"

"That's not fair."

"Oh, I think it is. Are you in love with that woman?"

Bastien threw his hands up and stood, the fire creating dancing shadows across his face in the darkness. "You want to talk about Ashryn? Fine! Let's talk about Ashryn. She's the only one brave enough to stand by my side. Despite the scorn. Despite how her own reputation might suffer. She's my friend, but sometimes she was something more. That part of my life is over. It never had a chance to blossom into anything, and it never will."

"But if you weren't half-Forest Fae, you would have married her already."

"No," he argued back, "I wouldn't have. Because neither of us wanted that."

She opened her mouth to continue the quarrel but didn't get the chance when he hissed suddenly.

"Ow!" he cried, hand flying to his neck before pulling out a small dart. He glared at her accusingly, all while the blood drained from her face upon noticing the black and white striped paint on the dart. "Why would you do that? I thought we were getting along splendidly."

"That wasn't me." And then a dart shot into her own neck despite her attempt to dodge the attack. Bastien slumped to the ground in a heap. Her hand flew to her dagger, but she barely managed to unsheath it before she lost control of her limbs, and the weapon fell limp from her fingers.

She struggled with all her might against the poison seeping into her bloodstream, but her attempts led nowhere when even her fingers couldn't move the slightest bit. She tried to kick, thrash, scream, but all that escaped was a garble of curses.

This would not go unpunished. These blasted Ember Fae were about to get a knife in the back—

A black boot stomped into the ground in front of her face, and she glared at the offending item and the man it belonged to. Black boots. Red trousers. And then the person stooped to reveal the red and white paint on his face. "Good evening, Your Highness."

Dread tightened in her gut, and she attempted to swallow the lump in her throat as she gazed back at eyes lined with black paint.

Blazes.

TWELVE

astien scowled at the offending sky that stared back, seeming to laugh at him as his body swayed with each step his captors took around him. He hung upside down beneath a large wooden pole, his wrists and ankles tied to the thick wood. His skin burned from where the scratchy rope cut into him, but he tried to maintain a brave front.

Especially when Seraphina hung upside down from her own pole, only an arm's reach away. Her glower was directed at the men carrying the poles like sacrifices to the slaughter.

When his body swayed close enough for her to hear him, he said quietly, "Doesn't feel so good when you're the one getting dragged around, does it?"

"Shut it, Bastien!" she hissed while giving him a warning glare. "These people will kill you."

Although she said nothing more, her swift glance toward his ears told him everything he needed to know. They would kill him simply because he was a Forest Fae.

Shite.

He was in really big trouble.

Especially as they neared the border of the woods, his gut telling him it was only a few paces to his right. If they crossed the line, he would drop over dead.

Mother-blasted blood oath!

He willed his ears to straighten rather than for them to droop near the pointed tips, but no matter how hard he wished for it, they remained the same. Fortunately, his ears were far less droopy than those of other Forest Fae. But they were still shapely enough to incriminate him.

Unwilling to reveal the uneasiness coursing through his blood, he feigned carelessness and grinned at her. "You're beautiful when you're angry. Which is a lot, I might add."

The sway of their captors' rocky steps moved her close enough for her to jab him in the ribs with her elbow as if she had gained control of her muscles for only a brief moment. He released a grunt and decided to hold his tongue when another retort wanted to escape.

Around them, their captors each wore face paint in varying designs of red, black, and white, and Bastien couldn't tell if they were readying for war or if they always wore such paint. The Ember Fae, who usually fought with the Forest Fae, had wings and black hair and lips. None of these people carried wings on their backs.

From his vantage point, he couldn't see much other than the sky, but his head somehow managed to roll to the side to view little huts made of black silt with straw-thatched roofs. Women and children stared at them as they passed, but mostly at Seraphina. Their eyes were wide, filled with horror and confusion. Bastien realized they were not too keen on their clan leader taking their queen hostage.

Their captors placed either end of the branches they were tied to between a pole that created a "Y" shape. Bastien's back dangled over dirt, nearly touching the ground but not quite.

The same man from before, the one Seraphina had referred to as Joram, stepped forward with a hand resting against a sword hanging unsheathed from his hip. Black metal gleamed beneath the light of a bonfire billowing a short distance away. The gray threaded into the man's black hair gave away his age. He was probably about as old as his father, in his early forties.

The other man stared him down, his gaze trailing over his hair, his clothing, and lingering on his ears. "What are you?"

What not *who*.

Seraphina gazed at him intently, attention flashing to his ears and then to his lips. In any other situation, he might have thought she was flirting. But this was no regular situation. She was sending a message, and he attempted to pick apart her meaning.

Although rusty, he switched from the Forest Fae tongue to his native Sun Fae language, trying his best to sound like he'd spoken it all his life. "My queen would have you release us."

Joram peered at him closer and answered in choppy Sun Fae speech. "Your queen?"

Seraphina huffed, and he didn't miss the clench of her jaw, which indicated he'd just said something stupid. But he was a talented liar, and she was about to find out just how well he could weave a tale.

"Queen Nova hired me as a guard in Heulwen, the Sun Fae city. An *outsider* to the clans given light of the current situation."

The man tilted his blade, and the bonfire caught as a glint on the smooth metal. "Why would she have need of *your* assistance? She has nearly every Ember Fae at her beck and call at the snap of her fingers."

"And yet, here we are, hanging upside down because her fingers are tied down."

Thankfully, Seraphina cut in next in her regular tongue. "Release us, Joram," she demanded. "Or I will punish you and your people for laying your hands on me."

Joram held up his hands as if in a show of peace. "No need to exercise your magic. I know you can drown my people in fire even with your hands tied behind your back."

"*My* people," she corrected. "You forget who rules over *you*." She scowled at him. "My patience is running thin, and I think you have humiliated me enough."

Discomforted feet shuffled around them as many Ember Fae glanced at each other uneasily. It almost seemed as if they were confused about whose orders they should follow when their clan leader and queen were issuing commands from opposite fronts.

Joram held up a hand to quiet them, and the crowd stilled once more. "What can you do?" He laughed as she glared at him. "I've been hunting you for days, Your Highness. And I finally found you nearly by your lonesome." He gestured to Bastien. "Some guard he turned out to be." But then he tipped his knife toward Seraphina this time and dragged the flat end across the side of her neck. "The dart you were struck with temporarily inhibits your magic. You are powerless here."

"What do you want?" she spat.

Bastien tried to struggle against the poison once again flowing through his veins, but his body remained limp. Quite frankly, he was getting tired of losing the ability to move. And not for the first time in his life, he wished he possessed the affinity for magic. His father's magical ability had skipped over him entirely, and his sister had inherited magic instead.

"What my son tried to accomplish twelve years ago." The man lowered his voice, and only the people within the immediate vicinity likely heard his words. "It's a shame he failed and died by *accident*."

Panic lurched through his stomach as his gaze shot toward Seraphina. Her fierce glare gave nothing away, but she likely knew as well as he did that something awful was in store for them.

"I deeply express my condolences for your son's death," Seraphina said in an even yet cordial tone. "I was only a child at the time, but I remember he was well-loved by the people."

Joram's expression contorted with anger as he grabbed a fistful of Seraphina's hair and pulled hard enough for her eyes to water. "It's funny how quickly alliances can change when a few threats are involved."

An elderly woman shuffled out of the crowd and stood with hands clasped in front of her, eyes fixed on the ground. The wrinkled and dull aged wings on her back indicated she was not originally from this clan. "Forgive me, Your Highness."

Seraphina gasped. "Alma, why?"

"My family comes first."

Now with the ability to move his head slightly, he glanced from Seraphina's horrified expression to the woman's hunched shoulders. If he could guess, he'd say the woman was the healer Seraphina had spoken of earlier in her tale about Pri. But the question was…how many people knew the truth?

Judging by the uncertainty and confusion in the expressions around them, very few people knew about what had happened. Surely, there would have been more outrage, no? But who would the anger be directed at? Joram or Seraphina?

Defeat melted the anger in Seraphina's eyes. "What would you have me do?"

The clan leader nodded toward a tall, bare-chested man with paint smeared across his face and torso. He wore a crossbow strapped over his shoulder, knives with black blades hanging in an orderly line from the strap. His black hair was cropped short, black lips curled into a snarl.

"There will be no more concubines but only one king. You will marry my son Zephyr." He lowered his voice once again. "And I will have no one question the legitimacy of the heir. Pri will have to be killed."

"No!" she screamed, and her outburst must have cut through some of the poison's influence when her body swayed against her struggling. Bastien glared when he could do nothing other than cast the man hateful looks. "You can rot in your grave like the spiteful man you are, you blazing, child-killing swine!"

Joram lifted his hand and, in a swift motion, struck her across the face. A collective gasp stole across the crowd, followed by enough shouts of disapproval and outrage that Joram's guards had to push their own people back.

The man simply grinned, his fingers tapping on the hilt of his sword. Once more, he lowered his voice, "*If* the girl isn't dead already." He chuckled darkly. Bastien hated the way he placed his hands on the branch she dangled from and leaned close. "I encouraged her from the goodness of my heart to seek out the healing water of the Glades. I reckon she didn't get far."

Seraphina spit in his face. "You sent her on a suicide errand."

"She chose to go. Her stupidity is not my fault." He nudged her side with the tip of his boot. "The joining will happen immediately. My son is ready to claim his queen."

Bastien hardly knew Pri. He knew little about Seraphina as it was. But he remembered that night. Pri had been scared. Helpless. And oh so young. At the thought of her terrified expression and the tears trailing down her face, anger coursed through him.

His thoughts drifted to Seraphina, alone and helpless and taken against her consent for the second time. He refused to allow it to happen.

He fought against the poison in his blood and won. He ripped his ankles free from their bindings, and with Joram's attention momentarily diverted, he slapped his feet over the flat ends of the man's black blade. Using his tied hands as leverage for his weight, he twisted the weapon sharply until it sliced the man across the torso.

Joram cried out and clutched his bleeding wound. Bastien wasted no time as he wrenched his hands out of the bindings he'd worked on loosening around his wrists and landed on the ground with a rather ungraceful thump.

He rolled over and snatched the same sword from Joram's belt just as guards rushed toward them with weapons drawn. He sliced the ropes from Seraphina's hands and feet, and when she, too, landed with an ungraceful thump, he realized she didn't have full control of her body yet.

Blade met blade as Bastien twirled in a frenzy of slashes, stabs, and blocks as he stood in front of Seraphina and protected her from the sudden onslaught of attacks.

A bolt shot toward him and barely grazed the tip of his ear. He realized with a start that the clan leader's son held a crossbow in his hands, loading another bolt as Bastien fought with the sword.

When someone brought an arrow to a sword fight, he knew it was time to run.

In his hands, the black blade fought ferociously, cutting down several enemies and driving back several more foes. When he created enough birth between him and the enemy, he drove the tip of the black sword through his clothing to create a makeshift sheath before he stooped before Seraphina.

Another bolt shot toward him, this time piercing his outer bicep and escaping completely through the other side. Blood gushed down his arm, followed by the fiery shock of pain. But he didn't pause as he picked Seraphina up, cradled her against his chest, and ran.

The position of her body quickly fatigued his arms, but he refused to throw her over his shoulders when the crossbow bolts could seek her as a target instead of himself.

A whizz shot past his ear, missing by a hair's breadth. Another grazed the tips of his hair in his pursuit of safety. He weaved in and out of the trees, using his vast knowledge as a patrol guard to his advantage.

It was as if the tree roots made way for him as he sprinted through the maze of branches, only to become winding obstacles behind him to block the enemies in pursuit.

When he no longer spotted them behind him but heard the shouting of their voices only, he transferred Seraphina from his arms and draped her across his shoulders.

"Hang on," he ordered. Her body weakly responded to his demand and tightened the smallest bit around his neck, making him realize he had to do this with her dead weight.

Using lower branches as his footholds, he jumped from one level of a tree to the next, only using his hands when absolutely necessary to keep himself from falling. By the time he reached the upper boughs of a tree, his legs shook in protest against the extra weight.

And then a bolt lodged into the trunk right beside his head.

He swore when he caught sight of the crossbow man below, now loading another bolt. Only three bolts remained in his quiver. Bastien had to dodge all three. Or die trying.

"Have you ever flown through the trees before?" he asked in a light tone, all while he focused on holding entirely still. It would be a bit more difficult to traverse the trees at night, but it wasn't something he hadn't done before.

"Not in the way Forest Fae do it," she answered with a nervous lilt to her voice. "Should I be worried?"

"Immensely."

Clink!

Bastien twisted sharply to the side, and the bolt flew past his shoulder and into the brush somewhere below. Without wasting another second, he took off down the thick branch at a sprint, silently cursing at how much smaller the trees were in Blackburrow. The branches sank beneath his weight rather than carrying him on sturdy limbs. But he'd trained on brittle limbs before. This would be no different.

He ran from tree to tree where they were tight enough together. For the others too far apart, he leaped as far as his legs allowed him, a few times only making it on a lower branch than one on the same level as before. He hoped he wouldn't slip because he'd trained for a situation in which he might fall. But he'd never trained when falling with another person in his arms.

The next tree was just out of reach, so he ran, jumped, and braced himself for the impact of the next branch beneath his feet. But then an arrow whizzed between his legs. He yelped at the narrow miss.

Only one bolt remained.

Preferably, he'd like to keep the family jewels intact.

His eyebrows drew together when the next tree was too far away to jump to. To leap the distance meant to put his and

Seraphina's lives at risk. But if he did nothing, they could risk getting shot.

At least he took heart in the fact that only one of them would take the bolt, and the other would live. But if he took it and left her to fend for herself, both of them could die. Or worse, the clan leader's son would take her back to his village as his bride.

"Don't do it, Bastien," Seraphina warned when she spotted the large gap. "Don't you dare."

"Hold on tight."

And then he jumped.

His heart soared when he realized he was going to make it. Not on the same branch level as the one he'd leaped from but one lower. It was good enough.

But then something sharp stung his leg, and the unexpected intense pain caused him to lose his focus. His stomach slammed into a branch, his body doing a disorienting flip. The impact flung Seraphina from his arms, and he found himself falling after her.

The ground approached at an alarming rate, fast enough to crack their necks or break a few bones. He reacted on instinct as he tucked Seraphina beneath his arm, and just as his feet hit the ground, they rolled into the fall together. Though instead of returning to his feet like a graceful feline, they rolled across the ground several times until they came to an abrupt halt in a mass of tangled limbs and disgruntled moans.

He gasped and sat up suddenly as he knelt over her, assessing her for damage. Her body remained limp from the poison, though it must have been wearing off because she moved an arm to brush hair out of her face.

"Please be all right," he breathed as he ran his hands along her head, her neck, her arms, and her legs. "Please, please, please." But nothing seemed to be broken, though she'd sustained several scratches from the fall.

A branch cracked behind him, and he leaped to his feet, only to hiss when placing weight on his leg momentarily burned. Blood ran down his leg and seeped into the fabric of his trousers. But otherwise, he remained mostly unharmed as he faced his foe where he stood beneath the shade of a tree, barely visible in the dark atmosphere.

The crossbow, now strapped to his back, was empty, and in his hands lay two small knives.

Bastien drew his obsidian sword from his clothing sheath and held it at the ready.

However, the man glanced from his sword to Seraphina lying on the ground to his knives before he huffed and turned back around, jogging out of sight.

He wasted no time as he sheathed his sword once more and slung Seraphina over his shoulders, much to her grunting protest. But he didn't have time to be careful with her. Not when the other man knew where they were and might come back with more soldiers.

Ignoring the pain flaring in his arm and leg, and yes, even his ear, he ran as fast as he possibly could while carrying Seraphina, making sure to cover his tracks whenever possible. Only when his body threatened to collapse from exhaustion did he finally set her down against the trunk of a tree within a small clearing far away from the Ember settlement.

"Why is it that we're constantly finding ourselves in a tight spot?" he grumbled as he paced back and forth in front of her. He tore several strips of cloth from the bottom of his tunic and wrapped his leg and then his arm over his clothing, tying the knot off with his teeth. He attempted to staunch the bleeding from his ear next. It was a shallow cut, at least. "*You* were supposed to be my enemy. Not an ice wraith. Not some Ember lunatics. *You*. And now you are far closer to an ally than I'm comfortable with."

"You saved my life," she murmured.

"They weren't going to kill you," he scoffed. "I probably only saved my own hide."

She stood on shaky feet and approached slowly, the intensity in her eyes freezing him to the spot. "You. Saved. My. Life. And you had no reason to."

Only then did he realize she wasn't talking about her actual life but the life he'd saved her from. One she desperately hadn't wanted. But it still didn't change the fact that she would still have to choose three concubines eventually.

Seraphina took a step toward him. And then another. Intent lay within the depths of her eyes, and he couldn't help but back up as she advanced.

"Oh ho ho." Bastien held a cautioning finger between them. "Don't you dare kiss me again. I don't trust you not to breathe your dragon fire into my lungs."

His back brushed the tree behind him, trapping him against Seraphina's slow advancement. He swallowed as his gaze roamed over her. Black hair fell over her shoulders in a beautiful, knotted mess. Her wings draped down her back like a waterfall of gold and green leaves, the color barely visible in the darkness. And her eyes... They captivated him with their shape, their color, their intensity.

In all his life, he suddenly found something he wanted to paint more than anything. To capture her on paper. To immortalize the alluring way she stared him down.

She was an Ember Fae. The enemy. But he could no longer think of her as *his* enemy. Because in the past several days, something had developed between them. A mutual trust, perhaps. Though, of course, he couldn't disregard the way her proximity caused his heart to beat faster, his pulse to race, his breath to escape more rapidly.

Which was why he held still as his fists clenched in anxious anticipation, not knowing whether she would sear him alive or offer him a gentle heat.

Her fingers cupped his chin and turned his head to the side before she stood on her toes and placed a kiss to his cheek.

The warmth from her lips lingered long after she pulled away as if it seeped into his skin and latched onto the deepest recesses of his soul.

A breath stuttered from his lungs as he lifted his hands and cradled her face. His thumbs rested on her cheeks, a hesitant touch. Despite the warning flashing through his mind, despite the impossibility of their situation, he liked the Ember Queen far more than he had any right to. And autumns, he wanted to kiss her.

But he wouldn't step over a line she didn't want to cross. Which was why he asked permission with his eyes alone.

Seraphina's gaze flitted from his eyes to his lips, and when she leaned into him, it was all the permission he needed.

He dipped his head and softly captured her lips, wanting to be as gentle with her as possible. She'd mentioned her desire to be touched with a gentle hand. He would not squander the hesitant trust she gifted him, the willingness to let him touch her.

Her hands lifted from her sides as she placed them on his hips. An unnatural heat sparked from her fingertips, from her lips. Her kiss was hot. But pleasantly so. He relished the burn.

A sigh escaped him as she slid her hands upward until they rested against his chest. More than anything, he wanted to catch fire beneath her sparks, but he forced himself to move leisurely like damp wood smoking instead of bursting into flame.

He kissed her softly. Slowly. And he only removed one of his hands from her face to wrap his arm around her waist. But he didn't pull her closer. He simply held her, suspended in a moment of time too precious to burst with hurried passion.

When his careful control reached its threshold, he broke the kiss and only then pulled her close, wrapping his arms around her shoulders while avoiding touching her wings. Some species of winged creatures often couldn't fly again when someone touched their wings. He didn't want to find out if that were the case for Ember Fae, too.

"I am going to get killed for this," he murmured into her hair.

"Me too." Her voice barely registered when smothered by his shirt. "Though, preferably you first."

He chuckled and breathed in deeply before releasing the scent of sweet flora and autumn winds from his nostrils. "Do you remember the night you captured me?"

"Mmmhmm."

"You were downright terrifying. I think I almost shat myself."

She laughed against him, inspiring a smile to his own face.

He continued, "Why does that feel like a lifetime ago?"

"Because it was."

Silence fell between them at her declaration. Only days had passed, but he didn't feel like quite the same person anymore. And he suspected she felt the same way. Well, *of course* she felt the same way. They were enemies holding each other close. Bastien didn't know what to do next. Although he craved her touch, her kiss, her whispered words… That didn't change the fact that there was no future for them. Ever.

At the revelation, he didn't know whether to hold her tighter or put distance between them.

"Have nothing to say?" Seraphina asked, breaking the silence with a layer of uncertainty in her voice. "That's so unlike you."

He ran his fingers over her hair, and foreign excitement jolted through his stomach at the simple but intimate touch. "Oh, I have plenty to say. But my thoughts are jumbled."

"Why?" she whispered, fingers trailing up his arm and resting lightly over his shoulder.

He closed his eyes and focused on breathing deeply. "Because I shouldn't want this."

"Yet you do."

"So do you." He waited for a reply, but none came, as if she, too, were experiencing jumbled thoughts. "We should find Pri."

Her wings drooped at the mere mention of Pri's name. "It's too dark to search for her, especially when we don't know where she is. We have to wait for the morning." She paused before continuing. "How competent is Ashryn?" Seraphina bit her lip, distress in her eyes as she stared over his shoulder to the darkness behind the forest.

He slipped his hands down her arms and lightly squeezed. "Ash is resourceful. She's likely got the village in an uproar by now." But when she gave him a look that suggested she didn't appreciate his jesting tone, he spoke the truth. "Ash and I have very similar ways of thinking." He winced. "If it were me, I would have staged an *attack*. The council knew you were in the forest. I would have created a rather fiery diversion and made it look like your doing before stealing Pri away from the prison while everyone's attention was occupied elsewhere."

"And then what?" she asked quietly. "If you managed to get Pri out of the village, what next?"

Bastien ran a hand over his face as he followed her gaze to the forest behind him, trying to envision what she might be imagining. "The patrol guard would be the first on our tail, and it wouldn't take long. I'd give them an hour at most before they realized Pri was gone." When the skin between her eyes crinkled with worry, he tried to reassure her. "The first thing I would do is hide my tracks to make pursuit difficult. Similar to how you did it when you first captured me."

"And if you ran into the guards? What then?"

He swallowed and dropped his hands from her arms. "I would have to choose where my loyalties lie."

"And what would you choose?" She finally met his eye, a burning intensity within.

But it wasn't a question he knew how to answer. "I don't know."

She shook her head and pointed to his chest. "Yes, you do. You would give her up. Because you've done it before. You had a chance to save her. And you chose to imprison her instead."

"She meant nothing to me then!" he shouted suddenly but winced and lowered his voice. He repeated in a softer tone, "She meant nothing to me, only that she was a child from the enemy clan." He took her by the shoulders and tried to convey his sincerity with his gaze alone. "But now she means everything to me. Because she means everything to you."

Her shoulders slumped in defeat. "But you still 'don't know' where your loyalties lie."

"This is a complicated situation. And you know it." Releasing a long breath, he brushed a finger along the earrings in her ear and tucked a strand of her hair behind her shoulder. "Luckily for you, Ashryn's loyalties lie with me and not the settlement. She would fight the patrol guard to save your—to save Pri."

"You don't sound too happy about it."

"Because *you* put my best friend in danger!"

Seraphina huffed and turned away from him with arms crossed. "Like you said—this is a complicated situation."

He slumped to the ground, weary from the events of the past several days, but most especially from so much running with aching, festering wounds. "Get some sleep," he said, even though he was ready to drop himself. However, she looked far too ready to drop as well. "I'll take first watch."

"You really have the patrol thing down, don't you?"

"Uh-huh."

"How about *I* take the first watch?"

The distrust in her eyes washed away any hope he might have had about her concern for him. "You still don't trust me after everything." When she didn't answer, he held up his palm to show her the small slice across his skin, now formed into a scab. "I am bound by an oath. I cannot leave you." He swallowed as he gazed up at her. "And I do not want to."

For several long moments, she simply stared back at him before she turned in a circle, and then another circle, as if to survey the danger of their surroundings. And then she stretched her wings out to either side of her, mesmerizing him with the shape, the color, the birth. What would it be like to fly? To soar through the air? To fly above the treetops?

She lowered herself to the ground and curled into a ball with her wings draped over her like a blanket. He started to chuckle but inhaled quite suddenly when she laid her head on his thigh, face turned toward his feet.

"Oh." He stared at the sheen of black hair cascading over his knee. "All right. Yep, that's fine."

"I still hate you," she grumbled.

Though, he didn't miss the slight twitch of her mouth as if she tried to hold back a smile. "I hate you, too."

It didn't take too long for her back to rise and fall with the deep breaths of sleep. He soon found it difficult to keep his hands clenched at his sides, refusing to touch her while she slept. He wanted to run his fingers through her hair, feel the scales on her shoulders, touch the thin membrane of her wings.

But he would not be like the other men in her life. He would not take but only be given with consent.

Forcing his attention away from her, he surveyed the forest with careful eyes. The faint rustle of mice scampering through the undergrowth occupied his attention, as well as the hoot of a distant owl.

He kept an eye out for the silhouette of an Ember Fae waiting in the shadows but found nothing more than dark branches and bushes.

The patrol guard part of him wanted to get to his feet, to patrol the area for threats without blind spots, such as the entire area behind him. But he also didn't want to leave Seraphina without a pillow for her head.

Besides, he admitted to enjoying her nearness far more than he should.

However, after a few minutes, he sighed, gently moved his leg out from under her head, and placed a pile of leaves beneath her. He was no fool. During patrols, all personal feelings and relations must be left behind in order to keep one's charges safe.

He winced when he put weight on his leg, and the soreness in his arm and shoulder was nearly too great for him to lift a hand to brush his hair out of his face. But he pushed through the discomfort and slowly made his rounds in the area directly surrounding Seraphina.

With each pass, he moved farther out but always made sure to keep the woman within his sights.

He fingered the palm of his new obsidian sword, the only weapon on his person, as he surveyed the area around him. Nearly four days had passed since his capture, which meant only three remained before they needed to reach the Burning Cliffs. They should have reached them by now. But he imagined having to drag someone through the forest, getting attacked by an ice wraith, and getting captured a second time might slow down someone's journey.

A sudden hush descended upon the forest, and Bastien internally groaned. What was it this time? Crossbow man? Fae-eating spiders? A pack of chupacabras?

The thought of facing down one more enemy pressed on his weary shoulders as he drew his sword. His body screamed for rest, and his mind begged for peace.

If he could make it only three more days, he might know both again.

But for now…

He scanned the boughs above him. His ears twitched as he listened for anything out of the ordinary. But the only things he noticed were the stirrings of nocturnal creatures, the groanings of trees around him, and the hum of a whispering forest.

However, he knew there was a predator about from his years of experience walking the forest. And gut instinct. Plenty of that, too.

He slowly turned around as his gaze glanced about. But then the tree to his right groaned again. His eyebrows furrowed as loose dirt skittered about his feet, and he leaped backward when a root snapped upward from the ground.

"What in the…"

The tree groaned again, this time louder, as the entire thing rocked back and forth. But instead of falling, the roots pulled out of the ground enough to reveal a pair of knotted legs made of dirtied roots and twisted branches.

Two yellow eyes opened on the upper trunk, blinking several times before they focused on him. Dread fell to the tips of his toes when he realized what he faced.

An ent.

"Sera—" he tried to shout a warning as he ran in the opposite direction, but then a tree limb grabbed his foot and yanked hard enough for him to smash his head against the ground. And then the world turned black.

Thirteen

He was gone.

Seraphina cursed as she darted into an upright position, the fog of sleep disorienting her for mere moments as she glanced around the vicinity. Morning had approached already, and Bastien hadn't woken her for watch.

An early morning fog crept into the forest, bounding across the ground like a prowling feline ready to pounce on its prey.

"Bastien?" she called out, hoping he might have disappeared to relieve himself or to hunt for breakfast. But only silence answered back.

She lifted her hand and stared at the scabbed cut created from her blood oath with Bastien. If he had left her like he'd sworn he wouldn't do, then he would be dead. Simple as that. But if he wasn't dead…then where was he?

Digging her hands into the damp, decaying leaves scattered across the ground, she pushed herself to her feet and scanned the area once more. Leaves layered the forest floor, along with the tracks of several larger animals that must have passed by during the night while she'd slept. And then...

Oh!

Sprinklings of dirt created a path several paces from the tree she'd slept beside. She stooped beside the trail in search of fae tracks or something to indicate Bastien had followed. No footsteps. No imprints in the ground. Nothing.

She followed the trail of dirt until she came across a large crater in the ground, almost as if a tree were missing from—

"Blazes," she murmured under her breath when she spotted Bastien's obsidian sword barely visible beneath a mound of dirt.

Giving little caution for herself, she scooped up the sword and sprinted down the opposite side of the trail on light feet, making hardly a sound as she searched in vain for the end of the tracks. But they kept going and going, becoming more difficult to locate as the amount of dirt lessened with each pump of her legs.

But as the dirt dispersed, large footprints became more noticeable. Following the tracks proved easy when the object in question didn't bother to hide its whereabouts.

Breathing hard, she burst out of the cover of the trees, only to find an ent hovering over her. Its eyes were closed, limbs outstretched on all sides and roots buried beneath the ground. And from one of those branches...

Bastien hung precariously upside down with several thin vines wrapped around his ankles. His body swayed beneath a light breeze while his face turned red from being held head-first. He crossed his arms and glared at her.

Seraphina burst into laughter at the absurd scene in front of her but quickly slapped a hand over her mouth as her gaze darted toward the ent. The tree creature remained asleep, a deep, groaning breath escaping its mouth with each exhale.

Bastien's scowl deepened as he swayed once more beneath the breeze. "This is not funny."

"Yes, it is!" She doubled over, unable to help the guffaw from escaping her mouth. "I thought you were supposed to be a ruthless patrol guard. What about getting captured thrice screams formidable and terrifying?"

A huff left his lips. "It took me by surprise. I was expecting something...else. Not for a tree to come to life before my eyes."

"You've never seen an ent?"

Another huff. "We don't have these creatures in our neck of the woods. I admit I didn't immediately jump to the conclusion that it was the threat I was facing at the moment."

"Oh, Bastien," she tsked as she approached slowly, wary of the giant creature who could wake up at any moment. "What am I going to do with you?"

"Uhh...cut me down? Preferably before it wakes up again."

"It likely won't. They're like cats. Sleep most of the day and play at night."

He snorted. "Play? Is that what it's doing with me? It strung me up like an ornament."

"It thinks you're pretty."

"Me?" he laughed. "Then it clearly didn't catch a glimpse of *you*. Otherwise, we would find ourselves in opposite roles."

Her cheeks heated at his confession, and she slowly approached until their faces were almost level, as he was still a bit higher off the ground than her. "Count yourself lucky that it strung you up by your feet rather than your neck. People who encounter an ent are often found too late."

Before he could reply, she spread her wings and flitted to the branch he hung from, landing lightly on her feet. The branch shuddered, several leaves falling to the ground, and she held perfectly still until the shuddering ceased.

She released a tense breath and turned her attention back to Bastien.

Small vines wrapped around his ankles, each holding firm. If she cut into the vines, the ent would surely wake, and they would find themselves in a predicament. But if she used magic?

"Get ready to fall," she said quietly and grimaced. "And run if necessary. This might not be pretty."

He stared up at her from where he dangled. "But I thought you said I was pretty."

"I said the *ent* thought you were pretty, you conceited man."

Down below, he chuckled but otherwise remained quiet. She reached within her for her magic, and a tingle surged down her arm and into her hand. A flame lit in her fingers, warm and inviting but not burning her skin. Taking a deep breath, she held the flame below the vine, not to burn but to make it uncomfortably hot.

Like a hand reflexively snatching itself away from the fire, the vines released Bastien, and he fell the remainder of the way to the ground with a satisfying "oof!"

She stifled a laugh, which promptly turned into a gasp when a large branch swung at her head. She ducked beneath the swing, only to slip when the movement knocked her off balance.

A cry of alarm left her lips as she fell right as Bastien climbed to his feet. She smacked into him. They both went down, and she found herself sprawled on top of his back.

Crash!

A branch smashed into the ground beside them, large, prickly, and destructive enough to shake the earth and kick up dirt in its wake. They held perfectly still, waiting for the tree to strike again. But it only groaned.

Slowly, she turned her head to find the ent's eyes still closed and its leaves swaying on its branches as it slept.

Bastien placed a finger to his lips before grabbing her hands and helping her to her feet. She handed him his sword, and together, they quickly and quietly snuck out of its resting place.

She couldn't help but notice the agile way Bastien moved and how he made very little noise as he traversed the forest floor. Getting captured three times wasn't quite so impressive. But the way he moved as if the forest was a part of him certainly was.

"Come on," Bastien murmured, nodding toward a break in the trees. "We're almost at the Burning Cliffs."

Seraphina paused in her step, glancing at the way ahead with uncertainty. Of course, she wanted to see her sister more than anything. But…what would happen to Bastien? Would he leave with Ashryn?

The thought created a pit of ache in her belly.

Before they exited the tree line, she tugged on his hand and turned him to face her. She glanced back and forth between his silvery blue eyes, begging him to stay but not knowing how to inevitably let him go.

"What happens now?" she whispered, her thumb trailing along the back of his rough hand.

He shrugged and lowered his troubled gaze to his feet. "I suppose we'll go back to being enemies. The next time we see each other might be on the battlefield."

"I cannot accept that."

"We don't have a choice."

She frowned as she stared at a button on his vest halfway fastened, slightly skewed like the rest of his clothing. She wanted to suggest they run away together. But he had his father to think of. And she had her entire clan to care for. The

Ember Queen couldn't abandon her people. Even if some of them wished her harm.

The only difficulty would be getting herself and Pri back to their own clan before Joram and his men intercepted her.

Within the small amount of time they wallowed over the future, raindrops pattered one by one on the leaves above them. Several drops fell onto her hair, one on the tip of her nose, before the storm began in earnest. The trees sheltered them from the majority of the rain, but the drops that managed to break through the barrier disguised the drip of tears down her face.

This wasn't fair. This just wasn't fair.

In a swift movement, she sliced her palm enough to draw blood and watched as a red droplet dripped from her hand and onto the floor. "I release you from your oath, Bastien Dalena." Her voice wavered, but she pressed on. "You never needed it to begin with."

"Ser..." he murmured, almost in protest, as he reached for her.

The idea of saying goodbye in any capacity gutted her, so she quickly turned away from him and strode out from the cover of the trees.

Only to be met by the roar of falling rain and nothing else.

Red and orange silt and rocks created a pathway from one edge of a steep cliffside to the other. Once upon a time, the water from the Glades had traveled through these parts, creating a thrillingly dangerous coursing river. But now?

The Forest Fae had dammed up the river, so only a trickle slithered across the red earth and over the cliffs to the expanse of emptiness below.

Oh, how she missed the refreshing water, pure enough to drink and sacred enough to be used in countless rituals. And when the sunset hit the water just right? The river looked like billowing fire. There was hardly anything left for them anymore.

On the opposite side of the dried-up river lay an expansive tree line, and she carefully watched for any sign of Pri or Ashryn. After several long minutes, Bastien sidled up beside her and took her hand.

"We are still two days early," he reassured. "We may have to wait for their arrival."

Of course, he didn't mention the fact that Ashryn might not have been able to free Pri from prison. But she refused to abandon what little hope lived within her heart. "Then we will wait. Until then…" She smiled softly as she met his gaze, the relief in his eyes mimicking her own, as guilty as she felt for wanting more time with him.

Pulling him by the hand, she led him across the dried river and into the trees on the opposite side. They traveled for another few minutes until they reached a tree with ladder rungs leading into a poorly crafted treehouse.

He followed her up without hesitation and stepped inside the small space barely large enough for them to stand. She shut the door behind him, though it partly hung off its hinges. "My friends and I built this when we were young when the river still flowed with magic and healing." She smiled as the memories of sweet, happy summers surfaced in her mind. "I don't remember it being so small."

For having been abandoned for years, the treehouse was in decent repair, aside from a few loose shutters and the door hanging off its hinges. Blankets made from animal furs lay across the bed, obsidian sconces rested across several small walls, and four chairs stood around a circular table tucked into a corner.

The treehouse was cozy. Perfect for a place to reside while they waited out the rain and Pri's arrival.

One by one, Seraphina lit the sconces with her magic until the flames bathed the treehouse in a warm light. She took Bastien by the hand and urged him to sit in one of the dusty chairs beside the table. And then she rummaged through the special cabinet filled with drinks, herbs, and medicine, shocked that so many things still remained. Though, some of the food had long since rotted away.

Bastien laughed when she produced a hairbrush from the cabinet and stood behind him while working to unravel the ribbon tying his hair back.

"Why in the seven winds do you keep a hairbrush in here?"

Her eyes sparked with amusement as she met his gaze in the dusty, antique-freckled mirror across from them. "An ember secret." And then, little by little, she began brushing out each knot in his hair and pulling out chunks of dirt and leaves.

She couldn't say she'd ever brushed a man's hair before, and by the barely restrained amusement on his face, she reckoned no one had ever brushed his hair either.

The methodic movements of her hand helped soothe the worry tying her stomach into knots. Worry over Pri. Over her safety. Over her future. She wanted to burst outside into the rain and track the young girl down, but she hadn't the slightest idea where to look first. She could only hope Ashryn's friendship with Bastien was enough to keep Pri safe.

Halfway through her administration, she glanced at his reflection in the mirror once more, only to find his brows furrowed and his mouth puckered into a frown.

"You are being quiet," she remarked softly.

He met her gaze in the mirror. "I'm worried about my father."

"Ah." Another smooth stroke of the brush. "He's in a wheelchair?"

He nodded. "He can take care of himself just fine for the most part. But...I don't like being away for long periods of time. It makes me uneasy. And..." He paused. "He's going to be so worried."

Her movements halted against his soft, white hair as she pressed her lips together. "Because he thinks I'm going to kill you."

He turned in his chair to give her a pointed look. "How many times did you promise to end my life?"

"That was before I got to know you." She resumed her fluid strokes with the brush, trying to be mindful of the bruise on his head and the cut on his ear. "I think I'd be horrified if I killed you now."

"Why?" he laughed. "Because you finally realize how charming I can be?"

Instead of answering out loud, a smile lingered on her lips as she set the brush down and rounded on him. "Hold still," she ordered and tried to ignore her shaky fingers as she began unbuttoning his vest and slipped it off his shoulders.

"What are you doing?" he breathed when she started on the buttons on his shirt next, overly aware of his piercing gaze watching her every movement.

"I believe you have several wounds you've received in the past few days. I'm not about to let them fester any longer."

Emotion clogged her throat when she helped shrug him out of the garment, only to face the muscles hiding beneath. Her fingers brushed against the hardened planes of his chest and down to the defined muscles of his stomach. She traced each dip and groove, relishing the warmth of his skin.

"Ser," he rasped, startling her out of her musings.

"Oh, uh, right. Bandages." She turned abruptly and knocked several items from the cabinet until her fingers closed around an old, rolled bandage and a jar of ointment. With far more concentration than she needed, she redressed the bandage on his muscled arm and took care in wrapping his shoulder.

"I apologize for doing this to you," she said, lightly tracing the skin around the place where she'd stabbed him.

"You are not forgiven. It hurt like hell."

But when she lifted her gaze, the twitch of his mouth gave away his jesting words. It seemed he had forgiven her, but it didn't appease much of her guilt. If it had been anyone other than Bastien, how differently would this scenario have ended up?

With a tug of his hand, she instructed him to lay face down on the bed while she inspected the quick patch job he'd done on his thigh over his trousers. From her vantage point, the cut didn't seem deep but rather shallow. It was a good thing the bolt Zephyr had struck him with hadn't been poisoned.

Because if it had been her, each of her bolts would have been coated with a potent poison. Much like the two knives currently sheathed to her thigh strap.

"Well?" Bastien asked as he rolled over, hands behind his head. "How does it look, nurse?"

She tipped her head and gave him a pointed stare. "I can't tell with your trousers on."

He waggled his eyebrows. "Do you want me to take them off?"

But instead of giving into his teasing, heat burned inside her core as she carefully climbed onto the bed with him, on her hands and knees, her hair draping over one shoulder like an ebony waterfall.

His playfulness turned to seriousness in an instant moments before she closed the distance between them. Their lips collided in a rush of sparks, of emotion, of passion. Not at all similar to the sweet kiss Bastien had bestowed upon her earlier. But a kiss that burst every fiber of her body into flame.

"If this is how you say goodbye," he murmured against her neck, "then I've no complaints."

"I'm not saying goodbye." She threaded her fingers through his hair as she deepened the kiss, loving how his touch on her arms, her shoulders, her waist stirred the cauldron of flames within her belly until every breath that escaped her was fire. She was fire.

Bastien's mouth trailed across her jaw, to her throat, and then her collarbones. She took that time to control her breathing, knowing any mistake might hurt him if she burned too hot.

But then she gasped when his fingers brushed against her wings. He quickly snatched them back.

"Sorry."

She shook her head, unable to form words, as she grabbed his hands and guided them along the edges of her wings. The membrane was thin and sensitive, but he was so careful and gentle.

A shaky breath left her lips as she ran her hands over his shoulders, down his arms, and along his chest. When she reached the waistband of his trousers, she wanted to throw caution to the wind. To give everything to this perfect moment in time, one which she might never get to experience again. Not like this. Not with him.

But then Bastien startled her when he grabbed her hands, breathing heavily as he shook his head. All too suddenly, she noticed the rain pattering on the rooftop over their heads and tree limbs groaning beneath the howling winds.

"*No,*" he said adamantly as he held her at bay by the shoulders. "You told me what your people will do if you don't remain untouched. I will not put you in such a position."

"I have already been put in such a position, and not by your doing." She released a long, sad breath as she thought about what her future might hold. "I want to choose my own path. Just once. Before the rest of my life is forced upon me in some way or another. And…" Her voice wavered. "If I had to choose, I would choose you."

Bastien's lashes fluttered closed, followed by a swallow. He remained quiet for far too long, and only then did she realize he was wrestling with his emotions. Finally, when he spoke, his eyes opened to reveal an unmistakable sheen, and his words escaped as a rasp.

"Those are not words I thought I'd hear in my lifetime. Not directed at me."

"Why not?" she whispered, resting her hand on his chest.

"Because…" He lifted one shoulder. "I'm a half-breed. Imagine the lowliest position you can be within your clan. That is me."

"Surely not."

"Surely yes. I'm not worth loving." He cleared his throat as if to rectify his words. "I'm not worth risking your life nor your future for."

She gazed at him in an attempt to convey the sincerity of her words. "You are worth it to me."

His lips parted, disbelief staring back at her but also…hope. He wanted to love. He wanted to be loved. And she was willing to risk everything for this moment. Perhaps he was, too, as he didn't stop her as she trailed her thumb over his lips, memorizing the shape of them. The softness. The laughter always waiting on the corners of his mouth. The way they eagerly drank in her fire.

"Love me today and let's forget about tomorrow," she whispered, placing herself on the edge of a cliff, not knowing if she would fall or soar.

He lifted his hand, and she sighed as he trailed the back of his fingers over her cheek. "You are going to be the death of me."

"Get in line," she laughed, which was promptly swallowed when their lips crashed together again within a passionate yet gentle embrace.

For a moment, everything was perfect. Because no matter how impossible a future was together, here in this moment, they had each other. If only for a short while, she had a choice.

And this was her choice.

FOURTEEN

R ain pattered relentlessly on the roof shingles a short distance above them, a calming, methodic rhythm that drowned out the rest of the world. As Bastien held Seraphina in his arms, he realized he could never feel cold or lonely in her presence. Her heat wrapped him up within the warm cocoon of the furs they lay beneath, thoroughly tangled up in each other.

He ran a finger along her arm and released a contented sigh. Although he would never admit it out loud, he cared for this woman. Immensely. But speaking his thoughts, his feelings, would not change the outcome of the future.

"Let's run away together," Seraphina murmured against his neck as if pondering the same things going through his mind. His only response was to squeeze her hand where it rested against his chest. His father's words echoed in his head.

You need to leave in the dead of night. Get far, far away from the settlement. Go somewhere they can never find you.

He wanted to. So badly. But...

"Pri?" he asked in a hoarse voice.

"She's in trouble if she stays. She will have to come, too."

"And my father?"

Silence.

Both of them knew hiding him, let alone getting him out of the settlement, would be impossible.

Bastien ran a hand over his face. To secure his own happiness, he would have to let his father go. And he wasn't sure his conscience would allow it. But he wanted to live this fantasy, no matter how fleeting. And he suspected she did, too, even though he knew she wouldn't abandon her people.

"Where would we go?" He caressed her shoulder with the tips of his fingers, admiring the tough scales blended into soft skin.

"Far away from here. We could live in the shadow kingdom. No one would look for us there."

He shivered. "That place seems...backward. Nocturnal fae? Terrifying creatures everyone thinks are normal?" Yet, he grinned. "Sign me up."

Her answering smile filled the cavern of his chest with happiness. "And we'll live in a cute little cottage at the edge of the woods. Perfect for a Forest Fae like yourself to feel at home."

"With a waterfall nearby," he added. "One that faces west to make Ember Fae feel at home during each sunset."

She stroked the skin at his neck. "And we'll have five children."

He swallowed the rising emotion in his throat, fighting back the internal torment raging inside him. It was impossible. But this was only a fantasy. One he wanted to come true with his entire being. "Six," he corrected. "Always an even number."

A laugh escaped her. "Five," she insisted. "Always an odd number."

"All right, five," he relented. "And Pri. Bringing us to an even six."

Beneath the furs, she kicked his foot, and he retaliated by capturing it between his and silencing her protests with a kiss. Her heat immediately seeped into him, creating a pit of longing. Because he wanted her forever. He didn't know how it was possible, but he never wanted to let her go.

When they broke apart, a look of uncertainty stared back at him as Seraphina bit her lip. "And you would be all right with it?"

"With what?"

"With the...Pri situation."

He picked up a strand of her hair and inhaled the sweet floral aroma. The black tresses were a knotted, tangled mess, but he loved the way it gave her a wild look. Wild and passionate and untamed. He wanted to paint her. Just like this. To never forget this beautiful moment.

With a shrug, he answered, "Why not?" And then he grimaced. "I can't say I'm the best fatherly influence..."

"Oh, blazes," she laughed, and warmth filled his entire body when she kissed his bare chest. "I can't say I'm the best motherly influence. But I do my best."

They stared at each other for a long moment before jesting in unison, "Grandfather."

Bastien's chest rumbled as he chuckled. "We'll leave the child-raising to my father. He seems to be good at it."

She pinched his side. "Is he? Because he raised you, after all."

Although he wanted children someday, he wasn't ready for them. And from how it seemed, neither was Seraphina.

In an alternate world, of course...

The thought broke his smile until it disappeared altogether in favor of the sobering feelings of reality. Because this wasn't their truth, only a distorted sense of a happier life far out of reach.

He held her closer when he realized he was going to lose her. Forever. What would it be like to see her on the battlefield the next time their people went to war with each other? He couldn't fight her when all his instincts would scream to protect her.

"Can you...give your power to someone else?"

But the hope spurred in his chest deflated the moment she shook her head. "My death will transfer the power to the next female heir in line. I don't feel like dying." Her finger traced his chest and down to his belly button. "Rivers of magma run beneath our lands, and the heat gives life to my people. We cannot live without our fire. If my magic dies, then so do my people."

Frustration furrowed his brows as he glanced away from her. Of course, he'd known from the beginning that getting too close to her was a mistake. But the mistake was made. And he would fight the impossible the entire way to the next battle.

"Then why are they so strict about killing you if you were to have premarital relations?"

"Because legitimacy must not be questioned when the power passes to the next generation. The power must remain pure."

"Annnnd a Forest Fae will corrupt such purity?"

"Bas..." she murmured, lifting up on her elbow to gaze down at him. A sweet softness lingered in her eyes, a refreshing sight compared to the constant playful mocking and anger in her expression. He liked this side of her. "What do you think I could do? File down your ears? Dye your hair black? Change the color of your eyes?"

"I don't want you to have concubines."

He scratched behind his ear as frustration and hopelessness ate at him. Envy had never been a good look on him. But when he imagined her with her three future concubines, his blood boiled with rage.

She said nothing but rather slipped her fingers through his and stared at their hands while wearing a troubled expression.

After several long moments of silence, she finally spoke, "I should have gone after the other man in your party. Sylvain. It might be better if we were still enemies."

Bastien threaded his fingers through her hair and pulled her down for a kiss, which she returned with an eager mouth. All he wanted was to kiss her until all their fears and worries disappeared. But delaying the inevitable would change nothing. "I don't regret knowing you." His breath mingled with hers in the small space between them. "Not for a single second."

"Neither do I."

Over the rest of the day and into the early morning of their final day together, they made love several more times, each with more heartbreak than the last. Because they both knew they would have to say a final goodbye. And Seraphina knew she wasn't ready for it.

Perhaps she would never be ready for it.

Because she was falling in love with the one person she should have kept her distance from. Love was never supposed to be a factor when she'd stabbed him and dragged him through the forest.

But now?

She never wanted their time to end together.

Which was why she packed her belongings with languid movements and secured her sash around her waist before exiting the treehouse by her lonesome. Bastien had left over an hour ago to hunt for one last meal together, but he hadn't returned yet.

As she stepped off the last rung of the ladder, she glanced around at the red and green trees around her, inhaling the fresh near-autumn air and tucking her surroundings away in her mind to forever keep these treasured memories safe.

"Bas?" she called out, but he didn't answer.

She glanced around the treehouse and surveyed the immediate area, only to find him still missing when he should have been back by now. No doubt doing a parameter check as if he just couldn't help himself. Or...

Her heart skipped at the realization of his disappearance. Today was the day Ashryn was supposed to meet her at the Burning Cliffs. Bastien was trying to intercept them before Seraphina did.

"It's the smart thing to do," she reassured herself. But for whom? Did Bastien truly think she would hurt his dear friend after everything they'd endured together? Or was he trying to protect her from Ashryn?

Either way, she fingered her dart gun as uneasiness traveled through her. She couldn't wait for Bastien to return. This was *Pri*, and she needed to be ready for her. No matter what.

After taking one last look around her, searching for any sign of long, white hair but finding none, she trekked toward the Burning Cliffs on silent feet and senses alert. Her attention darted about at every bird call in the boughs above. Her wings flinched at every rustle and sway of the brush. And her gaze constantly scanned the area ahead.

Her lips thinned when she realized she had never told Ashryn to come alone. An entire army might be waiting for her for all she knew. But would Ashryn risk Bastien's life by bringing an army to her doorstep?

She should have asked Bastien before he'd disappeared.

A rapid pulse thrummed through her as she reached the tree line. She placed her hand against the smooth bark of a tree as she slowly peeked her head out and surveyed the dried-up river.

A trickle of water streamed through the middle of the riverbed. A bird flew overhead. Leaves fluttered in a breeze. But no other movement caught her eye.

Seraphina dared to step out of the trees and placed one foot on the hard red silt, and then another, until she stood in the middle of the parched riverbed, her entire body on full alert. Somewhere out there, Pri needed her. And she refused to stray from this spot until they were reunited.

She turned in a full circle as she surveyed the tree line and then the cliff edge, followed by trees behind her. Where was Bastien? She needed him today. Surely, he would return soon.

But as she turned back around to face the empty river, a figure with white hair now stood where it had been vacant moments before. But it wasn't Bastien.

Ashryn held a knife to Pri's throat, a snarl on her face. "Where is Bastien?" the woman growled, squeezing Pri's throat tighter with her arm.

Inhaling sharply, Seraphina drew her daggers as fury boiled hot within her blood. Her sister whimpered, and her remaining rationale dissolved like a candle beneath her flames until all she saw was red.

Pri...her Pri. A child. Threatened by knifepoint.

"Release her!" Seraphina demanded, stepping closer, but Ashryn only tipped the knife at a more dangerous angle in warning.

"Did you kill him?" The other woman glared in the distance between them. "What did you do with him?"

But the words were drowned in the rage pulsing through Seraphina's ears. She didn't care if Ashryn was Bastien's friend. If she harmed Pri in any way, she would kill her.

Bastien! she tried to call for him, but his name got stuck in her throat. Ashryn's knife now hovered over Pri's thin neck, close enough to draw blood if the girl moved even the slightest bit.

"Start talking!" Ashryn shouted, a dangerous glint in her eyes. She'd seen the glint often enough in her lifetime to know Pri was in grave danger.

She spotted the leaf-like brand on the girl's wrist, indicating her magic was being suppressed by Forest Fae magic. Pri was helpless. But she was not.

Seraphina dug the roots of her magic into the hard soil, the air around them getting hotter and hotter until it felt as if they were traversing an unforgiving desert in the middle of summer. Her magic latched onto Pri, traveling up the girl's leg, through her arm, and resting inside her hand.

Without Bastien to calm Ashryn down, Seraphina had nothing to offer. This was all she had. And by the look of understanding in Pri's eyes, the girl knew as well.

In a quick movement, Pri latched onto Ashryn's arm with a hand hot enough to scald like smelted iron. The woman hissed and flinched back, but the instinctual movement caused the blade of her knife to slice across Pri's neck.

Blood rushed over Pri's throat. Seraphina screamed. The air around them burst into fire. And she only wished the flames latched onto Ashryn's wet clothing, but it seemed the Forest Fae had been anticipating facing a fiery opponent.

Her surroundings passed by in a blur as she rushed forward with her poison-tipped knives drawn and met Ashryn blade to blade. Pri managed to scramble away despite the blood rushing over her skin. Seraphina pushed Ashryn back, away from her sister, until a large buffer lay between them. But the other woman fought back just as fiercely. As if she, too, had something to protect.

Bastien...

But the moment she thought his name, it fizzled out of her mind until her sole focus remained on the woman before her.

They fought in a dance of twisting blades and underhanded stabs. She blocked Ashryn's next swipe by smashing her forearm against hers hard enough for the blade to fly out of her hands and clatter on the ground between two large boulders. She blocked the other arm and stabbed toward the woman's unprotected side, but Ashryn twisted out of the way just in time.

Behind her, Pri gasped and sobbed, bringing her panicked attention away from the fight for mere seconds to find the girl bleeding through the fingers clutching at her throat. The distraction was enough for Ashryn to produce the spear from where it had rested against her back. She drew back with the weapon, and Seraphina's eyes widened as she attacked with one of her knives. Though, she knew she wouldn't hit her target before the spear pierced her chest.

"Ashryn, no!" Bastien screeched from across the river, and the other woman paused in her tracks. Seraphina couldn't stop the momentum of her blade fast enough before it sank into Ashryn's belly.

All the breath fled her lungs as Ashryn's eyes widened, her hand flying to her stomach. The other woman yanked the dagger out and threw it to the ground moments before her legs collapsed beneath her.

Seraphina backed up, horrified at what she'd done, just as Bastien sprinted toward them.

She spun around and rushed to Pri's side, where her sister now lay limp and unconscious. She sliced her dress at her knees with her remaining knife, bunched up the fabric, and pressed it to Pri's throat. No sound escaped the child. Not even a grunt of pain.

"No, no, no!" she gasped, shaking her to try to wake her. Pri's head flopped to the side, and another bout of panic raced through her when she thought she might be dead. But as she placed her fingers on the girl's wrist, she managed to find a pulse. She was alive. But for how long?

"It was not supposed to happen like this!" Bastien cried, his voice cracking as he hefted Ashryn into his arms and held her close. "Why didn't you wait for me?"

"You never told me where you were going!" Tears trailed down her face as she held Pri's limp body in her arms, the cloth pressed tightly to her wound. She needed a healer. Otherwise, she feared Pri would pass away on the dry riverbed that had once held healing properties that could have saved her life.

She didn't miss the look of absolute heartbreak he cast in her direction. And even in Ashryn's delirious state, it seemed she didn't either.

"Don't leave like this," she begged, but she knew he had no choice. Neither did she. The people they cared about were on their deathbeds, and they couldn't stay any longer to tempt fate.

Bastien turned his back to her. "Goodbye, Seraphina." His voice held a finality to it, a hollow permanentness that cut her to the core.

She watched with a heavy heart as he walked briskly away. "It's emberweed poison," she called out to him. "Do you know the cure?" He paused in his tracks and nodded his head once but didn't turn around, even when she apologized. "I'm so sorry."

And then he broke into a run and disappeared into a thicket of trees, racing out of sight and out of her heart. Because she knew he would never forgive her for what she had done.

She wasn't sure she could ever forgive Ashryn, either.

Seraphina held Pri tightly as she stood, making sure to staunch the bleeding with the fabric the best she could. Before she could dwell on the heartache festering in her soul, she spread her wings and leaped into the sky, flying to her settlement as fast as they could carry her.

FIFTEEN

"I need a healer!" Seraphina shouted the moment she landed in Blackburrow and tucked her wings behind her back. Her two older brothers landed with her. One of them, Eben, took Pri from her. The other, Jude, waited for orders. "Secure the borders. No one outside the clan is to come onto our territory without my sole permission. Especially no one from Ebonywatch."

Jude frowned as he fingered the hilts of his obsidian daggers strapped to his back. "What happened?"

Her brother followed as they rushed through the settlement, black leather creating a series of tents that ranged in size from small huts to enormous meeting houses. Her people exited their tents to watch them pass while wearing concerned expressions.

Lowering her voice, she answered, "Joram took me hostage. Tried to force me into a monogamous marriage with

Zephyr to make him King. I managed to escape before the ceremony."

"That idiot," Jude growled, his attention turning to Pri's limp form. "And what happened to our sister? Ugh, I knew I should have gone with you."

"I had the situation handled. Until the end. I faced an...unforeseen hiccup."

Bastien...

Never in a thousand years would she have imagined she would fall for a Forest Fae.

They rushed into a black tent made up of a series of leather flaps to separate the structure into divided rooms. Eben laid Pri onto a cot, and moving faster than someone his age ought to, the healer hurried to Pri's side and began his administrations.

Her breath trembled with each exhale as she watched the healer work. He used a series of ointments on Pri's neck until the bleeding promptly ceased. From this distance, she couldn't tell how deep the cut was, but it was deep enough for stitches.

A sob escaped the blockage in her throat as Pri received treatment. Both Jude and Eben wrapped a comforting arm around her, always her rocks during the times she felt like a tempest might sweep her away.

But Jude didn't stay, not when he still needed to secure the borders. And Eben left for several minutes, only to return with her two living fathers in tow. Each wrapped her in a bone-crushing embrace and helped the healer care for Pri.

They each loved Pri. Even though they weren't her fathers. Did they know the truth? Or did they live in ignorance just like the rest of her clan?

The man she thought might actually be her blood father out of her mother's three concubines whispered encouraging words to Pri's unconscious form. For all her life, she'd searched for the similarities, wanting to know who her blood father was despite loving each of them equally. But the man, Gavriel, had similar green and gold eyes to her own, and his red-black mouth often held an underlying smirk like hers did.

However, she was often left confused again when she noted Zar's shimmery black hair and the shape of his ears. He was less likely to be her blood father, but it was a possibility all the same.

At long last, the healer approached her, wiping the blood from his hands with a white cloth. "The cut wasn't deep," he explained, eyes weathered with life and skin wrinkled around his mouth and forehead. "She will live, but I recommend a week's rest to heal."

Seraphina crossed her arms and frowned. "A week's rest was what got us into this mess in the first place." And then her worried gaze turned back to Pri. "Are you sure there is nothing you can do to heal her wings?"

They lay shredded and torn beneath her, a sad reminder that she would never fly again. Not unless she received the healing waters of the Glades. Unfortunately, that was out of the question.

"I'm sure."

The healer bowed on a trembling leg and departed the separated room, leaving her with her fathers and Eben. A part of her knew she needed to choose her concubines soon and do it with a wise head about her in order to keep Pri safe and away from suspicion. But after knowing Bastien?

How could she possibly choose any other? If only he could be a choice. But it was possible she'd killed his best friend. Even if the laws allowed it, he would never accept her.

And then what of the other clans? One concubine from each clan. Even if she were allowed to choose Bastien, he would not want to be one of four concubines.

She pinched the bridge of her nose as she attempted to ward off the approaching ache. This situation was not ideal, but she knew she couldn't leave it the way it was. Goodbye or not, she wanted to see him one last time if she would never be able to see him again. But how?

"Watch over her for me," she said quietly to the others as she approached the tent flap leading to the exit. "I will return shortly."

As she left the medicine tent, those within the vicinity bowed to her and watched her curiously. Like her, they each had wings, though with slightly different shades and patterns than herself. Their black hair ranged from bald to cropped short to long enough to reach past their waist. Many had black tattoos. Others wore piercings.

Her finger brushed against her left ear and felt along the four piercings in her upper ear. Bastien had said nothing of the piercings, but now she couldn't help but wonder if he liked them.

Her bare feet padded along soft grass mixed with patches of black rock with trees sparsely spaced throughout the camp to offer shade during the hot days and the cold months. Energy coursed beneath her feet, her magic humming in tune with the lava providing heat for her people far beneath the rich soil.

She retreated to her tent, only to find the place littered with flowers and written notes from a variety of suitors. She knew each man by name, though not by temperament or heart. She didn't know any of them like she did Bastien. She understood his heart, his thoughts, his feelings, his hopes and dreams. And in such a short time, too.

She ran her fingers along one of the thin, red petals of a crimson bloom, her thoughts returning to Pri. Would her clan truly kill her if they found out the truth? Perhaps the other clans might want to, but she truly believed her own would protect her.

Several pieces of parchment lay on one of the tables, and she picked up each and sifted through the names and signatures of each offering. Hearts were bound to break, alliances tested, and she feared outright wars if she didn't choose correctly.

Why did such a responsibility lie on her shoulders?

And how could she achieve happiness without causing her people suffering?

Gavriel, the man she assumed might be her blood father, rapped his knuckles on the tent pole, bringing her attention to the entrance. He gazed at her with a sorrowful understanding in his eyes, and he needn't say anything when he seemed to guess the direction of her thoughts.

When he held out his arms, she embraced him tightly, needing something to keep her together when she felt like falling apart.

"What was it like?" she sniffed but cleared her throat quickly to try to disguise her wavering emotions. "Were you ever jealous of the other concubines?"

Her father shook his head, the gold hoops in his ears clacking together with the movement. "How could I be? There were two others who could help make your mother happy, and that's all we wanted for her." His chest rumbled as he chuckled. "I won't lie. There were a few fights and perhaps a couple bloodied noses... But in the end, we were all a happy family."

"Even when children came along?"

"Especially then."

She paused and took a deep breath to steady her nerves. "And what if there is one man I want more than the others? And what if that man can only accept a monogamous marriage?"

Gavriel stiffened, and she glanced up to find his eyes darkened with anger. "You're not talking about Zephyr."

"No, no, no. I have a particular punishment in mind for what they did to me." She shook her head and dropped her arms, stepping away to stack the flowers in a pile. She would choose none of these men as her concubines. But she still had no idea who she might choose in the end. "He's a…Forest Fae."

Her father's gaze darkened further as he pulled the leather flap shut between them and their clan. "You don't mean…"

"I do." She tossed another bouquet into the pile as she firmed her resolve and turned back to her father. "I am going to unite us with the Forest Fae, ending the wars once and for all."

"How will you do that?"

Her fingers grazed the stack of flowers, her expression troubled. "I don't know yet how to accomplish what I want. But I think it's time for this to end. No more wars. No more feuds. Only peace. Just like there used to be a long time ago."

"And…you're set on this man."

"I am." She nodded. "But how can he ever accept our culture?"

Because it was all she could do to keep the peace between the clans. Her power could only die with her. And choosing between death and Bastien seemed like a terrible idea.

Picking up a small bouquet of red and white cinderblooms, she inhaled their delicate scent of ashes and fire before setting it on top of the pile with the others. Too many scents blended together, bombarding her senses. Getting rid of them was for the best.

"You can't force our culture on anyone," her father replied at last. "It must be their choice."

"But…" Her voice trembled. "I don't want to lose him."

He pulled her closer to offer her comfort in his brief embrace. "It isn't love if you only take. Love is sacrifice. And sacrifice is difficult."

Zar, her other father, knocked next and lifted the flap. "Pri is awake. She's asking for you."

Seraphina gasped, unable to move fast enough as she dashed across the settlement and threw aside the tent flap as she entered the medical tent. After ordering everyone out for a few minutes, she knelt beside Pri's bed and caught her hand in her own, noticing that the magic-blocking brand no longer marred her wrist.

Tears of pain trailed down the girl's face, but relief settled in her eyes when Seraphina gently kissed both cheeks and her forehead.

"I thought I would never see you again," Pri croaked.

She smoothed down Pri's sticky hair. "I would never abandon you. No matter what. You are safe now."

Pri sniffed, tears trailing silently from the corners of her eyes. "I wish I had my mother. Someone to hold me and tell me everything will be all right."

Seraphina closed her eyes and released a long breath before opening them once more. "I need to tell you something." If the truth was circulating, even among the leaders of one of the clans, then she wanted Pri to hear it from her rather than someone else. "You have a mother. And she's alive."

The girl's teary eyes darted to her, unfocused but still alert. "What?"

She ran her hand soothingly over Pri's damp hair and brushed her thumb along her face to gather the fallen tears. After fortifying her walls, she spoke the truth of the situation in hushed tones. Pri listened intently, especially at the part when she explained why she and her mother had done what they did and why they still needed to keep it a secret for as long as they could.

"I was not ready to be a mother," she whispered, catching several more warm tears. "But I tried my best, Pri. And my fathers helped. I hope you will find it in your heart to someday forgive me."

In a languid movement, Pri wrapped her arms around her neck and pulled her into an embrace. Seraphina's eyes smarted at how quick her sister—no, daughter—was to love and forgive others.

"Everything will be all right," she murmured in her daughter's ear while continuing to stroke her silky hair. "I won't allow anything bad to happen to you ever again."

A sniff. "I'm sorry for sneaking away. I thought I could get past the guards. I was wrong."

"No one can get past the guards. Not even me."

"Is that why Ashryn broke me out of jail?" When Seraphina nodded, Pri sniffed again. "She took me on a secret path by the river so no one would be able to find us."

She stiffened, her heart beating rapidly with hope as she gently laid Pri's head back on the pillow. "Tell me exactly where to find this path."

SIXTEEN

Two days had passed since Ashryn had been stabbed. Bastien had stayed by her side the entire time through the tremors, the mouth foaming, the fevers, and finally when she opened her eyes for the first time and gazed back at him without being delirious.

Treating her from emberweed poisoning was difficult, but Sylvain had helped gather the necessary ingredients, and the Attleglade healer had stopped by several times.

But something still didn't seem quite right with Ashryn, even though he was certain the poison was gone from her body. Her eyes were still glazed over with confusion when she screamed out in her sleep and her forehead damp with perspiration.

And an hour ago?

Cranky Cricket had come by to question him thoroughly. What was the Ember Queen like? How did she capture them? How did she get into the settlement? Where did she take them?

It brought some measure of satisfaction to lie to the man's face.

But…he also told a few truths. Because he cared about the people of Attleglade. And if they were to get attacked again by the Ember Fae, he wanted them to have a fighting chance.

"I'm so confused," he whispered to himself from where he sat in a chair at Ashryn's bedside, gazing outside the window into the village below.

"Me too," Ashryn croaked beside him.

"Ash!" he gasped as he stood and hovered over her, trying to find something that might be wrong with her. A bandage still wrapped around her torso. Her mouth no longer foamed with poison. Her eyes gazed back at him with semi-lucidity. "How long have you been awake?"

"A while now." She winced as she shifted positions, though she continued to lie down. "I've been watching you frown and sigh and scrunch your eyebrows together like the way you do when you're frustrated. And…" She shrugged and winced again. "Didn't want Cranky Cricket to know I was awake yet. I heard him downstairs. I thought we should get our stories straight first before he questions me next."

After helping her drink cool water from a wooden cup, he set it aside and returned to his chair, going over the story he'd told Cranky Cricket nearly word for word. Ashryn stared at him with a calculated look, but she didn't cast any accusation in his direction, not even when he knew she knew he was leaving out quite a bit of the story.

"Soo…" she started slowly, still watching him carefully. "How much is true? How much is fabricated?"

He ran another hand over his face, the short bristles of his facial hair scratchy against his palm. He hadn't shaved in, well, nine days. And he'd hardly slept much in that time, either. "A bit of both."

The emotional energy to continue didn't present itself as he returned his stare to the window, his elbows resting on his knees.

"I have not seen you smile once since we returned."

A long exhale left his mouth as he gazed somberly at the leaves transitioning from green to yellow and red outside. "Get some rest, Ash."

"You truly care for her. Don't you?"

Another long pause passed as he fought off his emotions and the memory of Seraphina's sweet, hot lips on his, the silk of her hair beneath his fingers, the beautiful, melodic laughter that filled his heart with joy. "It doesn't matter."

The words cut another hole in his heart. He had never fallen in love with someone before, but he'd never imagined how much it would hurt to lose them.

"I'm all right," Ashryn insisted, though the corners of her mouth winced slightly as she gestured to herself. She blinked sluggishly. "Perhaps you should speak with Sera—"

"Don't say her name." He couldn't bear for the sound of her name to carve another hole inside his heart. "She's gone. I don't want to see her again." Unshed tears burned his eyes.

"She got what she wanted." She got Pri back, and although he hoped more than anything that the young girl would pull through her injury, Seraphina had still fought for what she wanted. And it wasn't him.

"Bastien—"

"Don't. Just...don't."

She lifted a trembling hand and placed it over his heart. The touch broke him. The unshed tears trailed down his cheeks. "You love her."

"It doesn't matter. You are my only friend, Ash. You come first. She is my enemy."

Ashryn winced again and closed her eyes, her fingers hovering over her belly where she'd been stabbed. "I made a mistake. I threatened Pri with a dagger even after I promised her I wouldn't. I was just so...angry. The sight of the queen boiled my blood. She had every right to attack me."

He ran a hand over his face. "I don't even know what to say."

"I injured Pri. I was going to kill Seraphina. You stopped me. She stabbed me. There is nothing more to say other than I'm sorry, Bas. I...didn't know how you felt about her."

"How could you have?" He swiped the back of his hand across his face.

The somber look in her eyes almost caused him to glance away, but then she spoke again. "She didn't mean to hurt me. I saw the regret in her eyes."

"I." His hands cupped her face. "Don't." His gaze burned into hers. "Care." And then he hung his head, dropped his hands, and pressed his palms into his eyes.

She lightly touched him on the arm. "I've been through worse. Believe me."

"I know." He squeezed her feverish hand but didn't look her way again.

Several long minutes of silence passed. Comfortable silence. Each trapped in their own minds as they tried to come to terms with what had happened. Bastien was simply glad Ashryn was overcoming the effects of the emberweed poison. He'd known other Forest Fae who had died from getting stabbed by a poison-tipped knife or impaled with a deadly dart.

"Do you want to talk about it?" she asked finally.

He shrugged. "What more is there to say? Talking about it won't change anything."

"No...but it might make you feel better."

Running his hands through his hair, he tried to find a way to convey his thoughts and feelings from the past week. It was impossible to share what he and Seraphina had experienced together. But he wanted to try.

"She's so...angry. And heated. And passionate. And I just love it. I really have to work for a smile, but when I get one...I can't think of a better feeling in the world. She makes me feel..." He gestured to his chest, not knowing how to form the words. "So much. She sees me. She understands me. And I'm devastated that it's over as fast as it began."

Ashryn ducked her head and released a long breath. "Because of me. I ruined this for you."

He snorted. "No. It never would have worked to begin with. We both knew it from the start."

"I'm sorry. I wish…" Her words trailed off, and he was glad for it. It was over. Done. And now he needed to try to find a way to move forward.

Another long silence passed between them, at least until his friend broke the stillness of the room. "Just tell me one thing," she said with a serious expression. But then her lips curved upward in a teasing grin. "How many times did you…you know…?"

His frown melted, and he couldn't help but laugh as he sheepishly held up four fingers. His time with Seraphina had quickly become some of his favorite memories, and he vowed to cherish them for as long as he lived.

"Speaking of *you know what…*" Bastien slapped his knees as he stood and made his way toward the door. "Sylvain has been hounding me to let him up here to see how you are faring."

"You've been denying him?" Ashryn growled. "You are not my gatekeeper."

"Yes, I am." He cast her a devilish grin. "And now he knows it. I'll send him up. But hear me when I say if he in any way makes you tear open your stitches, he's done for."

She picked up a spare pillow from her bed and weakly tossed it at him, but it flopped onto the floor halfway across the room. Laughter escaped his mouth as he ducked into the stairwell and shut the door behind him.

Only out of sight did he sober, his laughter dying away. For seven days, he'd had something more. Something special. And now he didn't. The promise of a brighter future was gone. Because half-breeds didn't get happy endings. He only wished Ashryn could find one in his place. One of them deserved to be happy.

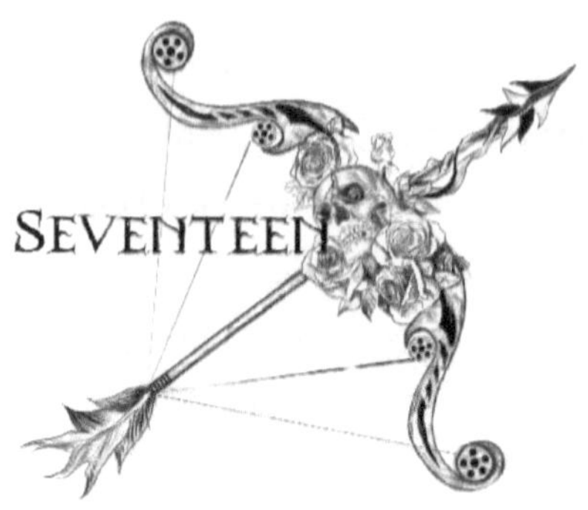

SEVENTEEN

The Glades rushing by stole her breath away.

Seraphina watched in awe as the gorgeous rapids cascaded down a steep waterfall and crashed into the river below. Sparkling blue waters reflected the moonlight while its passionate falls stung her face from where she stood on a small ledge, scaling the cliffside.

High above her, a wooden, rickety bridge stretched across one side of the ravine to the other. Leading to…

A part of her wanted to bow at the sight of the sacred place of her ancestors. The caverns that held the healing pool. Another part of her wanted to spit at the reminder of who stole their sacred land in the first place.

Stop, she urged her thoughts. The war would end with her, which meant she, above all others, must cast aside the toxic prejudices she held over the Forest Fae. Bastien was one of those Forest Fae. She must remember that.

She glanced down, barely fitting on the ledge as she scooted forward on slow but careful feet while her wings awkwardly hid her from view by camouflaging with the rocky cliffside. Thus far, she hadn't seen anyone. But after her many encounters with the patrol guard, she'd quickly learned that someone was always watching.

The crash of the water in her ears lessened when she positioned herself directly beneath the rickety bridge, which swayed with the breeze created by the crashing waterfall a short distance away.

She placed a hand around one of the ropes with the intention of swinging herself over but froze when two feet landed directly above her.

Her pulse quickened as she stared at the boots through the slats as well as the brown and white clothing of the person they belonged to. A patrol guard.

"You know you cannot cross the bridge," a voice warned, and for one terrifying moment, she thought the woman might be speaking to her.

But then a male voice answered, one her soul recognized, one she had missed with her entire being in the three days since she'd seen him. "Please," Bastien begged. "It's not for me. It's for Ash."

A pause.

"The council members have forbidden it. She was stabbed by an Ember Fae weapon. Such impurities will pollute the pool."

Are you serious? Seraphina mentally scoffed. Ember Fae were not dirty or impure. The healing waters of the Glades accepted all.

"Ash will not bathe in the pool," Bastien argued, and she only wished she could see him from her vantage point. But he wasn't standing near the rope bridge. "Just a cupful. That's all I ask."

The woman sighed. "You know I cannot allow it. Ash is my friend. This is hard for all of us to watch her suffer." Another pause. "How is she faring?"

Devastation clung to Bastien's voice, creating a pit of guilt in her stomach. "She was improving, but then the fits returned. I don't know…" He cleared his throat. "I don't know if she'll make it. So, *please*. I beg you. Only a cup. No one will find out. You have my word."

Through the slats, Seraphina noticed the woman bow her head and frown. "This is not up to me. You are trying to appeal to the wrong person."

A rock skittered over the cliffside as if someone had kicked it, and it fell a great distance before crashing into the river below, the sound drowned by the roaring water.

"When was the last time *anyone* bathed in the pool?" Bastien cried. "Cranky Cricket?"

"Shhh. You shouldn't call him that."

"I'm serious, Nathalie. Do you know why the Glades don't heal him? Because he is an unworthy leader. All of us are *impure* to him."

"Please, stop."

But Bastien didn't heed her warning. "That man deserves to die. But everyone is too cowardly to put him on trial."

"Hush," Nathalie murmured. "If anyone overhears you saying that—"

"Then what?" he challenged. "What will happen to me? If Ash dies, I have nothing left to lose."

The scuff of boots against grass announced Bastien's departure. Above her, Nathalie sighed, a look of regret on her face, before she started to climb the tree beside the bridge. Seraphina's heart leaped to her throat as she used the woman's momentary distraction to swing herself over the edge of the cliff and follow after Bastien.

The man stalked angrily through the woods, his footsteps louder than she'd ever heard them before, making following him easy.

She kept to the trees, using them as cover when she thought someone might discover her. But her wings helped camouflage her, and her feet made nary a sound on the forest floor.

At last, they reached a series of dwellings within living trees, and she barely refrained from gasping. The trees were taller and wider than anything she'd ever seen within the forest. They lived and breathed with beauty and vitality. Large, red leaves wound up the trunks and weaved through sturdy branches while rich, brown tree bark adorned every inch of them, untouched even by animals.

The rich scent of earth filled her nostrils, momentarily distracting her from the fact that she traversed enemy territory. If *anyone* learned of her presence in Attleglade, she doubted she would make it out alive with a hundred Forest Fae fighting against only her.

Not unless she activated the dormant volcano with her power... But hundreds of people would die. Men. Women. Children. And the Glades would be destroyed forever. Her life was not worth destroying so much goodness.

Hiding from passing fae proved difficult as she followed Bastien through the settlement. He stopped beneath a smaller tree, a mixture of anger and sadness on his face as he gazed up at a window, candlelight flickering through the small cracks in the shutters.

His jaw set as he rushed off in another direction. But this time? She didn't follow.

Glancing around her to make sure no one turned their heads in her direction, she stole through the darkness, opened the curved wooden door made of tree bark, and slipped inside the tree-dwelling.

She inhaled sharply at her surroundings, marveling at the *life* around her. The tree lived and breathed, its energy humming happily despite being hollowed out to use as a home. The entire structure was made of the tree's wood, from the walls to the tables to the chairs, but it was decorated with knick-knacks from books to paintings to glass vases and bowls.

She scolded herself for losing focus and began climbing the stairs. She winced when one of the stairs creaked beneath her weight but kept climbing when she felt far too vulnerable in the winding stairwell.

Finally, she reached the top of the stairs where it abruptly ended, almost as if unfinished, and to her right was a single door.

Her entire body remained alert as she pushed the door open and peered inside.

And then her wings drooped at the ghastly sight.

Ashryn was alone, though likely not for long. Perspiration slicked against her skin, her eyes unfocused as she gazed at the ceiling. Her face was flushed, and her breaths escaped as rasps with each exhale.

The woman was on death's doorstep. No wonder Bastien was so angry.

But was he also angry at *her*?

She pushed the door open wider, closed it behind her, and started toward Ashryn with purposeful strides. The other woman turned her head to glance in her direction before her eyes shot wide open. Her nostrils flared. Her hands weakly searched her person as if trying to find a weapon, and when she reached for the wooden cup at her bedside table, Seraphina hit it out of her hands, the small object skittering across the floor.

Unfortunately, she likely only had minutes before Bastien, or someone else, might return. After witnessing his anger, she wasn't sure if he would allow her to treat his friend.

A noise gurgled from Ashryn's throat, something between a distressed cry and a warning scream. But Seraphina grabbed onto the woman's chin and gazed into her eyes. Still unfocused. Her flushed skin was also feverish. And her wound…

As if realizing she wouldn't hurt her, or perhaps because she couldn't fight back, Ashryn didn't stop her as she unwound the bandage covering her torso.

She hissed.

Pus filled the stitched-up wound, the poison still festering within the woman's body. A white substance surrounded the injury, and she recognized it as an antidote to several other Ember Fae poisons. But…

"Bastien, you idiot," she murmured with far too much endearment clinging to her voice for the man who had stolen every inch of her heart. "You told me you knew the antidote. This is not the antidote."

Another gurgled cry left the woman's lips as she pulled out a knife from her belt, but this one wasn't tipped in poison. "Hold still," she ordered when Ashryn attempted to squirm away. "Unless you want a bigger gash than the one you have."

Ashryn ceased moving, and Seraphina leaned closer, holding the skin steady and ignoring her pained grunts as she cut each stitch one by one. Blood and pus oozed out of the wound, and she took a moment to wipe everything clean with a cloth, including the white serum.

Reaching into a leather pouch attached to her belt, she pulled out a vial filled with thick, orange liquid and pulled out the cork with her teeth.

"This is going to burn," she warned. "Breathe in and hold it." She poured half of the vial's contents into the belly wound, and the moment it made contact with the inside flesh, Ashryn gasped in pain, followed by a sob. But otherwise, the woman remained stoic in the face of the elixir's healing effects.

The remaining half of the elixir still swirled within the vial. She lifted it to Ashryn's lips, and instead of rejecting it, she swallowed the rest of its contents.

Agonized tears trailed from Ashryn's eyes as the antidote worked through her body. But after a few minutes, she began breathing easier, and the tears ceased flowing.

"There you go," Seraphina whispered reassuringly. She dipped a cloth into a bowl of water on the floor, wrung it out, and placed it against the other woman's forehead. "I wasn't sure if Bastien would have treated your wound correctly, but...I brought my supplies just in case."

She uncorked another vial of clear liquid, tipped it over a cloth, and dabbed at the wound. Ashryn hissed between her teeth but soon relaxed as the pain settled as the numbing took effect.

Wasting no time, Seraphina threaded a needle and began meticulously tying new stitches. Of course, the injury would scar. But perhaps not quite so much with careful stitches.

"Why are you doing this?" Ashryn asked after a few minutes, exhaustion in her voice.

"Ha." She shook her head wryly as she continued her administration. "Do you know how often Bastien spoke of you? I first thought him besotted. But no. I've never witnessed a friendship like yours." She swore under her breath when she cut one of the threads too short and had to start over. "When will Bastien return?"

"Soon. He will be happy to see you."

Again, she shook her head. "No, he won't. I'm going to have to hide somewhere in Attleglade until I can find a good way to approach him. He's livid. I'm afraid he will take drastic actions to save your life."

"But...you already did."

She lifted her head to find Ashryn gazing at her curiously. "He doesn't know that. And I hope you won't tell him. Not yet, at least."

This time, she cut the thread to the perfect length and tied off the last stitch.

"You still never answered me," Ashryn said slowly. "Why are you doing this? For me? Or for him? I killed your sister."

Seraphina covered the wound with a bandage, wrapped it several times around her waist, and tied it in a gentle knot away from the injury. "Pri will live. And I'm sure not doing it for you. Who threatens a *child* at knifepoint?"

Ashryn lowered her gaze. "Those desperate to see their friend alive and unharmed."

"Oh, I assure you," she chuckled humorlessly, "Bastien was quite content with me. But it's over and done with. Pri is fine. You will live. Bastien will forgive me? I have no idea. I came back for him. And I'm not leaving until he agrees to come with me."

"Where?"

She sat back on her ankles as she packed up her things as quickly as possible. "Home."

"This is his home."

She tipped her head and stared at her pointedly. "It sounds more like he's a prisoner here. He deserves to live his life to the absolute fullest, nothing and no one holding him back."

Down below, the front door opened and closed, followed by a creak on the stairs in the same place she'd stepped earlier. In a desperate attempt to hide, she touched the sconces on the walls, and the crystal light flickered out, giving way to darkness.

"Where can I hide?" she asked, her gaze darting toward the closed door.

"Bastien's father's home. Top floor. Bastien lives there now after Pri burned down his house, but I doubt he'll darken the door while I'm on bedrest."

Ashryn gave brief directions, and the moment the door opened, Seraphina squeezed herself out the window shutters and crouched low on a nearby branch outside, making sure her wings camouflaged her from nearby onlookers.

"What in the autumn winds?" Bastien said from within the dwelling, and Ashryn must have been feigning sleep because she said nothing. Moments later, the lights flickered back on, followed by a long, heaving sigh of relief. "Your fever is gone. Thank the stars. I was going to kill a man or two to get you that healing water."

Several seconds passed of silence, and Seraphina longed to hear his voice again, which was why she couldn't bring herself to move from her place on the branch. She'd missed him. Far too much.

"You scared me," he said after the pause. "I thought you were going to kick the bucket."

No answer.

"Sylvain will be back soon with fresh water. The man hardly knows you, yet he's still willing to stay by your side when you look like a confused pheasant who walked through the wringer."

"Ugh," Ashryn groaned. "I can hear you. Why are you so loud?"

Another sigh of relief. "This is my inside voice. Here, let me check your wound."

"No!"

"*Yes.* I'm not just going to sit here and watch you die."

Seraphina cocked her ears and leaned closer to hear his next words, which were nearly drowned by the leaves flitting in the trees above her head. "Who did this? These aren't my stitches. What is this orange stuff?"

More silence, but this time she knew Ashryn wasn't feigning sleep.

"Wait a second." He gasped. "Oh ho ho. No. *No!* Where is she?"

"I don't know who you are referring to."

"Don't play coy with me."

Movement below startled her from her eavesdropping, and she dropped her gaze to find a patrol guard scouring the village. If Seraphina stayed any longer, she might get caught. And this was the last place she wanted to be found.

Giving one last regretful look toward the window, she climbed higher in the tree until she stood on a sturdy branch. She had no idea how Bastien gracefully leaped from tree to tree, but she tried to mimic his movements as she made her way across the village by treetop. When the branches shook, she paused, heart in her throat as she waited to get impaled by a spear or arrow. However, when no such attack came, she continued on her way, but this time used her wings to keep most of her weight off the branches.

Soon, she found the house Ashryn had specified and climbed down several levels of branches until she reached the window. With one last glance around her, only to find a quiet evening, she slipped through the window and closed the shutters behind her, immediately met by silence.

She turned around and took in Bastien's room in the darkness, not daring to light a sconce to reveal her presence.

The room was...plain. Void of decoration but piled with an array of clothing and weapons on the bed and on the floor beside an armoire. She inspected each weapon and surveyed the sharp points of his rack of spears attached to the wall. She plucked the string of his bow, smiling at the satisfying *twang*. Two quivers of arrows lay on a table, several arrows scattered and two even on the floor.

She picked up the arrows and set them on the table next to the others. During their time together traversing the woods, he hadn't had a weapon on him for the majority of the time. Yet he still managed to be resourceful. She'd witnessed him with a sword, which she knew wasn't his weapon of choice, judging by the spears and arrows filling his room. What was he like in his element? If he had a bow and a spear at his fingertips?

Next, she opened the armoire door the rest of the way to find a mess staring back at her. Shirts, trousers, belts, cloaks. Some hung haphazardly off hangers. Others simply lay on the ground at her feet.

"Who are you?" she whispered, running her fingers over the soft fabric of a tunic. "Other than patrol guard?"

But judging by the disaster before her, she highly suspected being in the patrol guard *was* his identity. He had nothing else to look forward to in his future and therefore dedicated his life to protecting others.

Her breath hitched as she approached another table in the corner near his bed, this one layered with pieces of small, wooden spikes along with wooden circles.

She picked up one of the circles and inspected it in the darkness, only to inhale sharply. It was a wheel. More specifically, a wheelchair wheel. So, Bastien wasn't just a patrol guard. He was his father's caretaker, too.

A chill raked across her skin as a breeze entered through the cracks in the window shutters. She pulled back the bedsheets and slipped inside while igniting the flames within her body to keep herself warm.

And after a few moments? Loneliness engulfed her. Because she knew Bastien was with Ashryn and not with her.

"I have no right," she whispered, dragging her finger along the bedspread. "Because I have no choice but to take concubines."

She'd thought of every way to avoid such a scenario, to have Bastien and only Bastien. But she was the Ember Queen. And Ember Queens had the responsibility of uniting their people to avoid unnecessary bloodshed between clans.

Therefore, she had no right to envy Ashryn.

But then why did her chest ache at the thought of them together? What were they doing? What were they talking about? Was he holding her as she healed? Were they holding hands or sharing kisses like *friends* supposedly did?

With a huff, she tossed onto her other side to avoid staring at the empty space beside her. But when that did nothing to quell the ache inside her, she wrapped her arms around his pillow and inhaled his fresh, foresty scent lingering in the fibers of the cloth.

A part of her knew she should leave. To protect herself from being discovered.

But she refused to leave Attleglade without Bastien.

EIGHTEEN

"Y ou infuriate me. Do you know that?" Bastien paced back and forth across the small space of Ashryn's room, staring her down as she gazed back at him with her chin raised, defiance in her eyes. "If I catch you walking around one more time, I'm going to gut you."

"I wanted to visit Sylvain. You can't keep me bedridden all day, every day."

"I can and I shall." He threw his arms up. "You almost died, Ash! Twice! I don't care about how resilient you think you are. You have no idea what I endured watching you suffer like that."

The fire dissipated from her eyes, but the stubborn tilt of her chin remained as she crossed her arms and turned her head away from where she sat up in her bed. "You better be careful about making such bold, profound statements. Your beau might get jealous."

"Ha!" He rolled his eyes as he gestured to the empty space around them. "What beau? Besides, if Seraphina were here, I would—"

"You would what?"

An icy chill exploded through Bastien's chest as he spun around, only to find the woman in question standing in the shadows of the room, leaning a shoulder against the wall. Her eyes were determined and focused like a predator ready to strike.

But then his shock transitioned into fear as he crossed the room and slammed the shutters closed. "What are you doing here?" he hissed. "If someone finds out, you will be killed."

A smirk pulled on her lips as she stared him down. "Then I hope no one finds out. For your sake, of course."

"Why?" he snarled, still trying to recover from the shock of her presence. How did she get here? How did she arrive intact and unnoticed? Of course, he'd suspected Seraphina's presence in Attleglade because of the orange ointment that seemed to have helped his friend recover, but he had been doubtful all the same.

"Because." She stepped out of the shadows, and the first thing to draw his eye was the long slit in her dress, revealing her entire leg nearly up to her waist. "If history proves anything, you will be unable to help yourself as you leap to my rescue and take the brunt of the attacks."

His lips twitched as her humor hit him across the head like a mace, but he successfully reined back his smile. "You carried me on your back while my limbs were useless. I only returned the favor when you got a taste of your own medicine."

"How is your arm?" She touched his bicep, and it took all his self-control to jerk his arm away.

"Fine, no thanks to you."

"I'm glad." Her mouth smirked again. "My bandaging handiwork is parallel to none."

"Stop," he said as he fought hard against the smile wanting to appear before his expression turned serious. "This is not funny. How did you get here, anyway?"

Seraphina tipped her head toward Ashryn, who watched the exchange with wide eyes as if she didn't know whether to break up the verbal spar or cry out for help. "Pri told me how to enter the village without notice."

Bastien pressed his lips together. "And you came? Were you followed?"

"I took care to remain unseen. Besides, your dear friend would be dead without my interference. Next time, make sure you know the real antidote before you go running off, you infuriating man."

Her fingers lightly touched his chest as they glared at one another, and he found himself torn between sweeping her off her feet and putting more distance between them. But he'd craved her touch for days, and he couldn't find the willpower to push her away.

"I thought I knew it."

"I said *emberweed* poisoning. Not *emberwort*."

"How was I supposed to know? They sound the same!"

A breath shuddered from his lungs as she ran her fingers down his chest and to his abdomen, maintaining eye contact the entire time.

A soft yet silky tone clung to her voice. "I lied to you a week ago." She held up a pouch dangling from her fingers by leather strings, and his jaw slackened when she pulled out his chupacabra mask and his favorite bow. "I didn't really throw your weapons into the river."

He stared back at her with parted lips as he strapped the mask onto his back and his bow over his shoulder. "Why not?"

"Never discard anything you can later use as leverage."

"And now you're using it as leverage to get me to like you again."

A long sigh escaped her mouth. Long and weary and full of devastation. "Is it working?"

His mouth twitched from one side to the other as he studied her. "What else do you have as leverage?"

"An apology?"

"You?" He laughed. "Apologizing?"

She scowled and kicked his knee. The fact that he didn't stop her spoke volumes of how this situation might play out. He caught her foot, throwing her off balance. She turned into the movement and ended up behind him, poking him in the side with her fingers. "An apology," she repeated again. "I am sorry for hurting your friend." Feeling another pair of eyes on her, she glanced up to find Ashryn staring unashamedly at them, likely hanging onto every word.

The other woman shrugged sheepishly. "I'm not here."

Seraphina rolled her eyes. "Yes, you are." But there was no other place to hold this conversation unless she could somehow lure Bastien into the narrow hallway. But she assumed he would no sooner leave his friend's side than give her a few moments of his time.

"She had my sister," she tried to explain, gazing back at him to try to make him understand. "I didn't think. I just reacted. I'm so sorry, Bastien. Please forgive me. I never should have hurt her."

"You almost killed her." Fortunately, the cold edge melted from his eyes.

"And I deeply regret it." She ran a hand down his arm from his bicep to his wrist. "I cannot change what I did. All I can ask for is forgiveness."

He swallowed. "And is Pri...?"

With a shake of her head, she said, "She's alive and well."

The fight left his eyes, but a somberness remained. "We cannot continue this, Ser." He gestured between them. "It's forbidden for a half-breed like me to..." He glanced toward Ash, who suddenly found a book to occupy her attention. But she never turned a page.

"To what?" she urged.

He turned away from her and began pacing the floor while running his fingers through his hair. "For me to marry! To have children. I never told anyone this part. Not even Ash." He winced when he met his friend's eye across the room. Taking her by surprise, Bastien grabbed her arm and pulled her into the hallway, shutting the door behind him before he continued quietly. "The council forced me to take a blood oath to never have children. The alternative was sterilization. Why else do you think they allowed me to stay in Attleglade?"

Her mouth turned downward, and she swallowed a lump of emotion in her throat as her eyes misted over. If Bastien had truly been forced into a blood oath, then the moment a child was born, he would drop dead just from the magic of the oath. To be with him meant giving up so much. But after knowing him, she knew she wouldn't be able to pull herself away now.

Clearing his throat, he glanced away to stare at the top of the staircase rather than at her. "And a second blood oath to keep me grounded within the territory." He glanced at her but quickly looked away. "If I cross the border, I will fall over dead immediately. When those Ember lunatics captured us, I was only a few paces away from dropping dead."

Her lips parted as she stared at him, followed by a discomforting squeeze to her chest. The Burning Cliffs were *barely* within the Attleglade territory, which was why it had been abandoned over the years. She could have killed him.

Until now, she hadn't realized how close she'd been to losing him.

He stepped closer, a sheen of determination in his eyes. "If you know what's good for you," he said, pointing a finger at her, "then you will leave. There can be no *us*. You will lose so much."

But instead of retreating, she trailed a hand down his arm and slipped her fingers into his. "Or I will gain plenty. I never imagined wanting a Forest Fae so badly it hurts. You are weaved into the very fiber of my being. Into my body, my soul, my past, my present, and my future." She lowered her voice and brushed the back of her fingers against his cheek. "I love you, Bastien, and I cannot let you go. No matter how much you will it."

A sigh escaped him as he closed his eyes and held his hand over hers, where it rested against his cheek. "You are an Ember Fae. The blazing Ember Queen, at that. We will never work. You know this."

"You refuse to even try?"

Although she attempted to disguise her hurt, it must have leaked through her voice because he opened his eyes and looked at her with a somber gaze. "I have my father to think about."

"Yes, but perhaps someday, the bird might need to leave the nest." She cradled his face in both hands. "Run away with me. We'll find a way to make it work around the blood oaths.

We'll go somewhere else, to a place where our cultures cannot reach us. We can just be Bastien and Seraphina."

Silence echoed in the stairwell as they stared back at each other, and judging by the twitch of his mouth, she knew he was contemplating her offer. Finally, he spoke. "Running away will only offer more problems than solutions. Besides, it will not erase the danger of the blood oath. There is always a risk I will get you with child."

"Tell me you don't want me. Tell me you don't want me in your life."

Their hands dropped limply at their sides.

"I can't tell you that."

Seraphina's wings drooped as her hope slowly deflated. Throughout their dalliance, she had watched him fight for a lot of things. But he was unwilling to fight for her. No matter how difficult, love was always worth fighting for.

Wasn't it?

She released his hand and turned away from him. Her wings still drooped to the floor, betraying the heart within her chest melting beneath the hard flames of rejection. She never should have snuck into Attleglade. She never should have—

Bastien grabbed her hand and spun her toward him, and she grunted in surprise as she bumped against his chest, and their lips smashed together in a crash of blazing passion. She felt it then—he was refusing to let her go no matter how difficult and uncertain their future seemed.

She felt it in the way he claimed her waist with both of his large, sturdy hands. In the way he backed her into the wall and deepened the kiss. In the way his mouth devoured hers in a hungry embrace.

"I hate you," she gasped the moment she broke away for air, only to return for more.

His grip tightened around her waist. "I hate you so, so much."

Yet, she felt his love for her in every burning touch, in every tender kiss, in every murmur against her mouth. He was everything she should have shunned, everything she feared she could not have. But for now, he was hers. And nothing else mattered.

Someone cleared their throat below, and they leaped apart, only to find Sylvain paused on the bottom stair, eyes hard as he glanced between the two of them and then toward the closed bedroom door beside them.

"Ashryn told me you were here," the man said to Seraphina in an accusing, distrustful tone. "I worried she might be hallucinating." His eyes shifted between them once again. "Now I know it's true."

Bastien interlaced his fingers behind his head, adopting a casual demeanor. "Thank the autumns you're here. Ash was starting to get annoying with all her demands."

Thankfully, the jest eased the tension in the man's face and shoulders as he climbed the stairs. "How strange. She has not once demanded anything of me since her injury. It leaves it up to chance and guessing to figure out what's on her mind."

But then Bastien stopped Sylvain with a hand on his arm, and his jesting expression transitioned into something more serious. "I'm glad Ash has you." And then he scowled. "If you ever break her heart, I will hunt you down and gut you like a fat squirrel hoarding nuts in the middle of a blistering winter."

Seraphina wasn't sure what blazed in Sylvain's eyes. A challenge to prove himself worthy of Bastien's trust? A fervor to remain true and unyielding to Ashryn? Either way, the man simply nodded and entered the woman's room, followed closely by Bastien.

She leaned against the door frame and watched as Sylvain poured a cup of water from a jug on the opposite side of the room while Ashryn snatched Bastien's hand and pulled him close to speak in private. But by leaning a little closer, Seraphina caught every word.

"You do realize my door is as thin as bird bones, right?" Ashryn whispered.

He winced. "You heard nothing."

"Oh, I heard plenty." She raised a suggestive eyebrow, but instead of remarking on the heated kiss and the near tumble on the stairs, she said, "You never told me about the blood oaths. Did you not trust me?"

He shook his head. "Of course, I trust you. I didn't want the pity."

"I could never pity you, Bas. I never realized how serious your situation was. I knew it was bad, but not this bad."

However, Sylvain approached, and Bastien dropped her hand and murmured, "We can talk later." And then he turned and pointed to the other man. "Like a squirrel, Sylvain. Like a squirrel."

Bastien joined her at the door but kept it open as he descended the stairs, and she followed. She didn't like the serious note in his eyes nor the pinched skin around his mouth. To try to ease his worries, she slipped her hand into his and squeezed.

"Blood oaths can be unbound."

"Cranky Cricket would never allow it."

She raised both eyebrows. "Cranky Cricket?"

"Uhh...yeah. I suppose I need to catch you up on the hierarchy in Attleglade. I'll do it on the way."

He slipped a brown cloak from a hook near the front door and wrapped it around her, making sure it covered her wings. Her heart caught as he untied the ribbon from his hair, and his long white tresses tumbled over his shoulders and down his back. Unable to help herself, she reached out and trailed her fingers through the beautiful locks. Soft like powdered snow with a pure hue to match.

When she dropped her hand, her pulse jumped frantically once again when he stepped behind her and gathered her hair in gentle hands. Fingers brushed against her scalp and neck in the sweetest caress as he tied her hair back and pulled the hood over her face.

"Where are we going?" she asked quietly.

"To meet my father."

NINETEEN

Beside him, Seraphina jumped at every sound, seeming just on edge as they traversed the village in the open for everyone to see. Bastien wore a brown patrol cloak like hers to match, though he kept his hood down so everyone could view his face.

He wrapped an arm around her waist to make it look like he was supporting her weight, to make her look like Ashryn.

Autumn forbid anyone actually look beneath her hood or visit Ashryn's home. He wanted to prevent an outright war from breaking out within the village if possible.

Several people greeted him as he passed while casting a concerned glance toward "Ashryn." Thankfully, no one stopped him and thought it insignificant as he led her to his father's house. In the early evening, his father was likely home after a long day of council meetings and village audiences.

He opened the front door to his home, and they slipped inside. His father sat at the sink washing dishes, his back to them.

With an apologetic grimace, Bastien backed Seraphina up behind the corner to hide her from view. It was best to approach this subject...*delicately.*

His father's mouth was pinched, his eyes hard yet somber as he focused on his task. The last time he'd seen the man smile was when Nyana had come to visit months ago. A smile had not graced his mouth since.

Because he was unhappy in Attleglade.

Bastien blew out a long breath as he watched his father for a moment more, wondering if he realized his son had entered the house. Attleglade was beautiful. Good people lived here. But it was not the life his father had chosen for himself. And he'd lost so much because of it.

"If you got the chance to remarry..." Bastien ventured slowly as he leaned against the island table separating them. "Would you?"

His father paused his washing, his expression falling even more. "I loved your mother more than anything."

"But she's gone."

The man sighed again as he dried a plate and put it away, struggling for a moment with the task when he was bound to his wheelchair. "I don't know, Bastien. I just don't know." And then his worried stare fixed on his lap and, more specifically, on his lame legs. He was in his early forties, plenty young enough to find another wife and have more children if he married someone young enough to bear him little ones.

But like him, he was trapped in this village, unable to escape.

Finally, his father wheeled himself around but froze when they met each other's gaze. "Nuh-uh." He wagged a finger at him. "I know that look. You've been up to something that should see you to the gallows."

"Now, try not to burst a vein, Pops."

His father's eye twitched. "What did you do this time? I swear you will be the death of me, Bastien. The death of me, you hear?"

"Trust me. You'll be apoplectic about this one." He held out his hand, and hesitantly, Seraphina stepped out of the shadows in a swish of long skirts and uncertain wings.

The other man's jaw dropped, his eyes as wide as two silver moons. He abruptly wheeled his chair around, dropped his head into his hand, and pinched his nose. "What have you done?" he finally whispered after a long pause.

"What I think is right. Pa, this is Seraphina. The prisoner Pri's...uh...older sister. The Ember Queen."

When his father turned back around, his gaze lingered on their intertwined hands, and something between joy and sadness filled his expression. "The only road this leads to is heartbreak. I should know, Bastien. Heed my warning." But instead of expressing anger, he reached for her and cupped her free hand between his. "You are lovely, dear." Pa's eyes shimmered with emotion. "You will always have a place in our family."

Seraphina blinked several times, and when she spoke, her voice escaped as a raspy whisper. "Your blessing means more to me than you will ever know."

Wry laughter escaped his father's mouth as he shook his head and released her hand. "The Ember *Queen*, Bastien? Can't you ever do anything terrible halfway?"

"Nope." He stretched his arms behind his head and grinned. "Everything terrible all the way. Never anything half-baked."

Seraphina laughed, her eyes sparkling with humor, and he refused to admit how quickly his heart melted at the beautiful sight of her red-black lips pulled into a smile. He would follow this woman off the edge of a cliff if she asked it of him. Though, he hoped she would never ask him to do such a thing. He preferred keeping himself intact.

Wordlessly, his father locked the door before setting out three places around the table, accepting the new and dangerous situation with ease. After all, Bastien's upbringing likely had taught him to roll with the punches, each punch worse than the last.

"Are you sure I can stay?" Seraphina asked when his father pulled out a chair for her to sit, warm bread, steaming meat, and sparkling wine in front of them.

"Believe me. I have kept many of Bastien's secrets over the years. One more isn't going to damn me more than I already am."

Bastien shrugged sheepishly as they sat around the table and dined together. His heart warmed as he glanced between the other two making small talk across the table. The three of them...they felt like a family. If they'd had Nyana, Joel, and their two daughters with them, then the family would be complete.

He sobered at the thought of his sister. He might never get the chance to see them again because he doubted they'd step foot in the woods a second time after what happened months ago. If he crossed the border of the woods himself...

Seraphina tipped the wine bottle to pour him a drink, but he shook his head and smiled. "I'm fine, thank you."

Father answered her questioning gaze. "Bastien doesn't drink."

"Why not?" she asked, tipping her head curiously while she took him in.

Bastien scratched his chin, trying to find a way to explain their culture without going too much into it. "I'm on the patrol guard. We're not allowed to get drunk. And I prefer not to drink at all when I would rather have a clear head."

"Oh." She chuckled. "We are a bit more generous with our liquor in my clan. I'm sure if you visited our people, you would get more of a culture shock than you are prepared for."

He stared at her for several long seconds as he tried to dissect her words. It almost sounded like... "What are you saying?"

She set down her fork and turned to face him in her chair. "I can't allow you to stay here, Bastien. You don't think I came solely to cure Ashryn, do you? I want you to come home with me."

He and his father shared a concerned look over the idea of him crossing the border. Although he'd shared the danger it posed to him, perhaps she didn't truly understand...

"I can't visit you there." He shoved a piece of bread in his mouth to prevent himself from saying anything more.

"No, no, no. Not visit. I want you to become my concubine. From Attleglade."

At the same time, he and his father dropped their forks, which clattered to their plates. His father's mouth hung open. Bastien scowled. "One of four concubines?" He scoffed and pushed away from the table. "I must be extremely special to you then."

"One of three," she corrected, following him as he stalked toward the tap to fill his cup with water. "I will not take a concubine from the Ebonywatch clan."

He refused to glance her way as hurt festered inside his chest. "What about all your talk about running away together? I know it was only a fantasy but...a concubine? How could you ask that of me like I am some plaything to exist only for your pleasure?"

She stepped in front of him and glared, poking him in the chest with a finger. "That is not why the Ember Queen takes concubines from each clan. The exchange is meant to bring peace and harmony. Do you think I want two other men when I am in love with *you*?"

His heart jumped at the admonition, and for a moment, breathing became difficult as he stared back at her. But then he swallowed and turned his head to gaze at the floor. "I can't live that kind of life. Besides, it won't bring the peace you want with Attleglade. Don't ask me again."

For the first time since they'd met, her eyes shimmered with unshed tears as her wings drooped. "Then you will let me go without even a fight? I don't mean enough to you to try?"

"I never said that."

"I'm trying to learn your ways, Bastien. I don't understand monogamy. I just don't. In my culture, many men will have multiple wives. The Ember Queen will have multiple husbands, or concubines as we call them."

"And I believe in giving my life to one woman, and I expect her to do the same for me. I refuse to watch you disappear with your other concubines, tormenting myself as I imagine what you might possibly be doing with them."

His father coughed beside the table. "I think I left my carvings in my room. I'll be back in…umm…when your spat is finished."

The chair wheels squeaked in his departure before his father slammed his door closed. Only then did they resume their heated glares.

Seraphina poked him in the chest. "How else do you recommend me uniting my people? This is the way we've done it for generations."

His nostrils flared, and he clenched his fists at his side. "You told me you dreaded the thought of the night you were to take your concubines to bed. What changed? Did you meet someone?"

"No." She released a defeated sigh and ran her hands over her hair, turning her back to him. "I can't stand the thought of living life without you. This is the only way I know how to keep you."

Bastien crossed his arms and ankles as he leaned against the table, tucking his chin to his chest. "Why did you return?" he asked quietly. "We keep having the same argument. Nothing will change. We cut our ties rather messily in the riverbed, but you should have kept them severed."

"Ashryn would have died."

She did have a point there. No matter what, he was grateful she found a way to sneak into Attleglade. "Thank you for saving her life."

"You're welcome."

Seraphina rubbed a hand up and down her arm, and the sadness in her eyes cut him to the core. He didn't understand polyamory, but he was sure he could never share his wife with anyone. It wasn't right.

But the woman he loved was here. No matter how messy their severed ties might be, he had her now. And he didn't want to squander what little opportunity he had to spend time with her.

"Come sit on the sofa," he said softly as he gently took her hand and guided her across the room. She sat on one end, and he lifted one of her feet and rested it in his lap before gliding his hand up and down her foot from her ankle to her heel, over the arch of her foot to her toes. The rough, black scales fascinated him, and he would have assumed she wouldn't have felt a massage in the same way someone else of his settlement might if not for the rapture on her face.

"No one has ever done something like this for me." She sighed contentedly as she sank into the cushions.

"Never?"

"Never."

"Well then." He grinned when she sighed again. "I am glad to be your first."

When he finished the first foot, he moved onto the second until she started drifting off. He smiled when she shifted on the sofa to rest her head in his lap, and he switched his administration to her hair. The strands were soft beneath his fingers, and soon the repetitive movement lulled her to sleep, as her eyes closed and her breathing deepened.

I can't stand the thought of living life without you. This is the only way I know how to keep you.

His heart sank to the very roots of Attleglade as he recalled her words.

Then you will let me go without even a fight? I don't mean enough to you to try?

Could he truly let her go because of a bit of jealousy? Because she might come to love someone more than she could ever love him?

The pit in his belly grew as he faced his deepest fear. He was a half-breed. The lowliest person in Attleglade. Not worthy of friendship. Not worthy of love.

He didn't want to lose her love. Especially not to another man. Or multiple men. More than anything, he wanted to be loved unconditionally, despite being a half-breed, despite how little he meant in his society.

He didn't think he could survive the inevitable heartbreak he would feel if there were other men in their union.

Otherwise, he would try. For her. Because she meant everything to him. But this was not something he could endure. Not something he could survive.

It was better to lose her now before he lost her after giving her everything he possessed, including his heart.

The door on the opposite side of the room clicked open, almost hesitantly, before his father wheeled himself into the main room. He glanced over at him, then at Seraphina where she rested her head in his lap.

"Bastien," his father sighed.

Bastien's eyes watered as he stroked her hair but he smiled through the pain. "They sleep like this. Isn't it adorable?"

His father said nothing, only frowned as he moved closer.

"You never said how hard it was with Mum. Knowing you couldn't stay together."

More silence as his father steepled his fingers together and breathed deeply. "I got eleven glorious years with your mother. It was more than I had hoped for."

"But the council is stricter now. They'll never allow even a minute. Especially not with *her.*" Tears spilled down his face, but he didn't move to wipe them away as he continued stroking her hair. "I want to keep her."

"Then *run.* There is nothing more you can do."

"You keep saying that. But you know I can't."

Frustrating tension lingered in the air as his thoughts, and likely his father's, turned to the blood oaths that kept him in line. Unfortunately, he knew Seraphina's clan lay on the opposite side of the border. He couldn't seek refuge there.

"I will kill him," he hissed under his breath. If Cranky Cricket wouldn't release him from his oaths, then the only other way to break free of them was to kill the man.

His father reached out and stilled his hand over Seraphina's hair. "You are no murderer, Bastien."

"Cranky Cricket is a *tyrant.* I would be doing everyone a favor."

The man sighed, shaky fingers running over his face. His body had never quite recovered from getting his legs maimed. Even his upper limbs shook when under immense stress. "How close?"

"To the border?"

His father nodded. "Do you realize how terrified I was when I learned you were captured by the Ember Queen? She would have dragged you over the border without knowing it would kill you. Does she know?"

Bastien's gaze dropped to Seraphina, and for several long moments, he watched as her wings lifted with each inhale and dropped with every exhale. "I told her earlier today. At first, she was intent on killing me, anyway. There was no point in telling her until now." He lightly skimmed the edge of her wing, though she didn't stir at the touch. "We got as far as one of the three clans' territories. I was darn close to dropping dead. A bit scary, if you ask me."

The air whooshed from his father's lungs, and he rubbed at the stress gathered in his forehead. "I should never have taken you back to Attleglade with me all those years ago. You should have stayed with your mother and sister."

"Ma couldn't feed two children on her own. You did what was best for the family, given the circumstances."

A heavy silence pressed on his shoulders as he stared at the smooth skin on Seraphina's back. She never should have risked herself to come to Attleglade. Now he needed to find a way to get her back out.

"So…" his father started slowly. "What happens now?"

"The only thing that can. I'm just…not ready to say goodbye."

"Goodbyes are never easy. Especially when they're permanent." His father clapped him on the shoulder but said nothing more before he wheeled himself away and to his room located beneath the stairs.

"Permanent…" he murmured to himself. Unless he stained his soul black by killing Cranky Cricket and his lackeys and ran off with Seraphina to be her *concubine*.

The word left an icky taste in his mouth. But if the alternative was losing her?

What could he possibly do?

And was it worth destroying the man he was just to live that kind of life?

He hated himself for feeling so conflicted. A good man would put the past behind him and move forward, wouldn't he? But Cranky Cricket was responsible for the separation of his family, the death of his mother, his father's maimed legs, and Bastien's lack of freedom. His father had laid down and taken it. But how could Bastien do the same?

A pounding on the door startled both him and Seraphina upright, and his eyes widened as he glanced toward the entrance. Someone pounded on it again, and the wood creaked as if they were trying to break it down.

TWENTY

ide in my room, Bastien mouthed to her, his jaw set but his pulse racing frantically beneath her hand where she clutched onto his wrist.

Seraphina enjoyed her arguments with Bastien to some degree, but this was something she would never fight with him about. She slunk toward the stairs and climbed quickly but carefully until she slipped into his room and hid behind the door. She listened earnestly, hoping with her entire being that all was well.

Below, the front door opened, followed by Emeric's disgruntled tone. "What is all the ruckus about? I'm trying to read my book."

Several pairs of footsteps entered the house, and her heart shot to her throat.

One of the men answered, "The village healer saw to Ashryn's injuries when we questioned her. The stitches are Ember Fae in nature."

She swore in her mind. She hadn't expected anyone else to witness her handiwork. But she hadn't known how else to stitch Ashryn up within such a short time, especially because she hadn't studied Forest Fae healing.

"Annnd?" Bastien drawled. "All stitches are like the other, no?"

"We have reason to believe an Ember Fae is hiding within the village. Ashryn swears the only person who stitched her up was you."

Seraphina clenched her fingers as her heart raced and her knees wobbled. From what Bastien had told her, his leaders were cruel enough to kill him on the spot. She refused to let that happen.

Another male voice joined the conversation. "Either you learned healing practices outlawed in our culture…or you are harboring a fugitive. Where is the Ember prisoner?"

The logic suddenly made sense. They believed Pri hadn't escaped the village, and she had no other choice but to hide.

"What really happened when the Ember Queen took you prisoner?"

"I already told you," Bastien replied tightly. "Does your selective memory suffice? Or shall I repeat my story again?" A pause. And then, "Oof!"

Her fingernails dug into her palm when she realized they'd punched him in the gut. But his life wasn't in danger. Not yet. Which meant she needed to stay hidden.

"Your table is set for three," one of the men commented below. "Why would you need three places when only two of you live here?"

"We like to set the table for my deceased mother," Bastien wheezed. "Which is really none of your damn business."

"Watch your tongue, half-breed," the man growled. "Your thin ice has officially cracked. I have a witness who has claimed they saw you sneak your Sun Fae sister into the Glades last winter. Along with the evidence we found with the hair pin in the pool… You are under arrest, you will face the council, and we will thoroughly search your home."

"No!" Emeric sobbed. "You can't take him. The council will see him hanged no matter if he's innocent or not."

The man grunted, followed by a thump on the floor. Seraphina's eyes widened as she listened for him to get back up, to make another sound, but he didn't.

Bastien cried out in anger. Wood broke as furniture splintered. Blades whizzed through the air. A battle raged downstairs, and she waited on the balls of her feet to rush to Bastien's aid. She knew she should remain in her hiding spot, but her desperation for his well-being urged her to the stairs, and she descended just enough to peek her head around the corner.

Bastien stood in front of his father, who lay sprawled on the floor, taking on four other men with only a spear. One man lay on the floor. Another clutched his bleeding shoulder. But the way an older man stood behind, staring at the chaos with a grin, unnerved her.

Cranky Cricket...

Bastien's opponent struck him in the head, and he collapsed to his hands and knees. Before he managed to get back up, the men leaped on him and wrenched his arms behind his back before tying his wrists together.

"You will breathe your last breath for this!" Bastien screeched as he thrashed against his captors. "Mark my words."

Cranky Cricket simply chuckled darkly as he cast a shadow over Bastien. "To attack a council member, to resist arrest, will place you straight in the gallows without a trial. Tomorrow morning, you will hang."

"Father!" Bastien shouted as the men dragged him out of his home. "Father!"

One of the men stayed behind and began rummaging through drawers and searching the house. Seraphina rushed back upstairs, searching for a place to hide. The only way to help Bastien was to not end up in the same cell as him. No matter how cozy they might find themselves.

She threw aside one of the curtains, but it wasn't long enough to conceal her entire body. She pulled open a closet, but it was far too obvious. Beneath the bed was likely one of the first places the man would look, and not enough pillows lay on top of the mattress to thoroughly conceal her.

Realizing escaping through the window was her only option, she crossed the room in several purposeful strides but paused when the floor creaked beneath her weight.

Her gaze darted toward her feet, only to find the faintest cracks in the wood, ones she would never have noticed if she hadn't first stepped on the creaking spot.

Footsteps sounded on the staircase as her fingers frantically searched around the cracks. One of the stairs creaked halfway up just as her finger brushed against a small divot in the wood. Soundlessly, she tugged on the wood, and it came loose. Before she had a chance to think through her actions, she leaped into the darkness, replaced the wooden cover, and held perfectly still.

Her breath hitched as Bastien's door creaked open, and she didn't dare breathe further when she feared the faintest sound might give away her location.

The person searching the room moved above her head, but rather than crouching and finding her hiding spot, they walked toward the window area with an obvious limp in their gait, paused, and slammed the shutters closed.

"Finally," the man said, his voice sounding like Cranky Cricket. "You will die like you should have years ago."

Judging by the limping gait moving above, the man thoroughly searched the room before the stairs creaked once again, and he limped back down them.

Seraphina released a tense breath from her mouth, and when she was sure the man was gone, she sparked a flame inside her hand.

And then she inhaled sharply at her surroundings.

The small hideaway was barely large enough for two people to sit in. A small table was carved from the tree on one end while a bench rested beneath it. Papers lay scattered about the table, the floor, and they were also pinned to every inch of the walls.

Black and white drawings. Colored paintings. Quick sketches. People. Lots and lots of people.

With a start, she realized *this* was who Bastien was. Not just a skilled guard. Not just a caretaker for his father. But he was an artist. And by the looks of it, he didn't want anyone to know.

A colored painting of a woman pinned to the wall drew her eye, this one surrounded by similar sketches and drawings of the same face with different expressions and varying poses. But in nearly every picture, the woman smiled with a radiance that rivaled the sun. Her ears were long and flat, giving away her identity as a Sun Fae. In the colored picture, the woman's hair was blonde, and her eyes blue.

Another woman rested next to her, similar in appearance to the other woman but with an unmistakable caution in her expression. Unlike the first woman, her ears were mostly Sun Fae but with a slight droop, similar to Bastien's.

Nyana, she realized. His sister. *Then the other woman must be his deceased mother.*

The images momentarily distracted her from the immediate danger waiting outside as she turned in a slow circle to survey all of the pictures. There were plenty of Ashryn, which was to be expected at this point. But there was also an abundant amount of villagers from Attleglade from the looks of it.

She smiled at an extremely detailed picture of young Bastien with his father, mother, and older sister before Emeric's legs were maimed. They appeared joyful, trapped in this moment of time. Immortalized by Bastien's skilled hand.

She moved closer to the table but inhaled sharply at the masses of papers littering the surface. They weren't villagers or family members or random strangers.

Every single one of them depicted *her*.

With a pulse racing through her ears, she picked up page after page, glancing over the details of her wings, of her hair, of her face. Bastien had captured an image of her when they'd snuggled after their beautifully intimate time together. Her hair was a mess, a lazy smile on her face, but he had successfully captured a level of adoration in the sketch.

Her entire heart melted into a muddle on the floor when she picked up a colored sketch of the two of them, his arms wrapped around her waist from behind and her giving him a saucy look. They looked good together, their interaction perfect and sweet and left nothing to be desired.

"You will not fight for me because you can't," she murmured as she lightly trailed her finger over the corner of the page. "Then I will fight for you instead."

The acrid stench of smoke filled her nostrils, and her head snapped up when she realized it was not her own fire.

Someone had set the tree ablaze.

With heavy, panicked breaths, she began snatching piles of papers from the walls, especially those of Bastien's family members, and stuffed them inside the bosom of her dress. When she shoved the piece of loose wood over her head aside, she coughed when smoke entered her lungs. Although she knew Bastien might mourn the loss of his weapons and his clothing, she ignored them as she harnessed her magic and parted the smoke around her.

Without a care for herself, she sprinted out of the room, down the stairs, and through the smoky fog, searching desperately for Emeric.

Fire licked its way up the walls of the tree, the smoke so heavy around her that she couldn't see through the obstructive haze.

At long last, she spotted a shoe, and she rushed toward the figure lying prone on the ground, coughs and wheezes escaping his lungs.

"Emeric!" she shouted as she knelt by his side. With a surge of magic, she created a bubble around them to protect them from the smoke and the heat and the flames. Soot smeared the man's cheeks and forehead. Charred wood rained over their heads.

"Bastien," he coughed. "You need to go after Bastien."

"Bastien can handle his own for now. We need to get you out of here."

She glanced around the immediate vicinity for his wheelchair, but then her heart sank when she found it shattered into numerous pieces across the ground, nearly unrecognizable as the boon it had been only minutes before.

The strength ring around her finger had enough charge for her to stoop down and pick Emeric up into her arms, though the fit was far too awkward when he was larger than her.

Barely visible through the roaring fire and the gathering smoke, she heard frantic screams outside while Attleglade soldiers held civilians back from helping to douse the flames.

Too many witnesses lingered outside, blocking her path of escape.

"The cellar," Emeric coughed. "There's a door beneath the stairs."

"I'm not aiming to get us trapped in a place we will not be able to breathe."

"Trust me."

Having no other choice, she hurried toward the stairs and found the aforementioned cellar door, pulled it open by the metal latch, and struggled to fit them both inside while descending a wooden ladder. Tree roots weaved into thick dirt among various shelves of jars and boxes filled with food and preserves, and the air became colder in spite of the fire raging above their heads.

The smoke dissipated down here, but soon it, too, would not provide the refuge they needed to survive. But then Emeric silently gestured to the far end of the cellar and pointed toward the floor.

She grunted as she stooped and brushed the dirt aside, only to discover another trap door. She awkwardly leaned Emeric against the wall as she pried it open, this one much more difficult than the last.

Dirt scattered into the darkness below, leading into the pitch-black unknown. No ladders waited for her this time as she climbed inside the hole. But surprisingly, the drop was short, and she was able to pull the trap door closed behind them.

Silence.

A chill greeted her, along with a distant wind whistling somewhere ahead of her. And for one terrifying moment, she had no idea where she was nor where to go.

"Can I light a fire?" she whispered.

"Yes. We should be safe here."

After managing to maneuver Emeric into a more comfortable position in her arms which left more of her hand free, she sparked a fire between her fingers and lit up her surroundings. She inhaled sharply to find herself in a tunnel created with enormous tree roots weaved together on each side of her. If she wasn't mistaken, the shape and size looked deliberate, just large enough for a man to walk upright.

"What is all of this?" she gasped as she walked forward, wanting to put as much distance as possible between them and the burning tree above. "How did you dig such large tunnels?"

"Once upon a time," he winced, "I was blessed with forest magic. The trees were happy to do my bidding. When I was forced to move back to Attleglade with Bastien, I created many safeguards and escape routes within our home using tree roots and other species of plants." He grimaced again, and she worried he might be injured. "I only wish I had thought to escape earlier. I never realized it would come to a head so quickly." His voice caught. "Bastien is gone. Faster than I could blink."

Dread tightened her gut, but she attempted to maintain levity for both of their sakes. "From how it sounds, this was a long time coming."

"Yes," he half-laughed, half-sobbed. "It was. He has always been such a good boy. But he has never been able to lie down and beg when injustice stirs in the air. He fights back each and every time, *knowing* he will one day suffer for his actions."

"Do *you* think he should lie down and beg?"

Emeric lowered his gaze to the ground and swallowed. "No. Because that's just not how he is. It's what I have done to protect my family. I wish I had more courage to fight back. But Bastien means more to me than my legs, than my life. And

I will gladly give up everything I have, everything I am, to keep him safe."

"He is lucky to have you as a father." She smiled through her worry over what might be happening to him in his jail cell. "Of course, Bastien talks about Ashryn *all the time!*" She groaned exasperatedly but grinned to let him know she was jesting. "But the way he speaks of you... It warms my heart to witness how much he loves you. He would do anything for you."

The man chuckled and shook his head wryly. "I was fully convinced he and Ashryn would one day leave Attleglade and marry. But...you two suit each other. I have never seen him happier, never seen him more afraid to lose someone than he is to lose you."

When they reached several different tunnels that branched out in three directions, she placed Emeric on the ground to catch her breath. Next, she unstuffed her blouse and stacked Bastien's drawings and paintings into a neat pile beside him. "I am going to break Bastien's blood oaths."

His eyes hardened as he stared back at her. "If you kill any council members, the war will never end. Trust me."

But she simply grinned. "Oh, I plan on doing this another way, but it may include a blade and possibly even a hallucinating poison."

"As I often tell Bastien, don't be surprised if I feign ignorance."

"I expect nothing less." She nodded toward the tunnels. "Which way?"

He pointed to the left tunnel. "Bastien." He pointed to the tunnel in front of them. "The Glades." And then he pointed to the tunnel on the right. "The inner woods."

She peered down each tunnel, only to find darkness waiting. "How far does each lead?"

But he only shrugged. "Far enough."

Plenty of dead branches lay scattered across the ground for her to create a large pile beside Emeric. She gathered rocks next and created a contained pit in front of him before stacking the branches and what kindling she managed to find. With the tip of her finger, she used her magic to light a fire to not only keep Emeric warm but to provide light in an otherwise dark place.

When a fire flickered to life within the pit, she gazed across the flames regretfully. "I don't want to leave you here."

A weary breath escaped him as he waved her away. "If everyone thinks I'm dead, then I'm freer than I have been in a very long time. Several nights in the cold are not going to kill me."

"But what about food? Water?"

"I built these tunnels. I did not leave myself without a means to survive. Maneuvering about will be the difficult part. But don't worry about me." His expression crumpled. "Please find him. And bring him home."

"Where is home?"

"Where he is the happiest."

At this point in time, she still didn't know the answer. Where would Bastien be the happiest?

As she turned and started down the tunnel leading to where she might find him, she silently counted her inventory. Knives, dart gun, poisons, fire. She was not defenseless, but Bastien was.

"Seraphina."

She paused to glance back at Emeric, his face barely visible in the distance between him and her light. But she caught an unmistakable sheen in his eyes as he gazed down at Bastien's drawings in his hands. "Yes?"

"Traditions can change. It is never too late to start anew."

After a few moments of trying to dissect his words, she turned and continued down the tunnel leading to the man she loved. Attleglade could take their land, the Glades, their dignity, but there was hell to pay now that they took Bastien.

TWENTY ONE

I gnorant Imp backhanded Bastien across the face, the strike hard enough to bring him to his knees. But still, he fought back.

"No!" he screamed as Cranky Cricket threw a torch inside one of the windows and closed the shutters tight. He twisted against his captors' grips, barely managing to get free before two others jumped on him and pinned him to the ground. "My father is still in there. Please, I beg you. Please!"

The villagers around him shouted in outrage, demanding answers and a quick rescue. But the council's lackeys restrained them, keeping them from helping his father.

"He's done nothing wrong!" Bastien screeched, continuing his fight against the other men but losing when someone smashed his face into the grass. "I did it! I took Nyana to the Glades. No one else was involved, especially not my father. He's innocent!"

More outrage on his father's behalf, and when his father's cough sounded from within the tree, Bastien screamed as he managed to shove the others off him. He sprinted toward the tree now with flames and smoke billowing from the cracks in the windows and door.

Before he managed to reach the door, something slammed into the back of his shoulder, and he cried out in pain, dropping to his hands and knees. The warmth of blood seeped into his tunic, shock coursing through his body like it did every time he received a new wound. His arm refused to lift when he tried to push himself off the ground again.

Through the pain, he managed to get to his feet one more time, reaching for the door. The fire burned his hand, and he knew his father was gone long before he touched the handle.

And then someone pulled him back and shoved his face to the ground once more, this time tying his hands behind his back and securing a tight rope around his neck. They pulled him to his feet, and he obliged lest the air strangle from his lungs.

"You are all cowards!" Bastien yelled to the other villagers as they simply stood by and watched the debacle. The rope tightened around his throat, and he struggled for breath. But he wasn't done. "That man has done nothing but serve you for years! And when he needs you the most, you abandon him because someone told you to. Cowards! All of you!"

Some people lowered their heads in shame. Others stared with horrified expressions as the fire climbed the tree.

Ignorant Imp tugged him forward like an ox being led to the slaughter. Grief slammed hard into him as he realized he'd lost his father. With a snap of his fingers, it was all over and done. And it was his fault. This would never have happened if Bastien had stayed in line. If he hadn't snuck Nyana into the Glades to heal her from her deadly curse. If he hadn't fallen in love with Seraphina and brought devastation upon his family.

Although he didn't know where Seraphina was, he doubted the fire could harm her. But his father had been defenseless against the flames.

Behind him, someone pulled the arrow out of his shoulder. He screamed at the sudden agony, and his surroundings spun as he attempted to juggle the pain, the grief, the devastation, and the hopelessness.

One moment, he was on his feet being led by the bit. The next moment, he landed on a hard floor in a prison cell, dirt and dust tickling his nostrils.

A boot collided with his side. He grunted as a new wave of fiery pain encompassed his ribs. Through the pain, he still managed a glare at the three guards in the prison with him. It seemed they weren't taking any more chances after what happened when Ashryn broke Pri out of her cell. Though, he would take the secret to his grave.

Cranky Cricket peered at him through the bars and sneered. "Set up the gallows," he ordered one of his soldiers. "It's high time we see the half-breed hang."

"What are you so afraid of?" Bastien seethed as he forced himself to his feet, towering over the older man. "You've coveted my father's position as chief for years. Are you afraid the *half-breed* heir will ruin your chances to become chief?"

"Watch your mouth," he hissed.

"You've done everything in your power to see my father suffer, though I suspect you meant to kill him a couple of times. Now I'm the only person standing in your path."

After a nod from the old man, one of the soldiers punched him in the gut through the bars. Bastien grunted and doubled over as he tried to catch his breath from the blow.

"A half-breed can never rule as chief over Attleglade." Cranky Cricket casually fixed his sleeves despite the rage sitting on his face. "It's the law."

"Show me this law. Prove it."

The fist flew through the bars once again, too fast for him to dodge. This time as it struck him, he collapsed to his knees with his hand clutched to his stomach. Through gritted teeth, he climbed back to his feet and faced them down. If he were to die tomorrow, then they would have to fight him the entire way.

The stench of smoke permeated the prison house, reminding him exactly why he hated the council with every fiber of his being. His fists clenched at his sides. His blood boiled with rage. "Why couldn't you just let us be? Why did you have to drag my father back here all those years ago and make a scene? Why did you have to destroy my family?"

"Because," the man glared, "traditions must be upheld at all costs. Even if it means the death of the chief."

Bastien wanted to grab the man through the bars and snap his neck. But his father wouldn't have wanted him to stain his soul before his death. So he forced himself to step back and stare coldly through the bars.

"A person incapable of kindness should never be allowed in the chief's seat."

Instead of answering him, Cranky Cricket stormed out of the jailhouse, leaving him alone with the three guards. He was flattered, really, that they thought him equal to three men. And he wanted to prove them right. He'd escape through his father's tunnels and…

And what?

Die the moment he crossed the border of the woods? After they had dragged his father back to Attleglade, he realized they would never stop looking for him, even if he managed to escape.

He would never be free.

He sat crossed-legged on the ground as he stared down the guards, all while trying to ignore the throbbing ache in his shoulder. Only hours remained until dawn. If he didn't find a way to escape by then, he would be a dead man.

Seraphina was officially lost.

She started back down a fork in the tunnel on frantic feet when she realized this path led to a dead end, just like several others she'd tried. Emeric hadn't mentioned multiple obstacles, which made her believe the trees had done this on their own after years of disuse. Either that, or he'd created them himself so others would get lost if he were followed.

When she reached the fork in the road leading to five different tunnels, she paused as she tried to recall which ones she had already explored.

"Blazes!" she cried, cursing her stupidity. She'd been in such a hurry to reach Bastien that she hadn't bothered to mark which paths she'd already traveled.

One of the council members had said Bastien would be hanged at sunrise. How close was sunrise?

A tired ache settled in her eyes and in the slump of her shoulders. But she broke through the haggardness and forced herself to continue forward.

Holding up her flames, she stood in the center of the fork and lifted her hand, waiting patiently while intensely watching the fire. After several moments, the flames billowed to the right, indicating a slight breeze within the tunnel on her left.

She left a marker at the tunnel she had recently exited and started down the left tunnel. Instead of gnarled branches poking out of tangled roots, these tunnels contained smooth roots with an easy walkway beneath her feet.

Another breeze whipped through her hair, and she quickened her pace when she realized she likely traveled the correct path this time.

But then the tunnel ended far too soon, and she despaired when she stared back at a gnarled wall, mocking her in her failure. Should she turn back and consult Emeric? Was losing precious time worth it in the end?

Deciding to return to the man, she turned around but paused in her tracks when her flames billowed again.

Her heart leaped to her throat as she spun on her heel and faced the gnarled wall once again. This time, she approached and placed her hand on one of the tree roots. The walls around her shuddered as if the tree had woken from its slumber. And like a stretch during a yawn, the tree roots parted to reveal a rocky wall with the smallest slit for someone to fit through.

And through the slit, the light of early morning broke through the crevice.

"Bastien," she gasped as she raced toward the opening and peered outside. The faint blush of dawn decorated the skies with streaks of pink, orange, and gray-blue. From her vantage point, she noticed the fissure lay within the side of the mountain, with numerous trees blocking her view of the village below.

Wary of the possible patrol guards within the area, she slipped out of the crevice and traveled nimbly from tree to tree, keeping her wings close to herself to camouflage as much of her movements as possible. Brown and green with veins of black to blend in with her surroundings.

At last, she crouched behind a cluster of boulders and peered over the top, and her wings transitioned to gray and black to match. Down below, a scaffolding lay erect while a large audience surrounded the wooden platform as if they couldn't help but witness an unjust murder. Because that's what it was. Bastien wasn't sentenced to die because he'd done something awful. But because he'd done something good.

You are all just going to stand there? She wanted to shout at them, take them by the shoulders, and shake sense into them.

Slowly, she pulled out her blow-dart gun from her belt and loaded it with a hallucinogen. But even as she placed the end against her mouth, she knew she was too far out of range to hit her target. She needed to get closer.

But how without drawing notice to herself?

Everyone's attention lingered on the currently empty scaffolding, and she took advantage of their distraction to slink closer while attempting to stay within the bounds of the underbrush. She could do nothing to disguise the color of her hair nor the color of her lips, but her wings did a decent enough job at concealing her.

Every fiber of her body thrummed with anxious tension as she scouted the boughs overhead, as she peered around trees, as she watched the waiting noose hanging dangerously as it lay in wait.

And then a hush fell over the crowd as the first rays of sunlight peeked over the distant mountains.

Seraphina's jaw clenched as she surveyed the distance between the tree she hid behind and the scaffolding. From her vantage point, she might not hit her target. And in that case, she would use her magic. She wanted to light up the scaffolding immediately, but she would sooner find herself with an arrow through the head before she managed to break Bastien free.

What am I supposed to do?

She swallowed uneasily as she spotted five archers standing at the front of the audience, arrows nocked but bows not drawn quite just yet. If the noose failed to do the job, she didn't doubt the archers would finish the feat in its place.

The red Ember gem hiding within her blouse burned against her breastbone, and she jumped as it startled her.

Seraphina, her brother Eben's voice entered her mind, and even a more startling realization…he was close.

Where are you? she asked as she held up her blow-dart gun. If she created a distraction with her magic, perhaps she could swoop in and run off with Bastien without being discovered.

Near the Glades, he answered. *We followed you, and now we're waiting on your command.*

A relieved breath trembled from her lips, and she braced herself against the nearby tree to keep from collapsing to the ground. *There is a man...*

Father mentioned as much.

They are planning to hang him. What can you do?

She almost saw the shrug in his voice. *Light the forest on fire?*

Alarm bolted through her chest, and she nearly dropped her dart gun when her fingers fumbled with the weapon. *Not so close to the Glades. You might activate the volcano. How many men did you bring?*

Eben chuckled through the gem. *A small army. I'm almost disappointed they haven't seen us yet. If we had discovered this path years ago, we would have already secured the Glades for ourselves.*

But Seraphina didn't want to hoard the Glades. She'd always wanted to share it. But she would take what they could get. But first...Bastien.

Suddenly, Eben swore through the gem bond.

What is it? she cried out through the connection.

Zephyr.

Seraphina ran her fingers through her hair as stress ate away at her. If Zephyr was here, then she might as well kiss Bastien goodbye. But she refused to give up. Not unless he was cold and dead in her arms.

Icy dread climbed up her legs when her attention darted toward the scaffolding just as three men dragged Bastien out of the prison with his arms tied behind his back and a gag secured around his mouth.

The three men shoved him forward, and without the use of his arms, Bastien stumbled and crashed to the ground. Gasps surrounded them, followed by several cries of injustice. But those cries quickly quieted with one warning look from a man carrying a cane, who she assumed was Cranky Cricket.

Angry heat coursed through her when she spotted the bruise on Bastien's jaw and the blood staining his shirt. What other injuries were hidden beneath his clothing?

She barely managed to tamp down her fire before it set the area around her ablaze. Instead, she focused on what she *could* do rather than the things she couldn't control as she scanned the area around the scaffolding. Giving away her position seemed like the only plausible action. But she couldn't help Bastien if she was dead.

She glanced above her to find another vantage point but froze when she spotted a familiar face in the boughs to her right, barely concealed by the foliage. Ashryn held a bow pointed toward the scaffolding, but instead of a slack string, she pulled her string taut as if the effort of holding the bow in such a position didn't faze her muscles in the slightest.

Quickly, Seraphina loaded an empty dart into her gun and blew through the mouthpiece. The dart whizzed through the air and embedded itself into the tree trunk nearest the other woman's face. Ashryn jumped as she glanced at the dart and then down toward where Seraphina stood on the ground.

Ashryn's eyes widened momentarily before she nodded in acknowledgment. Seraphina nodded back. They were on the same team. For once.

And if she were honest, she wondered who Ashryn meant that arrow for.

The three guards dragged Bastien up the steps and toward the waiting noose. He fought against them and managed to land a kick to one of their stomachs, but in a swift motion, they captured his head with the noose and pulled tight.

Alarm shot through her at seeing him in such a vulnerable situation. She stepped forward, but the slight shake of Ashryn's head held her back. Only then did she allow her gaze to follow the arrow's path, and she realized it was pointed at Bastien. Or rather, just barely above his head.

Was she planning on snapping the rope with her arrow? Could her aim possibly be true enough to hit the rope without killing Bastien?

She didn't want to find out.

What choice did she have?

Bastien glared at the audience, shouting grumbled words muffled through his gag. Another wave of rage coursed through her. How dare they silence him before they planned to hang him! Even criminals deserved their last words. But it seemed Cranky Cricket didn't want anyone to know what he had to say.

The archers pulled back their arrows. Premature grief rained down on her head. And judging by the defeated look already in Ashryn's eyes, she likely didn't think Bastien could pull through this time. But the woman was going to try anyway.

Seraphina could take on a half-dozen patrol guards on her own. But not a half-dozen guards plus a hundred more regular villagers.

She reached for her necklace and felt the warmth burn against her skin as she called to her brother. *Eben, I need a distraction. Now!*

We are still trying to subdue Zephyr and his men.

She clenched her fist around the necklace. *This is not a request from your sister but an order from your queen.*

A pause. And then, *Consider it done.*

Seraphina stood upright and stepped out of the foliage behind the tree. She spread her wings wide to draw attention to herself. Across the distance between her and Bastien, his eyes shot open when he caught a glimpse of her, and he rapidly shook his head just as the hangman stepped up to the platform and placed his hand on the lever.

The next few moments happened quickly, but they also felt like a lifetime.

Seraphina lifted her blow gun to her mouth and shot a hallucinogen toward the hangman. The dart embedded in his throat. The man screamed and dropped to the ground, writhing as he faced whatever nightmares lay within his mind. Another man rushed up the stairs faster than she could reload her weapon and pulled the lever.

The trapdoor beneath Bastien's feet gave way. His body dropped. But a half second before the rope could snap his neck, it was severed by a well-aimed arrow.

Bastien disappeared beneath the scaffolding as he fell. Screams erupted around her as heads whirred in her direction. But she only managed a smirk as her hands lit up in flames. The fire climbed up her arms, her shoulders, and bathed her wings in a magnificent, magical blaze.

At best, Seraphina had hoped for a negotiation. At worst? To be fighting every member of the village. Luckily for her, half the village ran. The other half trained their weapons on her.

No woman or child would die today if she had a say in the matter. But she also had herself and Bastien to think of. These people had betrayed him. They had thrown his meaty carcass to the dogs without stopping to consider the consequences of their actions.

Arrows whizzed in her direction faster than she could blink. But not quite fast enough.

She snapped her wings closed and dodged two arrows, drawing upon the ancient magic coursing through her blood. Her senses sharpened until she heard every rustle, noticed even the smallest movement, and tasted the very tension in the air.

She heard the *twang* of an arrow before it whistled toward her, giving her just enough time to twist to the side and dodge the attack. It lodged into the tree behind her.

With her wings still blazing at her back, she rushed forward with nearly inhuman speed, pulled her knife out of the sheath filled with hallucinogen poison, and stabbed the archer in a barely inconsequential place in the gut.

Leaning close to his ear, she whispered, "Sweet dreams," before she pulled her knife back out and pushed him by the shoulders. He stumbled backward, and before he crashed to the ground, the nightmares hit him as his eyes glazed over with terror.

More than anything, she wanted to utilize her deadlier poisons. But she had no idea who these people were nor their relationship with Bastien. If she could spare him pain, she would.

Despite the power flooding through her, there were still too many opponents circling her, drawing in closer with their bows and their spears and their daggers. Short of blasting each of them with a wall of fire, she was thoroughly trapped.

And she loved it.

She laughed at their audacity to face the Ember Queen in combat as she dove in and out of thrusting spears like a ritual dance to welcome in the blood moon at the start of each new year. There were spears then, too, but the ends were blunted rather than sharp and dangerous. Still, it would be no different than dressing in her blood moon outfit and dancing without a care in the world.

One of the spears thrust toward her, and she grabbed it by the handle and lit it on fire. The man on the other end screamed as his sleeves caught fire. He dropped and rolled across the ground to put them out.

She ducked beneath the swipe of a blade, moved in closer, and stabbed the woman in the leg. Immediately, the woman screamed and fell to the ground as she held her hands above her head to ward off an unseen threat.

Two down. Twelve dozen more to go.

But she didn't need to defeat all of them. She only needed to fight long enough to save Bastien.

Tree roots shot out of the ground, taking her by surprise as they attempted to grab her. But one blast of her fire had them retreating like a well-trained dog fleeing at the sight of a predator.

As she twirled and fought and felled her opponents, she caught sight of Bastien beneath the scaffolding, desperately trying to cut his rope restraints with a nail jutting out from the structure. Her heart soared when Ashryn leaped from the boughs above and landed gracefully before him. With one slash of her knife, the woman freed his wrists, and next, his gag.

Seraphina stabbed another man in the shoulder, sending him into a wheezing panic attack as he curled into a fetal position. Between the distance separating her and Bastien, they locked eyes. Horror filled his expression. But she only grinned.

Run, she mouthed.

Never, he mouthed back just as she heard a blade whizzing toward her from behind. She ducked beneath the attack, and the man in front of her ended up getting slashed across the face.

Unexpectedly, Ashryn and Bastien took up positions behind the group. Instead of abandoning her to fight on her own, they fought beside her against their own people.

Her eyes unexpectedly smarted. Bastien had decided where his loyalties lay. And it was with her.

And even more unexpectedly, other members of the patrol guard dropped beside the two and helped them fight. A few of them even turned on the council members.

She officially had no idea what was going on anymore…

She reached farther inside herself until the Ember Queen's magic lay in wait for her command. To mold it. To shape it. To—

A resounding *boom* shook the air, and moments later, a fierce wind tugged at her and threatened to drag her away. All at once, her surroundings fell silent as the wind died down, and each turned to watch the volcano above the Glades erupt in a shower of molten sparks.

Weapons lowered. Mouths fell open. Her fire died as if doused with water.

"The Glades!" those around her shouted, followed by, "The villagers!"

What did you do? she shouted through her gem.

We did nothing! It was Zephyr's doing.

Swearing under her breath, she abandoned her fight and sprinted toward the erupting mountain. Behind her, the Attleglade soldiers shouted orders to evacuate the women and children, Bastien among them.

"Seraphina, no!" Bastien shouted and grabbed onto her arm. "Surely, even you can't survive a volcano."

"Everyone will die if I don't hold it back." She gripped his arm and tried to smile reassuringly. "I can handle this."

"Ser..." But as if realizing she might be their only chance, their hands slowly slid out of each other's.

"Go! The heat will be too much for you to bear."

And without another backward glance, she sprinted toward the heat and the flames and the molten lava, spread her wings, and leaped into the sky. Her clan quickly joined her, no longer keeping themselves hidden by the cliffs.

She shouted orders to her people, and they were quick to obey. "We need to redirect the lava away from Attleglade!" Those who were capable of magic flitted toward the spouting lava. To those not capable of magic, she said, "Protect the villagers. Protect the land—"

She hissed as pain seared her arm, and she glanced toward the edge of the cliffs to find Zephyr staring her down while loading another bolt, not with the intention of capturing her this time, but with the intention to kill.

He stood with several of his guards, and her heart shot to her throat when he pointed his loaded bolt at her once again and aimed.

She braced herself for pain. For a swift death followed by an unforgiving fall. But then a Forest Fae arrow lodged into the man's neck. Her eyes widened as the man choked on his own blood and stumbled over the edge of the cliff. He swiftly fell the great distance and smacked hard into the lava below.

Across the ravine, she met Bastien's hard eyes as he lowered his bow. She nodded her thanks to him, her relief. He nodded back before rushing off once more while her clan met the rest of the enemy Ember Fae in battle.

Once again, she called upon the ancient magic running through her veins, gritting her teeth as she latched onto it. Energy drained from her body, but she didn't dare release her hold on the lava as its trajectory obeyed her.

But without a clear path down the mountainside, it was spilling. Everywhere.

The heat from the volcano washed over her as if trying to bake her in an oven. Usually, her skin enjoyed the extreme heat. But today? It was nearly too much for even her to handle.

Lava moved closer and closer to the Glades, and she realized she had no choice but to maneuver the lava directly.

She braced herself for severe heat as she flitted toward the roaming, crackling magma that sounded like breaking glass as it moved. Landing on warm grass far enough from the Glades, she planted her feet, raised her arms, and gasped as she created a wall of magic to keep the lava at bay. Her arms shook with the effort. Her feet slid across the ground as if from an unseen force.

I can't do this. I can't do this.

"Bastien!" she screeched as she turned her head, searching frantically for a white-haired man across the bridge on the other side of the cliffs. Unfortunately, there were many white-haired men. But only one of them glanced in her direction.

Remembering Emeric's tunnels made of tree roots, she called out, "Gather your magic wielders! We need to create a path for the lava."

As if he understood her intent, he nodded and rushed off in the other direction.

Ember Fae joined her side, each taking turns directing the flow of lava when the heat proved too much even for them. But not once did Seraphina yield to the crackling and explosions and powerful force of the volcano, even as her skin glistened with perspiration and her head threatened to explode from using far too much magic than she thought she was capable of.

Only minutes later, Bastien returned with a half-dozen Forest Fae, now taking orders directly from him despite almost getting hanged not even thirty minutes ago. Tree roots shot out from the ground, but instead of attacking the Ember Fae like they had done plenty of times in the past, the roots cleared a straight path down the mountainside and into the empty creek below.

The water from the Glades was redirected by a dam, leading to a dry creek that ended in Ember territory. But even if the magma flowed down the empty creek, it could still take days, even weeks, to cool. Animals would get hurt. People would die. The land would suffer.

She gritted her teeth as she put all her focus into pushing the lava out of the top of the volcano and streaming it steadily down the path created by the Forest Fae.

Never in her life had she ever suspected they might one day work together. But the Glades were important to both of them.

Lava now flowed through the dry creek, kept steady by others in her clan so it didn't seep out of the riverbed. But it was still too hot. And the toxic fumes were beginning to leak through her wall. It would destroy the land and everyone within it.

Her feet slid back again as she fought against the wall of molten red, black, and orange threatening to swallow her whole. Exhaustion crackled through her body. Her limbs shook with the effort. Her strength was depleting and fast.

And if she lost consciousness, no one could take her place. It had to be her.

She glanced around frantically for Bastien, and she found him barking out orders to the magic wielders with a cloth tied around his face to protect himself from the fumes. She hadn't the strength to speak when they met each other's eye, so she mouthed, *Break the dam.*

He didn't question her, not for a single second, as he spun around and shouted out new orders to those not capable of magic.

A smidge of smug relief passed through her when Forest Fae rushed off to fulfill his orders, even as Cranky Cricket screamed at them to stop.

Darkness crept into her vision as her consciousness could no longer keep a steady foothold within the abyss of her magic.

She had to finish this. *Now.*

Magic surged out of her as she leaped into the skies, just as the volcano exploded with vicious anger. She channeled her magic around the explosion, grasping the remaining magma and pulling with all her might.

The lava cascaded down the root-lined path, both Ember and Forest Fae leaping out of the way of its untamed trajectory. There was too much of it. Someone was likely to get hurt.

The darkness pulled her farther out of her consciousness until only a speck of color remained in flashes of orange and red and white. White hair. Lots of it. Below, the Forest Fae hacked at the dam, breaking the large branches piece by piece until spurts of water squirted out between the cracks.

Where was Bastien?

Where was he?!

Finally, the last of the magma burst out of the volcano, and her magic swallowed the poisonous gasses emitted from the eruption.

But she left nothing for herself.

Midair, her wings ceased fluttering. Her world blacked out. And she started to fall.

Twenty Two

No one had ever leaped the distance between one side of the cliff to the other without magic. At least none who had survived to tell the tale.

Bastien didn't think. His instincts reacted as he sprinted toward the cliff's edge as Seraphina fell through the air from above, her body limp and her magic exhausted. He knew the leap was impossible. He knew it was more likely they would both die than for him to manage it successfully.

But the knowledge didn't stop him from taking one last sprinting step at the edge of the cliff and leaping the gap with every muscle available in his body.

Wind tore at his hair. Nearly unbearable heat consumed his body. But his focus rested solely on the Ember Queen, falling too fast for even her clan members as they dropped to catch her.

His arm connected with her waist halfway across the gap, but like he suspected, he missed the opposite side entirely and started to fall with her with his arm wrapped around her waist.

His feet slid down uneven, crumbling rocks. Dirt rained over his head and into his eyes. And with his free hand, he felt blindly along the cliffside as they fell at an alarming rate toward the magma and sharp boulders below.

Breaking rocks echoed in his ears as tree roots shot out from the cliffside as if in an attempt to catch them. He whipped his arm through a loop in one of the roots, which heaved them to a sudden stop a short distance from the lava racing through the creek.

He screamed as his shoulder and possibly even elbow were ripped from their sockets, leaving him momentarily blinded with pain while the heat from the magma wafted up from below in a sea of orange and black. He nearly dropped Seraphina in his haze of agony but barely managed to keep his grip on her.

He breathed heavily through gritted teeth, realizing he would have dropped both of them toward their deaths with the immobility of his arm if it hadn't been for the tree roots hugging him against the cliffside. Someone in his village had caught them. However, he didn't know who.

More tree roots wrapped around their bodies to hold them steady. He was vaguely aware of shouts from above over the din of crackling magma below him. A flit of red and green wings caught his attention from the corner of his eye, and he soon found himself facing a man with black hair and piercing green eyes.

For just a moment, they stared back at each other before the man wrapped his arms around Seraphina. The tree roots released her, and he flew away with her limp form.

Two other Ember Fae flew toward him. Each wrapped an arm around him to support his weight, and they also lifted him away from the danger the lava posed below.

A cool breeze settled over his skin in their short flight toward land above, a small relief in comparison to being bathed by eternal heat.

The moment his feet touched the ground gave him little reprieve because the two Ember Fae grabbed his arm, and in a swift movement, they jolted his elbow and shoulder back into their sockets.

The cloth around his face muffled his scream of agony and swallowed his tears of pain. He collapsed to the ground in a heap while focusing on breathing in and out, in and out, instead of allowing the darkness to overtake him.

"Seraphina..." he murmured as his head shot up. "Where is Seraphina?"

But he didn't get an answer before wood splintered far below, and the river gushed out of its restraints. He peered over the cliffside to find a trail of ferocious water overtaking the broken dam and swallowing the magma. The rapids buried it beneath its unforgiving tempest as it crashed against the sides of the ravine, trying to find its path downstream.

His mouth fell open as the water hissed and sizzled while steam wafted upward, quickly bathing the ravine in a watery fog and obscuring everything below.

"Is anyone down there?" Bastien shouted as he pushed the cloth over his mouth down, glancing around him at both white-haired and black-haired fae.

The same Ember male from before who had taken Seraphina shook his head. "The way is clear. Our people are away from harm, and your people are nowhere near the destruction other than at the dam."

If they were at the dam, then they likely reached safety.

His gaze dropped to a group of Ember Fae huddled in a circle around a limp figure. Ignoring the pain in his arm, he rushed over, only for one of the Ember Fae to spin around and push him to the ground.

Bastien froze with his hand tenderly cradling his arm as he stared back at the people he had called his enemy throughout his entire life. With the snap of their fingers, they could simply light him on fire or poison him with a blade.

"Let him pass," the man behind him ordered.

After several uncertain glances between the clan members, they parted for him. This time, he cautiously approached the circle until he spotted Seraphina lying on her back, eyes closed, with an elderly man kneeling at her side. The man placed blued crystals across Seraphina's breastbone, and when they touched her skin, each lit up with a dim light.

"Ser," he murmured, dropping beside her. No one stopped him as he cradled her face in his hands. She didn't respond. "You are brave but incredibly stupid. You are no match for a volcano."

A faint cough escaped her mouth, and although she didn't open her eyes, her lips twitched with the faintest smile. "Then why am I the one who came out on top?" she asked weakly.

He closed his eyes as he fought off emotions of relief. To hide the moisture gathering at the corners of his eyes, he leaned over and pressed his forehead against hers. "Never do that again."

"It saved your life, didn't it?"

"I was managing fine on my own."

"Says the man who had a noose around his neck."

When the healer placed a rock against Seraphina's throat, Bastien moved aside but kept a steady hand closed around hers. He didn't plan on leaving her side for a single second if he could help it.

"Please tell me you won't die from this," Bastien murmured as he brushed a black strand of hair from her face. He was overly aware of a dozen pairs of Ember eyes following his every movement, but he cared more about Seraphina than he did about getting stabbed through the back.

She almost imperceptibly shook her head.

All while keeping a cautious eye on him, the healer explained, "Our queen has exhausted her magic. These stones will help her recharge her stores. She will gain back her strength then."

"Chief," a hesitant voice called out from behind the group of Ember Fae. They parted to reveal his patrol guard comrades huddled together, their expressions filled with discomfort as if they weren't sure whether to attack the enemy or flee.

"Don't you call me that," Bastien scoffed. "All of you tried to hang me."

"You didn't really think Ashryn was the only one with the mind to fight back?" Tobie asked, casting a suspicious glance toward one of the Ember Fae. "The council is over and done with. The next in line is you."

Slowly, Bastien stood and winced when his entire arm felt like it was engulfed by flames. "What happened to the council?"

"We rounded them up inside the jailhouse. We are waiting for you to tell us what to do next."

He hardly believed his ears. The entire situation seemed far too suspicious. And quite frankly, he felt safer on this side of the Ember Fae than on the other. "A half-breed? It's against the law."

"That law died the moment Alban got chained up in a cell."

It took a moment for him to remember that Cranky Cricket's actual name was Alban. He preferred the latter.

Well, shite...

He scratched his cheek as he surveyed the waft of steam rising behind him, then at the slew of villagers watching the

Ember Fae with wide, uncertain eyes in the distance. His heart cracked when he didn't see his father because Cranky Cricket had killed him. It was up to him now to lead these people.

Unless…

His gaze fell on Seraphina lying at his feet. The thought of losing her hurt. Because to be together, one of them had to give up their home.

And he certainly wanted nothing to do with being concubine number four. Or three. But still.

"Clear out the meeting house," he ordered. "We are far more civil than to allow our new *friends* to camp outside while their queen recuperates. They can stay there."

"But Chief…" Gael frowned.

"But nothing. She saved all your sorry hides. The least she deserves is your appreciation, a soft bed beneath her head, and a warm bowl of broth to fill her belly."

"I'd rather go to your home," Seraphina murmured behind him.

While the others begrudgingly followed his orders, he turned around and smiled at Seraphina, where she now lay with her eyes open. "I currently find myself homeless. Pri burned down my home. Cranky Cricket burned down my father's home…"

He trailed off, and his smile slowly fell as he thought of his father. He hadn't yet found a chance to mourn him. He desperately wanted the man at fault to pay, to burn like his father had. But…

"Bastien." Seraphina rolled her head to the side until she met his gaze. "Your father—"

"Chief!" another villager cried out, winded as he approached. Though, the man slowed to a stop when he caught sight of the Ember Fae. Like the entirety of his people, they didn't seem to know what to make of them. "Your presence is needed in the jailhouse."

"All right," Bastien scoffed. "Now I'm starting to feel like this is a joke. Who in their right mind named me the chief?"

"Uh…" The man glanced between Gael and Tobie. "Ashryn. She's got all the hostages at knifepoint."

"Of course," he breathed, running a hand down his face. Ashryn could be very persistent with a knife in her hand.

He turned back around, and the Ember Fae guards allowed him to pass once again until he knelt on one knee beside Seraphina and took her hand. "Queen to Chief, perhaps we can come to some sort of…peaceful arrangement with the Glades."

Gasps of surprise resounded on all sides of him, and Seraphina's eyes grew wide. "But…but…our people have been fighting over the Glades for as long as I've been alive. It can't just…stop."

He chucked her chin and grinned. "I can't see why not. Without you, they'd be gone altogether. I think that should be taken into full account." More than anything, he wished to pull her into his arms and kiss her until her strength returned. But he forced himself to stand and step away. "Get some rest, Ser.

My people will show you where to go." *I hope.* "But I'd still keep one eye open if I were you." He grimaced and shrugged as he glanced at their group of dark-haired fae again. "Or two."

And then to himself, he murmured, "Autumns knows I'll do the same."

As he walked toward the jailhouse with his patrol guard comrades at his side, it felt odd when villagers stared as he passed, with a level of uncertainty in their eyes. And he suddenly realized they didn't know what to do. Without Cranky Cricket issuing orders after the Ember Fae had saved them *and* the supposed enemy wasn't attacking, no one seemed to know what happened next.

What was this? he wondered to himself. *A coup? Did Ash organize this?*

He stopped before the jailhouse and took a deep breath to try to calm the anger simmering in his veins. His fists clenched at his sides. His body temperature spiked despite his best efforts. Ever since he and his father were dragged to Attleglade, he'd wanted to kill Cranky Cricket.

Unable to dampen his anger, he threw the door open and strode inside, only to find the prison packed. Ashryn, Sylvain, and a handful of other people kept the council members inside a single cell. The six of them stuck up their haughty noses, but he didn't miss the underlying fear in each of their eyes.

Bastien pushed up his sleeves, but before he managed to approach the cell, Ashryn took hold of his elbow, steered him to the opposite corner of the room, and blocked his view of the cell.

"I could kill you right now," she hissed, one hand over her stomach as if the wound still pained her. "What were you thinking? Jumping the ravine like that?"

Obviously, she knew the answer because she didn't allow him to speak before pulling him into a tight embrace. He swallowed the emotion gripping his throat. Because he knew this was one of the last times he would embrace her. At least for a while.

He refused to remain in Attleglade for longer than necessary if he had a chance to flee.

"What did you do?" he asked when they finally pulled away from each other, though he didn't miss Sylvain's side-eyed glance in their direction as if he still might be unsure about the constraints of their relationship. "Why did I suddenly find myself the chief after nearly getting hanged?"

"After what happened to Emeric..." She lowered her gaze and squeezed his arm as if to offer reassurance in whatever way she could. "The villagers and patrol were outraged. And ashamed they allowed it to happen. I think it was a wake-up call. If the councilmen were willing to kill their chief and the heir, what would happen to them? To their children?" She nodded toward the others in her group, engaged in hushed conversations of their own. "Everyone thinks it's time for a change in leadership."

Bastien ran his hands down his face. "I can't stay here. I hate it here. Attleglade only holds chains and terrible memories."

"I know." She squeezed his arm again. "I didn't mean you. I know you can't do this job."

"Then who will?"

A secretive smile lifted her lips as she gazed back at him with a raised brow. He knew that mischievous look by heart because it always meant they soon after got into a great deal of trouble together.

"Not you." He scrutinized her, briefly wondering if he'd hit his head during his leap across the ravine.

"Yes, me."

"But you're…" He shrugged, not knowing how to form his words. Ashryn was his friend. His partner in mischief. He knew her inside and out. But she loved the people of Attleglade. And…well, perhaps she was the perfect candidate for this job.

"My mother used to be of noble Forest Fae blood before…" She lowered her gaze and frowned, not finishing her sentence, as her family history looked a lot like his own. "Between Sylvain and I, we will bridge the gap between Attleglade and Albrasia."

He raised an eyebrow. "With a…marriage?"

Surprisingly, her cheeks pinked, and he almost found himself gaping at the sight. Ashryn blushing? Sylvain must have quite the hold on her.

She nodded. "For allegiance purposes and whatnot."

He seriously doubted that was all it was. "That woodpecker better ask for my permission first."

"Go easy on him."

"Never. You deserve only the best."

Her mouth twitched as if holding back a smile. "Go on. Be the chief for just one day. This punishment is yours." She nodded her head toward the councilmen clustered in the cell. "I suggest you act sooner rather than later while the volcano is still hot."

Fury boiled in his blood again, and lest he strike his spear through the tyrant's heart, he turned around and avoided glancing their way at all. "Bring them all outside to the firing tree. I'll deal with Sir Crankiness first."

He marched outside toward the tree, and as if feeling the tension in the air, the villagers followed, murmuring amongst themselves. The Ember Fae followed farther behind, two men supporting Seraphina between them.

His anger simmered to jealousy when he glanced between the two men. Were they both the concubines she'd chosen? Who were they? How did she know them?

A matter for another time, he reminded himself and turned his attention away.

The councilmen were lined up in front of the tree, leaving a larger space in the middle for Cranky Cricket.

"You can't do this!" the older man snarled, his knee creaking as he took a single step forward. "I am the new chief.

Not you. You will be tortured and hanged for this. Guards! Arrest him!"

No one moved to follow orders. Not this time.

"Seize him!" the man shrieked, a wildness in his eyes. The ropes binding his arms behind his back pulled against his movements as if he were trying to free himself.

Nothing.

Ashryn stepped forward and handed Bastien the bow Seraphina had taken from him what seemed like ages ago. He strapped a quiver to his back filled with six arrows. He pulled a single arrow out. Because all he needed was one.

A deadly silence descended upon the forest as Bastien nocked the arrow and lifted his bow. His arm screamed in agony at the motion, but he pushed the pain back and focused on the present. The weapon was like an extension of his body. Well-practiced and unfailable. He never missed his target, and he didn't plan on doing so now.

Like himself, it was as if everyone held their breath, not daring to make a sound as they waited for his judgment. He felt Seraphina's gaze on him, but he didn't turn to look at her. He needed to focus. Otherwise, he might miss. Probably not, but it was possible.

He planted his feet and stared back at the man who had wreaked havoc on his life, on his family.

He released the arrow. Several gasps and screams echoed around him. The arrow whizzed through the air, flying toward Cranky Cricket faster than a blink. But instead of striking him through the eye, the tip of the arrow scratched the side of his face before embedding in the trunk of the tree behind him.

Bastien lowered his bow, even as Cranky Cricket stared back at him with wide eyes. The area hushed once again as everyone leaned in to hear him speak. "You are responsible for the death of my mother. For the maiming and death of my father. For the separation of my family. You are responsible for dozens of deaths of good people, and I'm not only speaking for myself when I say we have rolled over and let this happen. But no more. No more ceaseless bloodshed. No more lives lost." He gestured with his bow to the path leading out of the forest. "You and your lackeys are hereby exiled from Attleglade and are never to return again, lest you seek a worse punishment to fit your crimes."

"You can't do this!" Cranky Cricket cried in outrage. "This is *my* home. You are the outsider, half-breed."

The title spurred anger through his body, and he blindingly fast reached for a second arrow, took aim, and released.

The arrow shot through the air and scratched the man's opposite cheek. Droplets of red trickled down his face.

He reached for a third arrow and aimed, but this time he didn't release it. "I suggest you make haste and pack your things. The third arrow might not be so kind as the last two."

The other council members scrambled away, with patrol guards acting as their shadows. Cranky Cricket stayed behind.

After a brief, disbelieving scan of their people making no move to help him, the older man asked, "Where will I go?"

"Anywhere as long as it's nowhere near the forest."

"But…but…winter is fast approaching."

Bastien waved Ashryn and Sylvain closer until the three of them stared the man down. "These two will take over as Chiefs when I leave the forest myself. I think they should have a say in your sentence."

He stepped back but made the mistake of meeting Seraphina's gaze. Devastation lingered in the position of her parted lips, and disbelief lit in the fiery ring around her eyes. He couldn't bear to lose her. But a concubine? Could he truly live such a life?

Ashryn's response pulled him back to the situation at hand. "I will give you two choices. You can either stay in the forest, living as a hermit away from the village. Or you can leave the forest entirely. The choice is up to you."

Cranky Cricket glared at all three before pointing a finger at Bastien. "Your mother was a dirty Sun Fae harlot. She deserved her fate—"

Bastien released the third arrow, and this time it struck the man in the shoulder, bringing him to his creaky knees. "Never speak of my mother again. Unless you want a fourth arrow to hit true. Now, release me from my blood oaths and be on your way."

This time, the tyrant flicked his own blood to the ground at his feet to break the oaths, stumbled away, and paused only once to scream when a patrol guard broke the arrow in half and pulled it out of the man's shoulder.

Bastien strung his bow around his shoulders and clapped his hands together to rid himself of a dirty job. "I'm done. That's it. I'm out of here. You're the chief, Ash. Don't bungle this too badly."

She offered him a smile and gripped his arm in hers, and he swallowed a lump in his throat when he realized they would part ways. For good. But their friendship wouldn't end because of distance. He planned to visit often. And perhaps she might visit him, too, with her soon-to-be husband and maybe even some strapping young children.

"Take care of yourself, Bas."

"I will." And then he took Sylvain's arm next.

The other man's eyes hardened with determination the same way they had days earlier as if he wanted to prove himself. "I would like to ask permission—"

He pulled Sylvain into a headlock and playfully roughed his knuckles along his skull. "Of course, you can have Ashryn's hand in marriage. Duh. If I declined, I would sooner find two daggers in my back faster than I can run."

When he released him, Sylvain grinned from ear to ear as if the anxious weight on his shoulders had been lifted. "I'll see you two soon, I hope," Bastien said with a final wave before he marched over to Seraphina.

Ignoring everyone watching him, especially the two men still holding Seraphina between them, he cradled her face in his hands, pulled her to him, and kissed her with as much passion as he could muster despite their audience and to convey all his conflicting feelings churning inside his belly.

He broke the kiss faster than he wanted to, and not giving her a chance to speak, he whispered a breath away from her lips as he made his final decision. "If the only way I can be with you is to be your concubine, then I'll make the sacrifice." He gazed into her beautiful green and orange eyes. "I'll go with you wherever you need me to go. My home is with you, wherever you are, if you will have me." He sucked in a breath and pushed the words from his mouth before his courage fled as he nodded to the two men still holding her. "Even if I have to share you."

The two men glanced at him, then at each other, and then they burst into laughter, one elbowing the other in the ribs. Seraphina grinned unrepentantly as if what he said was hilarious. It certainly was not. The farthest thing he wanted was to be her concubine. But he would take what he could get.

Seraphina pushed away from the two men and linked her arm with his, though her weight sagged against him as if she still hadn't gained back all her strength. "Bastien, I know we all have black hair and look a bit similar to you. But can't you see the family resemblance?"

His jaw dropped as the two men guffawed. "Family?"

"Yes." She laughed. "These are two of my brothers, Eben and Jude. They're tolerable, I suppose." His skin prickled as she ran her hand up his arm. "I would like to speak to you privately." She shot her brothers a look. "Come with me."

295

TWENTY THREE

Bastien was not accustomed to being followed by guards, especially not guards who were family members. But as he supported Seraphina by the waist as she led him up a hill within a copse of trees, the two men followed at a distance, though still too close for comfort.

"In here." She grabbed his hand, now walking on her own, as she led him through a crack in the rocky hillside, which led into a dark tunnel with branches from floor to ceiling in an unnatural weave.

He inhaled sharply as he recognized his surroundings. "My father built these tunnels. He showed me them long ago. How did you…"

Eben's and Jude's hands burst into flames to light the way, light flickering across the tunnel and casting shadows within every crevice. And instead of answering him, Seraphina continued to lead him forward.

"I spent far longer in these tunnels than I should have, I'm embarrassed to admit." She squeezed his hand. "Trees certainly are not my element."

Their footsteps made no sound as they continued down the tunnel, and when they reached the five forks in the road, she pulled him down one of them.

When he was younger, his father had forced him to learn which tunnel led where, and he never forgot it. If they continued this way, they would find themselves in the woods. If they turned down a left tunnel, it would lead them near the Glades.

He squinted his eyes when he caught sight of a flickering fire up ahead. He cautiously slowed his footsteps and unstrung his bow from his shoulders. But as he reached for an arrow, his hand froze when the flicker of light caught on familiar white hair.

"Father?" he choked.

Instead of finding a dead body, his father's head jolted up in response to his voice.

Bastien's sob stuck fast to his throat. He dropped his bow and sprinted down the remainder of the tunnel leading to his father. When he reached his side, he skidded to his knees and threw his arms around him while burying his face into his shoulder.

He sobbed. "I thought you were dead. I thought..."

His father's voice broke as he spoke. "I never thought I'd ever say I owe my life to an Ember Fae. But here we are."

He turned his head from his father's shoulder to find Seraphina twiddling her thumbs, her mouth moving as if searching for something to say. He grabbed her hand, and mindful of her lack of strength, he pulled her down beside them and wrapped one arm around her and one around his father.

"You are magnificent," he whispered in her ear. "I owe you my every breath." He would gladly become this woman's concubine after everything she had done for him because of how much she meant to him. "I love you, Seraphina."

Her breath hitched, and she pulled away to look into his eyes. He hoped sincerity stared back at her because he meant every word.

A small, almost shy, smile pulled up on her lips as she sat back on her heels. "Perhaps I should do this somewhere more private. But I'm just too tired to move." She held out her hand, and one of her brothers—Bastien still couldn't tell them apart—handed her a black obsidian box as large as his fist.

She unlatched the box and pulled it open to reveal a smooth, red gemstone similar to the one hanging around her neck. She lifted it out of the box from its chain and dangled it in front of him. Firelight caught on its smooth surfaces, creating a dazzling effect as the gem slowly turned where it hung.

"What is this?" he asked reverently, his finger hovering over the gem but not touching. "Well, I know you can communicate with others using it. That's all I really know."

After one more rotation through the air, Seraphina laid the gem flat on her palm. "Everyone I would like to communicate with receives an Ember gem cut from the same stone. This allows communication to happen freely between all who have a gem. My fathers… My brothers… Pri… They all have one." She pointed to a golden pendant attached to the chain with an etching of fire on its surface and then pointed to an exact replica of the one she wore. "These are the ones meant for my concubines."

Bastien released a shuddering breath as he accepted what it meant to have her in his life. It would not be an easy life, and he feared it would destroy him. But he would never know unless he tried.

She dangled the gem again, this time using two hands instead of one. "In my culture, it is customary for the woman to propose." A nervous, shuddering breath left her lips, similar to his own. "Bastien, will you *not* become my concubine? Will you become mine as my one and only husband?"

"Huh?" Eben and Jude said at the same time, sharing a confused look. "That's not how it works."

"It is now," she laughed, and he caught her sharing a twinkling, knowing look with his father. "I'm changing the tradition. I brought back the Glades. I negotiated peace with the Forest Fae, or at least Bastien did on my behalf. I think I should be rewarded for doing so much good for my people. I am taking only one husband. If he will have me."

Bastien snapped his gaping jaw closed and glanced between her and her confused brothers. "I don't want to cause any trouble for you."

"Believe me." She cradled his cheek with a soft hand. "When the creek fills once more with the healing water of the Glades, my people will rejoice. All three clans. They will understand, from a political viewpoint, why I would choose to marry you, the prior chief from Attleglade. No one will argue with my decision."

When his father raised a questioning eyebrow at the mention of "prior chief," Bastien only shrugged and silently promised to tell the story later.

"Except, perhaps, Father," one of the brothers protested. "He's been breaking up suitor fights for the past several months."

Seraphina chuckled weakly and shook her head. "One of my fathers told me love is sacrifice. And sacrifice is difficult. I want to spend my life with you, and I will weather any storm to make it happen. I can't weather it alone."

Once again, she held up the Ember gem, waiting for his answer with her lip wedged between her teeth.

Why didn't the answer pop out of his mouth immediately? Why didn't he shout a resounding *yes* and spin her around until they were both dizzy and drunk on love? He had everything he'd ever wanted at his fingertips. Love. Freedom. Someone to share his life with. But the realization only left him dazed.

"Pops?" he asked quietly, glancing to where his father was staring at a pile of drawings. *His* drawings. Seraphina must have saved them from the fire. Just one more thing he was immensely grateful for. "Would you come with us?"

His father shook his head. "Everyone thinks I'm dead. I'm *free*. I want to spread my wings. I am not going to find what I'm looking for in the Ember clans."

Bastien ran his fingers through his hair as the weight of his decision crushed him. His father needed help, whether or not he would admit as much. The man couldn't walk, for autumn's sake! Bastien couldn't just leave him to fend for himself.

"It's all right," his father urged. "Don't let your worry over me affect your choice. I will be fine."

Seraphina lowered the necklace until it rested in her lap. Her lip all but disappeared between her teeth. "If you need more time to see your father settled, I will give it to you. You deserve to be happy, whatever that looks like."

"How fast can we marry?" he asked suddenly, startling her. "How...fast?"

He nodded, new plans working through his mind. "My father will come with us to your home. He needs a new wheelchair, no? He's not getting anywhere without one. We marry. And then we'll take him to my sister's home in Ebriel on a honeymoon trip. Surely, your people would let you go long enough for that."

Her smile grew back slowly but surely, and she shifted until her knees rested against his. "You can't rush these things, Bas."

But he shook his head, hearing none of it. He pointed to the gem. "Yes to this." He pointed to her. "Yes to this." And then, he included all of them within a circle drawn by his finger. "And yes to this. As long as your people won't roast me alive."

"They won't." She laughed and shook her head as she draped the necklace over his head. A new connection to her sparked within his chest. Even without touching her, he felt like he could simply reach out and take her into his soul.

"Are you sure?"

I am, she replied in his mind, giving his hand a squeeze. Then out loud, she said, "No one kills my husband without my permission first."

"I think brothers are the exception to the rule," one of the Ember males said, each laughing and elbowing each other in the ribs.

Seraphina rolled her eyes. "I think not, Jude." And then to him, she said, "Just ignore them. They're typically harmless until they're not. They won't hurt you. Much."

Bastien snorted. *I'm not going to lie. I'm looking forward to having siblings again.*

You'll regret you said that by the end of the week.

Likely not. But only time will tell.

He untied the patrol guard cloak from his shoulders and held it up with one arm to block the others' view as he threaded his fingers through Seraphina's hair and drew her in for a kiss. Heat sparked between their lips, and he drank it in as if he were frozen over by an ice wraith all over again and needed her warmth.

He could hardly believe it, even as he held her against him and felt the solid, warm touch of her hands and her lips. For many years, he'd believed he'd never get the chance to have a wife, children, and a life away from Attleglade. But now he would get all three. With the *Ember Queen* of all people.

When they broke apart, he gazed back at the orange flames burning around the pupils of her eyes. His gorgeous Ember Fae.

"I wish we were alone," she whispered as she used her finger to trace his eyebrows, his nose, and then his lips, the action still shielded by his cloak barely separating him from the others. Thankfully, the other three engaged in conversation to pull their attention away from them. "Thank you for saving my life when I fell. My brothers told me if you hadn't done what you did, I wouldn't have made it."

He ran a flustered hand through his hair. "I suppose you owe me now."

"Owe you?" She raised an eyebrow. "At the very least, we're even. At the most? You owe *me* twice over."

"No, no, no. You have this backward." He began counting on his fingers. "The first time I saved your life was from myself in the cave. I could have stabbed you."

"But you didn't," she pointed out. "And what about that incident makes you think you came out on top? You were one giant icicle. You never would have thawed out without my fire."

"Are you so sure about that?"

His father sighed heavily. "Here we go again with the bickering."

He and Seraphina stared back at each other before snorting with laughter. Bastien dropped his cloak only for a moment to frown at his father. "As the Ember Queen's concubine, I declare that you must pretend you can't hear us."

And then he raised the cloak again while the other three were clearly trying to hold back their laughter. Seraphina clamped her hands over her mouth as if to stifle her own.

"If we must," he started again, "we can swipe the slate clea—"

Her lips crashed into his again, stealing the words from his mouth and fogging his mind until his train of thoughts dispersed into the most beautiful chaos. Without a doubt, he knew he had made the right choice. He would go anywhere with Seraphina. Now and forever.

"I don't know about you," he breathed the moment they parted. "But I'm ready to go home."

Home...

Home was wherever she was.

Seraphina smiled and rested a hand lightly on his chest. "There is just one thing I need to do first."

Seraphina refused to admit how much lingering in the Forest Fae territory unnerved her.

The silence of foreign uncertainty garbled up the quiet birdsong in the giant boughs above as she held tightly onto Pri's hand. Bastien held onto her other hand. The young girl glanced nervously about, watching each Forest Fae with suspicion. Seraphina couldn't blame her after what had happened. Nor did she completely trust that no one would jump out at them with a weapon raised.

But Forest Fae created a path on either side leading to the Glades, with Ashryn guiding them forward only a few steps ahead. No one attacked. No one reached for a weapon. Rather, they wore hopeful expressions, as if they wanted the war between their people to end as much as she did.

The war over the Glades.

Pri whimpered and hid her face in Seraphina's shoulder as the roaring falls echoed in their ears. Her gaze shifted back and forth across the line of Forest Fae, and she knew if any one of them attacked, not only were she and Bastien capable of defending Pri, but the Ember Fae following behind would defend them to their dying breath.

They stopped at the edge of the rickety wooden bridge, and for a moment, she watched as it swayed back and forth, a misty breeze scaling the steep ravine walls and clinging onto the rope and boards. Her breath caught when she spotted the sheen of green far below, a layer of volcanic glass beneath the water rushing down what used to be a dry riverbed.

Ashryn turned to face the villagers. "This day marks the truce between Forest Fae and Ember Fae alike. By sharing the Glades with our friends, we vow to put anger and bloodshed behind us."

Murmurs of agreement lifted into the air, though most of the fae remained quiet.

Ashryn nodded, and Seraphina, Pri, and Bastien moved forward. She tested her weight on the bridge, and thankfully, it held. Although she wanted to trust her previous enemies, she also feared the road to peace was weaved with a few thorns.

Together, they crossed the bridge, and with each sway, Pri's whimpering grew louder. The poor girl must be terrified. But she vowed to never let anything harm her again.

When they stepped off the bridge and onto soft grass, she exhaled a breath of disbelief as she stared at a large boulder formation etched into the mountainside. A peaceful stillness washed over her as she gazed in awe at what used to be the pride of her ancestors.

Bastien released Pri's hand, and without a word, he stepped aside to let them go in alone together. Likely to watch as a lookout as well.

She gave Pri's hand a reassuring squeeze as they stepped through the door carved into the boulder and entered a series of corridors, almost like a maze, leading into different rooms of the sanctuary.

It was as if a magic called to her, beckoned her forward within the dim light of the rocky corridor until the air turned cold and humid. The stone hallway opened into a larger cavern. Her feet froze, her eyes widening as the sight struck her with awe.

A reverent hush settled upon the cavern, aside from the gentle lull of the pool of water in the center of the room. A blue light pulsed gently at the bottom of the pool, creating a mesmerizing sheen beneath the surface of the sacred waters.

Their movements created the faintest scuffs of a whisper as she helped Pri undress and then took several hairpins out of her hair until she lay bare, her tattered wings hanging limply against her back.

"You will come with me?" Pri asked, the faintest murmur of her voice nearly shattering the reverent atmosphere.

She shook her head and ran a hand over her daughter's dark hair. "The healing pool is not for me. It's for you."

Pri exhaled a long breath before she descended the stone stairs leading into the sacred pool. She inhaled sharply at what must be frigid water before she took a deep breath and dunked her entire body beneath the surface.

Please, Seraphina begged, her fingers clasped together. *Please heal her.*

Of course, she knew the healing properties of the water did not always heal immediately. Sometimes it took days. Other times it took months. But mostly, the Glades chose not to heal those afflicted with their infirmities. Would it shun Pri? Or accept her with grace?

Pri gasped as her head reemerged from the water, and she shivered from head to toe as she scrambled for the stairs. The moment she stepped foot out of the pool, Seraphina wrapped her in a large drying cloth and held her tight.

I beg you, she murmured within her mind. If the waters didn't heal Pri, it might only prove to the Forest Fae that Ember Fae were unworthy of the Glades. She refused to believe her people were any lesser than their counterparts.

Pri stiffened against her and threw the cloth off herself. She spun around, and Seraphina's breath caught. The pulsing blue light of the pool illuminated the shimmer of Pri's wings. The torn, tattered pieces healed back together while the holes were filled with new membranes. Slowly, Pri lifted her wings. They were whole. Healed. Beautiful.

"Thank you!" Pri sobbed as she threw her arms around her once more. "You did this for me."

"I did this for our people," she corrected, but then she smiled. "But especially for you."

After Pri dressed, they exited the Glades and stood at the base of the bridge, Bastien now at their side while all the others watched from the opposite end of the ravine. Pri's face glowed with happiness as she lifted her wings, and both of their people alike cheered at the miracle that had taken place.

Seraphina reached for Bastien's hand, her heart fluttering at the beaming smile he sent her way. As much as she wished to take the credit, this was his doing. And although she would only ever admit it to herself, she owed him a thousand times over.

TWENTY FOUR

A heavy, reverberating beat echoed around Bastien as Ember Fae pounded on their drums in a mesmerizing rhythm. Fire burned brightly from long torches stuck into the ground, lighting up the night of the full moon.

He sat cross-legged beside Seraphina on a large, red rug laid outside with mountainous gifts piled on both sides of the rug. He wore half his hair tied back, with a plait on each side of his head. Like most of the other Ember Fae, he was bare-chested, wearing some sort of loin cloth around his waist that barely reached his knees. Something about union traditions. The other clothing he would wear would be far less exposing.

Bastien had never worn so little clothing before, but if he were to integrate into Seraphina's culture, he wanted to do a fully baked job of it rather than half-baked. Although he'd hated almost everything about his time in Attleglade, there were some things he couldn't let go of. One of which included his long hair. Despite everything, Attleglade was a part of him, and he refused to let go entirely.

Two women approached with bowed heads, one with a bowl of red paint and the other with black. He watched in fascination as they painted his new bride with intricate patterns across her skin, including her neck and face.

For their union day, she wore a two-piece outfit, a deep red in color. The top dipped low, cut off to show a good portion of her stomach. And her skirt cut off at her lower calf, a slit on either side of her leg.

Seraphina explained with her eyes closed, "In Blackburrow, it is a tradition to paint the bride and grooms, or groom and brides, to symbolize a powerful union of togetherness, happiness, and good luck." Her mouth twitched. "And it is also used to determine the luck on a union night."

He furrowed his brows as he tried to make sense of it. "How so?"

Her grin grew into something a bit more sultry and teasing. "The more smudged the paint, the better chance at conceiving offspring."

The moment the meaning clicked, he slapped his knees and laughed out loud, drawing plenty of attention in their direction. "Well," he wheezed, "I'd have to say if our firstborn doesn't come out with white hair, I might be a little concerned."

"Ha ha." She shoved his shoulder just as the women moved onto him next. But when the first woman ran a finger over his chest with red paint, Seraphina swatted her away. "*Chchch*! No one touches him except me."

They bowed, leaving their bowls behind as they backed away. When Seraphina knelt in front of him, several hoots and whistles rounded in the audience, one particularly loud whistle coming from Ashryn, where she sat on a rug beside Sylvain and his father in the large circle. On other rugs, Seraphina's fathers and brothers sat beside Pri. No one knew the truth about Pri yet, and until they deemed her safe from harm, they planned to keep it that way.

In the middle of the circle of rugs, several performers danced with flaming balls on the ends of a rope, dangerous and foreign and fascinating all at the same time.

Heat spiked his blood when Seraphina dipped her fingers in the paint, drawing whorls and designs across his skin.

"How could you possibly think I could have handled *you* having several concubines if you can't handle the thought of another woman touching *me*?"

She huffed as she dragged her finger lazily across his face next, and just the simple touch burned his soul in the most pleasant way. "Perhaps I was not made for the traditional polyamorous life."

Her fingers dipped lower until she drew designs across his belly and then the portion of his visible legs. As she finished the designs on his arms, the beat of the drums intensified. The dancers twirled their fire ropes in mesmerizing circles, and not for the first time, he was struck dumb by the beauty of the flames.

Servants passed by with drinks and plates of food. He passed on the drinks but took a sample of white cheese and roasted meat.

"Wait," Seraphina said before he managed to pop them into his mouth. She nibbled on a corner of each of his offerings before nodding. "Can't be too sure someone might not try to poison you tonight. The food is fine."

Unable to keep his hands completely to himself, even with an audience, he ran a hand up her arm, uncaring when the paint smeared as he did it. "Is this how life is as the Ember Queen? People dance for you, feed you, wait on you?"

She shrugged and rested a hand on his knee, smudging the paint there, too. "Not always. But a union day is a special event in everyone's lives, an important occasion for all clans. The party will last all night and well into the morning. Even if we are absent."

A fiery yet mischievous twinkle gazed back at him in her eyes, and he couldn't help but meet her heated stare.

But the arrival of two more servants with trays of food broke the heated tension between them. Not until after they bowed and backed away did he ask, "How are the clans taking this change of tradition?"

"Better than I expected, I admit. After what happened with Zephyr, their clan has been groveling at my feet ever since. The other two clans are disappointed to be left out of the choosing, but not terribly much now that the Glades flow through our territory once more."

Seraphina perked up beside him at the change of tempo of the drum and the accompanying music and chanting of her clansmen. To him, the new beat sounded heavy, almost like a dare.

"Our turn," she breathed excitedly, pulling him to his feet.

"Oh ho ho!" He pulled back. "No one said anything about dancing. I know exactly zero Ember Fae dances."

However, she simply squeezed his hand reassuringly. "This is not a set dance. It is a joining with nature, with the elements around us." Her mouth twitched as she traced his jaw. "It would have helped if you had a drink or two."

"Never. Especially not tonight."

She laughed as if expecting his answer, and when she pulled him onto the dance floor, he didn't resist her this time. She spun him in a circle, and he followed her lead until they reached the middle of the dance floor. Cheers erupted around them. He grinned sheepishly, still not having a clue what to do.

Especially when Seraphina placed a spear in his hand. The obsidian end was blunted, useless as a weapon. But the shaft felt familiar in his hands, as he'd trained with a spear day in and day out until his fingers bled.

She swung her own spear at his side. He reflexively blocked.

What in the...

She attacked his other side. He blocked.

And then her actions became quicker as she swung and thrust and spun until her body swayed like a leaf floating down a river with each movement. Taking her cue, he relaxed and mimicked her, their sparring becoming a dance rather than a skirmish.

The beat of the drums invigorated him. The chanting filled his soul with an energetic balm. And with his new bride at his side, they joined in a dance of oneness and love. He knew that despite how many hardships and storms they might have to weather together, he was right where he was meant to be.

The drums ceased beating, and he and Seraphina faced each other, each holding both spears in two hands as they breathed heavily, inches away from the other. Shouts and cheering were drowned by his pulse beating wildly through his ears as he closed the distance and kissed his wife.

"Had enough yet?" Bastien murmured as he leaned away just enough to look her in the eye.

"Hardly." She dropped both spears, and they clattered to the ground as she pulled him in for another kiss. Deafening whoops and hollers filled his ears, the ground seeming to shake with energy around them. Normally, he might care enough about people's stares and opinions to kiss her in private. But on their wedding day? Who could resist such a fiery, beautiful woman?

When they broke apart, Bastien grinned from ear to ear and gave a thumbs-up to his father and Ashryn. She rolled her eyes, but his father gazed back from his new wheelchair with a warm, happy smile, his eyes glistening with unshed tears.

All his father had ever wanted for him was to find happiness. And although he found it in the most unlikely places, he was the happiest he'd ever been, and he wouldn't trade it for anything.

"How long until we can smudge our paint?" Bastien asked Seraphina, waggling his eyebrows.

She playfully smacked his arm and pulled him back toward the rugs, where they settled to watch more fire dancers. "Sit for a few more performances, at least."

He opened his mouth to continue jesting with her, but the words halted on his tongue as she rested her head against his shoulder. Warmth spread through his chest, and he swallowed thick emotion as he wrapped his arm around her waist and pulled her closer.

After the performance finished and another one started with people enacting a play in another language with large, painted masks, he glanced sideways at her.

"Ser?"

"Hmm?"

The quiet rumble of her voice sent a pleasant shiver down his spine. "Thanks for kidnapping me all those weeks ago."

Her voice rumbled again as she laughed. "Let's make it a tradition, shall we?"

"A tradition, eh?" He turned his head and raised an eyebrow. "Can we leave out the part where you stab me?"

"What's a new tradition without a few surprises?"

He laughed along with her and pulled her even closer until his arms rested around her waist, his mouth against her soft hair. "This time, I'll be ready with a few surprises of my own."

She nuzzled into his chest. "I look forward to it."

EPILOGUE

Stepping outside of the forest entirely unnerved Bastien in many different ways. First, he feared he might drop dead at any moment. But as he wheeled Father down a frozen dirt path lined with apple orchards on either side of them, he didn't lose consciousness. The blood oath was good and broken.

But he still felt a bit jumpy.

"Are you nervous to visit your sister or nervous to drop over dead?" Seraphina asked several steps behind him.

"Both?"

He grinned as his eyes raked her up and down. She wore black furs from the hat on her head, the cuffs on her arms, and the triangular skirt reaching her knees, while she wore leather pants underneath. Ember Fae did *not* like the cold, and the queen was no exception.

"She doesn't know we're coming..." Father wrung his hands resting over the blanket in his lap. "We should have sent a letter beforehand or some forewarning."

Through his musings, he seemed to be talking to himself. But ever since leaving Attleglade, he hadn't been the same. Distant. Distracted.

Lost.

Bastien wished he could help, but like the man had said weeks ago, he wouldn't find what he was looking for in Blackburrow. What, exactly, was he looking for?

Because obviously, he hadn't found it yet.

Trying to remain cheerful, Bastien released one side of the wheelchair to squeeze his father's shoulder before resuming their bumpy trek over the frozen road. He breathed in the crisp, chilly air and said, "It will be more fun this way. Just imagine the look of surprise on their faces!" He leaned over the chair to grin at his father. "Besides, they showed up on our doorstep unannounced last year. I doubt they would be anything but kind and hospitable." His lips pursed. "Well, they *did* steal from my stash of wine."

Father tipped his head to give him a pointed look. "You don't even drink wine."

"I might someday!" he defended. "It was sitting there, aging to perfection until I was ready for it. But then Pri had to go and blow it up."

He winked at the girl dressed similarly to her mother, walking close to her side. Pri's face blushed before she hid it beneath a fur scarf. "Sorry," she murmured.

But then the girl's eyes crinkled with a hidden smile. He was glad for it, that she could now look back on her capture with some level of amusement rather than outright fear.

He momentarily reached for her and gave her a sideways embrace before they continued their long trek. Finally, two houses appeared at the end of the road, one straight ahead and another to the right. It had taken a good amount of asking around to figure out where Nyana now lived. He hoped he wasn't wrong because wheeling his father around proved tougher than he thought, especially during the chilly autumn days.

"Which do you think it is?" Seraphina asked.

He surveyed each yard. The house on the right contained items in the front, such as shears, clippers, crates, and a doll collecting frost on one of the porch steps. The four of them wordlessly opened the gate leading to the property, and Pri picked up the doll and smoothed its yarn of hair back on its head.

To confirm their choice of house, children's laughter echoed from within, muffled by the door standing between them. But before anyone managed to knock, the door swung open, and a tall figure stepped outside onto the porch with the lingering traces of laughter still on his face.

Joel stopped short, and his eyes widened as he took in their group of four. Bastien's brother-in-law still looked the same as a year ago—golden brown hair curled around the ears, careful green eyes, and a physique that spoke of outdoor labor.

Although he didn't know Joel well, Bastien met his brother-in-law in an embrace once the man recovered from his shock.

"Nyana!" Joel shouted over his shoulder. "Come out here."

Light footsteps rushed toward the door as if she thought Joel was in trouble, and then a small woman appeared with blonde hair, blue eyes, and ears more Sun Fae than Forest Fae. The moment her gaze landed on them, she burst into tears.

"Papa! Bastien!" She braved the dirty, cold ground without shoes and embraced their father first and then him. When she pulled away, she swiped a hand across her eyes. "I never thought I'd see you again. After the Ember Fae attacked while we fled, I worried the two of you might be dead."

Bastien winced through a forced grin as he took hold of his wife's hand and pulled her closer, watching his sister's eyes slowly widen and her face pale.

"Nyana, I'd like you to meet my wife, Seraphina. Ser, this is my sister, Nyana."

The two women shook hands, but he didn't miss the way Nyana cast a nervous glance toward Joel as if she were uncertain how to proceed in such a confusing situation.

"And!" Bastien added to chip the tension away from the atmosphere. He draped an arm over Pri's shoulders. "This is my stepdaughter, Pri. But we keep that information on the hush-hush, if you know what I mean. Everyone thinks she's Seraphina's sister. And for now, we'll keep it that way."

At last, the anxiety in Nyana's eyes melted into warmth as she clasped Pri's hand. His sister had always had a weak spot for children. "It's wonderful to meet the two of you. You are all welcome to our home." She opened the door wider and ushered them inside. "You came a long way from the forest. How was your journey here?"

"Cold," Seraphina answered. The first thing she did was shed her coat and huddle up beside the hearth, where a trickle of fire dwindled away. With a gesture of her hand, the fire grew until it once more licked at the firewood and created a steady blaze.

His nieces, Maisy and Eva, scrambled into the room. Maisy immediately jumped into his arms, and he spun her around as she screeched with giggles. Eva touched Seraphina's wings with awe in her eyes.

"Are you a fairy?" the girl whispered.

Seraphina laughed and nodded. "A fire fairy. But one of the bigger ones."

Father wheeled himself inside and took up a position beside the couch. His mouth was pinched, his gaze wary and uncertain. Bastien quirked his mouth to the side as he once again faced the dilemma of the change in his father.

He reached for levity as he grinned. "I'm dumping Father on your doorstep. He's your problem now."

Their father rolled his eyes. "I'm fully capable of taking care of myself." He turned to Nyana and Joel. "I'm only asking to stay for a couple of weeks until I find my own footing."

Nyana gingerly touched his arm and offered a warm smile. "Papa, stay as long as you need. We're your family." She motioned for him to wait while she disappeared up the stairs and returned a minute later carrying an envelope. After handing it to him, she bit her lip. "I'll admit I was tempted more than once to use this before I married Joel. But it's yours. I never could have taken it."

Bastien peered over his father's shoulder, curiosity probing at him as he opened it. Simultaneously, he and his father inhaled sharply at the wads of money tucked inside, along with a note covered in achingly familiar scrawl.

For Emeric, it read. *If you ever escape, make the most of your life. I wish you every happiness. Always and forever, your loving Meredith.*

Father swallowed and stared at the offering in his lap for far too long. "Where did she get so much money?" he finally rasped. "We were so poor."

"Mother received the money from a distant relative after his passing before she died. As far as I know, she never spent a wick of it. She thought you might need it more someday." Nyana then held out another envelope, and with shaking hands, their father opened it. She continued, "It's the deed to the man's house. It's a nice home located in Ebriel, about ten minutes away from here by horse."

His heart broke for his father when the man dropped his head into his hand and failed to form a response. Without a word, he wheeled himself across the room and down the hallway, followed shortly by a *click* as a door shut behind him.

"I hate seeing him like this," Nyana murmured, staring after him.

"He hasn't been the same since we left Attleglade." Bastien ran a hand over his face. "He resigned himself to dying a lonely life. And now that he's free? I don't think he knows what to do with himself anymore. He doesn't know where to go from here."

Nyana squeezed his hand reassuringly. "We'll help him figure this out. Truly, you can all stay as long as you need."

He crossed the room and wedged himself in the chair with Seraphina, and his heart soared when she eagerly accepted his close proximity by wrapping her arms around his shoulders and warming him with her magic.

"We'll only stay until tomorrow. Technically, it's our honeymoon, and I'm taking her to see some of the sights outside the forest."

She raised a brow. "Have you even seen the sights outside the forest?"

He laughed and placed his hands on his hips. "Nope! It's just a bumbling adventure for all of us. I have no idea what I'm doing or where I'm going."

His sister smiled warmly at the two of them. "Congratulations on your wedding. I'm so happy for you." But before she said anything more, a gurgle sounded from the corner of the room, followed by a tiny squeal.

A cradle rocked back and forth with movement before Nyana picked up a bundle of blankets with a baby face poking out. Joel joined her side, and together they smiled down at what must be their love child.

As if noticing his stare, she asked, "Do you want to hold him?" Nyana offered her son to Bastien, and he shook his head.

"No, thank you. I'll pass."

"Seraphina?"

His wife tucked her wings in and crossed her arms while she shook her head, and he couldn't help but laugh at the pair of them. Children weren't on the agenda anytime soon, and he was perfectly content with that. But he was happy for his sister, especially after the terrible past she'd suffered through, only to find a better future with Joel.

His gaze moved to the hallway where his father had disappeared. More than anything, he hoped his father might find happiness in Ebriel. A second chance at a new, joyful life. Because he deserved it more than anyone.

ABOUT THE AUTHOR

Sydney Winward is an award-winning fantasy and paranormal romance author who dabbles in the occasional historical fiction. She loves building complex worlds filled with magic, strong characters, and emotional stories that can make you laugh and cry.

Sydney is the author of the Sunlight and Shadows Series and the best-selling Bloodborn Series, and when she's not writing, she's reading, thinking about stories, or going on adventures with her children. She lives in Utah with her husband and three amazing kids.

www.sydneywinward.com